ALSO BY RANDALL SILVIS

THE
DEEPEST
BLACK

A NOVEL

RANDALL SILVIS

Poisoned Pen
PRESS

Sourcebooks, Poisoned Pen Press, and the colophon are registered trademarks of
Sourcebooks.

Published by Poisoned Pen Press, an imprint of Sourcebooks
P.O. Box 4410, Naperville, Illinois 60567-4410
(630) 961-3900
sourcebooks.com

Library of Congress Cataloging-in-Publication Data

Names: Silvis, Randall, author.
Title: The deepest black : a novel / Randall Silvis.
Description: Naperville, Illinois : Poisoned Pen Press, [2022]
Identifiers: LCCN 2022011065 (print) | LCCN 2022011066 (ebook) |
    (trade paperback) | (epub)
Subjects: LCGFT: Novels.
Classification: LCC PS3569.I47235 D44 2022 (print) | LCC PS3569.I47235
    (ebook) | DDC 813/.54--dc23
LC record available at https://lccn.loc.gov/2022011065
LC ebook record available at https://lccn.loc.gov/2022011066

Printed and bound in Canada.
MBP 10 9 8 7 6 5 4 3 2 1

for my sons,
Bret and Nathan

"Human nature is not black and white but black and grey."
—GRAHAM GREENE

"For every veil lifted, another waits beneath it.
You can choose to be frustrated by
that truth, or enchanted by it."
—RANDALL SILVIS

Throughout this book, the author employs information gleaned from numerous print and online sources. For those interested in the full source citations for that material, or in reading further on the subjects discussed, an addendum is provided on the author's website at randallsilvis.com.

1.

The report

Dear Detective Smathers:

The narrative you are about to read will strain your credulity. It has certainly strained mine, even though I lived it. Included here is everything I learned over the past four weeks about not only the triple homicide in the Burchette house in Bell's Grove, but of the dark forces that might have precipitated that tragedy. Much of what I relate is unprovable, and the rest is unprovable by me but perhaps not by a department with your resources. At the very least, the following information, when reduced to its most elemental parts, will provide what you do not yet have, namely a motive for the murders, based upon a premise that can be verified by DNA, i.e., the paternity of Baby Doe. As I see it, and as I will attempt to illustrate, all of the following events, whether mundane or incredible, derive from Baby Doe's true identity and the ramifications thereof.

I want to emphasize from the outset that I cannot vouch for the truth of any of this information except for that which I personally experienced, and which you will find the most difficult to believe. Of the rest, some came to me directly through four interviews with Ms. Phoebe Hudack and one conversation with a woman named Holly who alleged to be quoting Justin Cirillo's older brother, Dennis. As you will see from my narrative, though, even I have reason to doubt the veracity of those sources.

As for the strange events that befell me personally over the past weeks, I can only assure you that they took place exactly as I have written. I felt, at times, that not only was my will being subverted, but that my mind had been hijacked. I was mind-jacked. Not possible, you say? I would like to believe that that's true. Unfortunately, numerous precedents for such events and the clandestine sources responsible for them are readily available online to any researcher persistent enough to do the necessary digging.

My interest in the Burchette case, and in fact my first awareness of the case, began on October 12 of this year, at approximately 2:00 in the afternoon. I was having a late lunch at Joy Chinese Buffet in Hermitage when a young man who introduced himself to me as Thomas Kennaday approached my table and invited himself to sit. I will be happy to provide a physical description of this individual, but that, and the contents of our single conversation, are all I can provide in regard to him. Numerous attempts on my part to verify his identity have failed. It is my hope that you and your department will be more successful. Phoebe Hudack, a tenant in the Burchette house, was my only direct source of information about Kennaday; I trust that you and your team will find her more forthcoming now than she was during your initial interview(s) with her.

The above is the introduction to a report I composed for a detective employed by the New Castle, Pennsylvania, police department, and as such it concluded my mostly reluctant participation in an investigation that at times imperiled my personal safety as well as my sanity. My participation, as it turned out, had little to do with the final disposition of the case, but more to do with the unseen worlds that intersect, overlap, and often undermine our own.

Six additional months of research and rumination followed my submission of that report. This book is the result. But not, I think, the conclusion.

Most names have been changed to protect the privacy and safety of those individuals.

2.

The encounter

guess you could say it all started with the baby," Kennaday told me.

"What baby are you referring to?"

"The one they found in the woods last month. Little girl? Four months old? Had a broken leg and concussion? Tested positive for meth?"

I shook my head.

It was a Tuesday, a few days shy of the middle of October. The day had dawned without promise, gray and cool. I put in my usual hours at the desk (though this time, and too many previous times, with nothing to show for it), but around 10:30 that morning, when I rose to dash the dregs of my coffee into the sink, I happened to glance out the window and was stunned to see the yard bathed in pools of sunlight. Western Pennsylvania sunlight is a rare thing from October through March, so the sight of it stopped me in my tracks. I pulled out my phone and checked the weather forecast. Mostly sunny till six, then cloudy and cooling, with a high temperature midday of sixty-six degrees. Sixty-six degrees! Suddenly all sourness evaporated from my stomach, all stiffness fled from my limbs. Twenty minutes later I was astride my motorcycle, where I remained through nearly three hours of aimless, blissful riding along the narrow country lanes of my home county.

Throughout that fall and all of the previous summer, riding one of my motorcycles was my only release from self-recrimination. I hadn't written anything new since spring, and that last piece was an unmarketable novella now consigned to the dark limbo of my hard drive. With that piece, I had, I told myself, "lost the music." Day after day since then I sat at my desk, starting one piece after another only to delete them in frustration. It was as if I had gone tone-deaf. I could no longer compose a single lyrical sentence or phrase. I honestly don't know what happened. Early in the year I had finished a five-novel series, and they were all good books, and well received. But apparently I had written myself dry.

To a writer, this is a kind of death. And an especially dire one when the writer has no other identity, no other way of ascribing meaning to his life. There was a time when I defined myself in multiple ways—as a father, a novelist, a teacher, a screenwriter, a playwright, and a writer of creative nonfiction. These were the feathers in my cap, and I was proud of every one of them. But then my sons grew up and moved to other states and no longer needed my advice or my money. And, one by one, each of the other feathers also molted and fell out, and nothing grew back in their place. Finally, with my completion of the piece-of-crap novella, and my inability to blow any life into it, I saw what I had become. A nothing. My future had run out of road at the edge of a cliff. There was nowhere to go but down.

Still, I sat at my desk every morning and leafed through my notes for all of the stories and novels and essays I hadn't had time to write when I wrote those notes. But instead of becoming immersed in one of those ideas, I would get lost in some memory sparked by one of those notes. A memory of when my boys were small and I was happy. Or when *I* was small and I was happy.

The irony of those memories is that I *wasn't* happy back then, not in the way most people understand *happy*. My sensitivities were raw when I was a boy, and if anybody around me was unhappy, even a TV character, I was miserable for them. And in my little village filled with families on welfare, where most of the fathers were unemployed alcoholics, where domestic violence was a daily occurrence, I was unable to jibe what I was taught in Sunday school about a merciful and loving God with what I saw happening all around me. Any God who would allow such suffering and cruelty was a monster, and I hated him for it. This quietly seething anger stayed with me for decades.

Fortunately, at around the age of forty or so, I had an epiphany. On assignment for the Discovery Channel magazine, I interviewed a roboticist whose dream was to upload his consciousness into thousands of robots and send them out into space to beam their experiences and knowledge back to him. And on the drive home that day, it hit me. That's why *we're* here! We are God's robots! With no body of His/Her own, and nothing to compare itself to, God had created us out of a vast, deep loneliness, gave us free will, and sent us out into the universe, and now, through us, was experiencing everything there was to experience, good and bad. Through the choices we make and the lives we live, God grows and learns.

The day I had that epiphany was the day I stopped blaming God for all the grief and suffering in the world. God has nothing to do with it. *We* started it, *we* perpetuate it. We can stop it if we want to, but not enough of us want to.

It was a watershed moment for me.

Yet nothing changed me more than becoming a father. In that role, I felt true happiness for the first time. And for a couple of decades, I basked in the joys of fatherhood plus enjoyed a degree of professional success and financial security. Then my creative talent abandoned me, though the creative urge remains as demanding as ever. And now it's the same routine every morning. I start with ambition, which soon erodes into nostalgia, which soon morphs into melancholy, self-loathing, and despair. The only thing that keeps me going, that keeps me from throwing myself in front of any passing bus, is the knowledge that an hour or two on the motorcycle will buoy my spirits sufficiently to get me through another day.

And that's the state I'm in, the person I am, when Thomas Kennaday comes walking toward me at the Joy Chinese Buffet. My plate is filled with Chinese green beans and California rolls. As is my habit, I am sitting in a booth as far removed from other customers as possible, thanks to a condition called misophonia, a hypersensitivity to certain sounds and smells and other sensory triggers. Even in the best of situations and without the exacerbating influence of misophonia, we introverts are never relaxed among others. We are never truly comfortable except when alone.

Unfortunately, I have been unable in my home kitchen to duplicate the umami of the Chinese green beans at this particular restaurant, and am forced now and then to suffer the clangs and clinks, slurps and chomps, the sinus-clogging breezes of too much perfume or cologne, the loud voices and squalling babies inherent to public dining.

So that's me. And there I was in a high-backed booth at Joy Chinese Buffet, intending to enjoy some sushi and beans before scurrying home again. I looked up just in time to see a young stranger, whom I would come to know as Thomas Kennaday, striding toward me with a plate of lo mein and phoenix chicken in one hand, a bowl of steamed dumplings in the other. Neatly dressed in a pair of pressed khakis, brown Skechers mocs, a dark-green Columbia nylon pullover, a black T-shirt underneath, he was a good-looking young man in his mid- to late twenties, blue eyes, thick blond hair neatly clipped and styled, parted high on the right side. At first glance, he looked taller than his five eight, had a slender but fit body and a healthy tan. In every way *not* the kind of young man who would frequent a serve-yourself eight-dollar buffet.

He stepped up to my booth and flashed a bright, expensive-looking smile. "You're Silvis, aren't you?" he said. "The writer?"

Although it is flattering to be recognized by a stranger—it has happened only three times in my life, and never more than fifteen miles outside of my home—I am immediately knocked off-balance by such encounters, especially when I have a mouth full of sushi. So I looked up at him just long enough to mumble, "Nope. Sorry."

"Yes you are. I recognize you from the photos on your book jackets."

"Sorry," I told him. "I don't read much."

He issued a little laugh, *haha*, two syllables, set his plate and bowl on the table, then plopped down across from me. "I'm Thomas Kennaday. I've seen you at Planet Fitness a few times. I thought that was you."

"Sorry, but it wasn't. It isn't. And if you don't mind, I just want to finish my meal and leave. I'm kind of in a hurry here."

Kennaday acted as if he hadn't heard my dismissal. "Just answer me this," he said. "Have you been following that case over in Bell's Grove?"

"No," I said, hoping I sounded annoyed, and also hoping that my mother didn't reach out from the spirit world and give me a slap across the head. *What did I tell you?* I could hear her scold. *Always be polite. To everybody!* So, to the interloper at my table, I added, "What did you say your name is? Kennedy?"

"Kenn-a-*day*," he answered. "We're supposedly an offshoot of the Hyannis Port Kennedys. Some family disagreement a couple of hundred years ago. Somebody shagging somebody else's wife, something like that. I can't believe you're not familiar with that Bell's Grove thing. I mean, you write mysteries. I figured you'd be all over it."

I said nothing. Poured more soy sauce into a little plastic cup.

He leaned toward me. "Four people murdered," he said. "That doesn't interest you?"

Yes, it did interest me. "Drugs?" I asked.

He chuckled. "Man, you don't know the half of it."

"And you do?"

"Intimately."

I dipped a piece of the California roll into the soy sauce and lifted it to my mouth. Had Saint Francis de Sales, patron saint of writers, finally gotten around to noticing me?

Kennaday, grinning, watched me as I chewed. "I see a lot of DeMarco in you," he said. Ryan DeMarco is the protagonist of the mystery series I had completed earlier that year.

His statement hit too close to home. As much as we introverts might resent our isolation, we fiercely guard our privacy, as if to be known is to be exposed, to be caught in public with our pants down. A statement as simple and well meaning as "I love your blue eyes!" can make us blush from our ears to our heels and look around frantically for the nearest exit. With Kennaday, I broke eye contact and spoke toward my plate. "No, you don't."

"Are you saying the two of you don't share a lot of qualities and traits?"

"I'm saying it's too easy to confuse a fictional character with his creator."

"That sounds like something DeMarco would say."

"It was Truman Capote. And thousands of other writers who get annoyed when people confuse them with their characters."

"Yeah," he said, still smiling. "I think they get annoyed because they *are* their characters. They just don't want anybody else to know it."

Cheeky guy, I thought. Perversely, I enjoy a certain degree of cheekiness. "You write fiction?" I asked.

"Me? No, I'm not a writer."

I couldn't help myself. "What do you do?"

He smiled, and his eyebrows went up, then down.

An inability to maintain eye contact can indicate either dishonesty or insecurity, but dishonesty can also be revealed by eye contact that never breaks, especially when accompanied by a smile that borders on cocky. Kennaday's smile was near constant, and though he would break eye contact long enough to lift up a mouthful of noodles, those clear blue eyes always returned to regard me with a confidence I'd seldom encountered in one so young, and one which I, well beyond youth, have never been able to exude. Actually, his was more than confidence. What I saw in those eyes, I'm sure, was a taunt, a challenge.

He said, "I'm especially curious about DeMarco's near-death experience. Pretty wild stuff."

Again his eyebrows rose. He was looking at me now as if I were a new kind of bug in a petri dish. And he was comfortable doing so, too comfortable interrupting my meal and my solitude. He considered himself my equal, or more, despite the difference in our ages. This spoke to his upbringing. Loving, supportive parents. He was probably an only child, denied little. The neatness of his dress, the pressed khakis and stylish haircut, it all harkened back more to my generation than to his scruffier one. Catholic school maybe, followed by prep school. Ivy League possibly. Nowhere visible was the ungroomed, careless, and frequently unwashed quality I had seen creeping into my male students over the past twenty years, and which was now evident at nearly every other occupied table in the restaurant. This kid seemed to have been plucked straight out of a 1970s issue of *Esquire* and dropped into my booth at Joy Chinese Buffet.

He asked, "Have *you* had an NDE?"

"No."

"You couldn't have made all that up out of thin air."

"Research," I said.

"Naw, I don't think so. You've been there. I'd bet money on it." Again, that challenging smirk.

"I've had some experiences," I said, and immediately regretted it.

"I'd love to hear them."

I wasn't about to discuss anything personal with him or any other stranger. "There's nothing worth hearing."

Not so much as a flinch disturbed his calm. "Hey, you know what else of yours I liked? *Mysticus.* A telepathic aborted fetus? That was sick, man. But in a good way, you know? I take it you believe that telepathy is also real?" He nodded in response to my silence. "Yeah, I bet you're into all of that paranormal stuff, aren't you?"

I saw through the trick he was using: get a person talking about himself or one of his passions, and that person won't notice that you're intruding upon his privacy. "I try to keep an open mind," I told him. Then, "I'll look into that local murder case. Thanks for the heads-up. Have a good day."

It was impossible to insult him. He leaned forward again, pointed a chopstick at me, and said, "Four people dead and you don't know anything about it? Honestly, I find that difficult to believe. It's been right there on your doorstep for what, three weeks now? Don't you pay any attention to the local news?"

"I do not." I had every intention of researching the murders online the moment I got back home.

"Me," he said, "I can tell you every sleazy little detail if you want me to. I can tell you stuff the cops don't know and maybe never will."

Sleazy details? Stuff the cops don't know? It was as if he had read an X-ray of my brain and knew exactly which pleasure points to probe. I allowed him half a glance, then asked, as nonchalantly as I could, "Why?"

"Why what? Why tell you?" He shrugged. "Because I'm here, you're here, and I don't know how to get in touch with John Connolly."

He flashed his beautiful grin again, which made me shake my head and smile in spite of myself. "Besides, this is your turf, dude. You got to claim what's yours."

My turf? I have never felt a true part of any community, not even the one in which I spent my first eighteen years. As a small boy I spent many nights crying myself to sleep, praying for the answer to the questions *Why am I like this? Why am I here?*

At that moment, though, I had a different question. "Seriously, Thomas. What are you looking for here?"

He turned over his hands, showed me his empty palms. "The truth, I guess. Yeah. I feel like it needs to come out. The whole truth and nothing but."

"The truth about what?"

Another shrug. "Change can't start without awareness."

"Awareness of what?"

"Of the need for change."

Either he was talking in circles or I was missing something. We seemed to be on different frequencies. Still, my interest was piqued. Initially I had viewed him as a nuisance, but now modified that description to a nuisance who just might save me from drowning in a very private, very debilitating despair. I tried not to let the eagerness show in my eyes. "How is it that you know more about this case than the police do?"

He grinned. Leaned back against the vinyl-covered cushion. "So we have this baby," he said. "They're calling her Baby Doe, still don't know who she is. It sure looks like the parents are responsible, seeing as how she was never reported as missing. But there's not a single trace of evidence, nothing to charge them with. Plus, nobody knows who the parents are! And then, not long after the baby is found, this kid named Cirillo—very weird guy, by the way—he shoots up the Burchette house in Bell's Grove, kills two adults and a little girl. The question is why, right? Apparently, nobody knows anything, and Cirillo's doing a good impression of a clam. The cops are clueless. They have no idea where to go next."

"But you do?"

Again he ignored my question. He finished off his dumpling, grinned, and shrugged. "So I come walking back from the buffet, see you sitting here and I think, *he* knows a thing or two about investigating a crime."

"Having never done so," I said.

"Maybe so, maybe not."

"What's that supposed to mean?"

"There's this theory, you know, that our thoughts create reality. And all possible consequences of those thoughts spin off into parallel universes, right? In which case the characters you create are *real* people in some other universe, and in maybe more than one, living out the lives *you* created for them. In other words, every time you write something, you're creating characters and worlds that are every bit as real as this one. And they are all a part of *you*. You're the god who created them. Have you heard that theory?"

I had not only heard it before, but that very theory had raised its head in a recent DeMarco novel. But I didn't want to give this kid any kind of corroboration. I said nothing.

"Which means," he continued, "that you not only created those crimes, but you used DeMarco and Jayme to solve them. They couldn't know how to do that unless you knew how."

"Unless they have free will once they've been created. After that I just watch. Benign neglect."

"Touché," he said. Another smug smile, as if he had scored a point against me or had obtained some secret understanding of who I was.

"A corollary of your theory," I told him, "would be that you and I and everybody else on this planet is nothing more than a character in somebody else's theory."

"I think because I am," he said, "unless I only think I am because somebody else is thinking me thinking I am."

He was quoting me again, from one of the DeMarco novels!

I responded with a little grunt, "Hmm," then slid out of my booth, more to get my head clear than to get another plate of sushi.

"Hey, let me know how the oysters look!" he called after me.

———

With five pieces of nori-wrapped avocado rolls on my plate, and having talked myself into letting this conversation play out, I returned to my booth. "Okay," I said to Kennaday. "Tell me about the baby. Start at the beginning."

"How did the oysters look?"

"The same way all oysters look. Like a big blob of mucus. The baby, okay? Start at the beginning."

"The beginning," Kennaday said, "was when a couple of

teenagers, boy and girl, were getting themselves a little afternoon delight underneath the pines. One of them heard a whimpering sound, so they got up off their blanket and started looking around. They found her wrapped up in beach towels."

"Where are these woods?"

"About a hundred yards or so behind an Amish farm. It's out along Route 168, I think. South of New Wilmington."

"She's Amish? The baby?"

"Probably not, considering the beach towels had beer ads on them. But the kids who found her were."

"And you said she had a broken leg and concussion?"

"And tested positive for meth. Well, the towels did. She'd been sucking on one of them all day, it seemed."

"Any indication of how long she'd been there? How she got the injuries?"

"They figure since sometime that morning. Middle of the night, that kind of thing. Otherwise, she appeared fairly well fed."

"How severe were the injuries?"

"Broken leg might be a bit of an exaggeration," he conceded. "It was a stress fracture. The concussion was mild. Laid down hard on the back of her head, that kind of thing."

Though I was wincing with each new bit of information, Kennaday seemed inured to it. He dragged his last dumpling through the brown phoenix chicken sauce and bit it in half.

"When did all this happen?" I asked.

"When was she found? Like I said, last month. About three weeks ago. Two days before the murders."

"And how do those two events tie together?"

He pushed his empty plate and bowl to the side and slid out of the booth. "Let me get some of those oysters first."

He returned a minute later with eight raw oysters in their shells, plus two lemon wedges. After sliding back into the booth, he squeezed lemon juice over the bivalves and immediately seized one in his chopsticks, placed it in his mouth, and swallowed.

I winced again. Just the thought of swallowing a slimy oyster activates my gag reflex. And there sat my new acquaintance sliding one after another into his mouth. I tried to keep my eyes averted, but that perverse part of me kept sneaking a peek. It was like trying to not watch a snake swallowing a slimy, bug-eyed frog.

His grin widened. Why was he enjoying this so much? I got the feeling that he was playing with me, and I did not like that feeling, not in the least. I asked, "What do you know that the police don't?"

He swallowed another oyster, then grinned.

I crossed my chopsticks along the edge of the plate. "If you want to tell me something, Thomas, you need to tell everything. Otherwise, I'm ready to pay my check and leave."

Again he shrugged. "I'm just an interested bystander here. I feel bad for the baby is all. She's going to end up with a foster family, a bunch of strangers. Maybe one foster family after another until she's eighteen. There's no telling what kind of so-called parents she'll be subjected to. Take it from somebody who grew up in the system."

Him, a foster child? If he was trying to make me as interested in him as I was in his story, he was, alas, succeeding. Although I already disliked and distrusted him, that, in truth, only made him more intriguing. What was he up to?

"You need to talk to Phoebe," he told me. "She's a boarder in the house where the murders took place."

"She knows something about the baby?"

"She knows just about everything that happened. She might be the only person alive who does."

"And why hasn't she told all this to the police?"

"Look," he said, and now appeared uncomfortable for the first time since he had sat down. "I'm, uh…" He glanced at the clock on the far wall. "Oh boy, late again," he said, and abruptly slid out of the booth. He stood for just a moment to look down at me. "Talk to Phoebe, man, seriously. She'll clear everything up for you. The Burchette house is right on the main drag, you can't miss it. Big wooden place, two stories and an attic, kind of an ugly green. She works the afternoon shift tomorrow so you can catch her at home until three. She's a good girl, she'll tell you what you need to know."

Then he was striding away, giving me no chance to ask the questions forming in my head. I watched him go out the door, then briskly along the glass front until he could no longer be seen. I hurried to the window, hoping to observe him getting into his vehicle and maybe get a quick look at the license plate. But he was nowhere to be seen. Had he disappeared into Planet Fitness? I would try to track him down there. Why had he been so candid, so straightforward, until he brought up Phoebe? What was his relationship with her? If he knew that she knew everything, didn't *he* know everything too?

He was orchestrating something, that much seemed clear. And if I was to be a player in it, I darn sure wanted to know what the hell was going on. Yes, I was intrigued, but my bullshit meter had kept up a steady beep all the while Kennaday was talking.

I returned to my table to find the server placing the bill for two lunches beside my plate, along with two fortune cookies. I thanked her, then stared at the fortune cookies, more than a little dizzied by the previous twenty minutes. I decided not to crack open the fortune cookies, seeing as how a small Pandora's box had already been tossed into my lap. And that was the last I ever saw or heard from Thomas Kennaday.

3.

A bit more backstory

I used to joke that I am a card-carrying thirty-third-degree introvert, but that's not a very effective selling point for a woman in search of a romantic partner. And all but one of the women in my life have moved on to more fertile ground. How many women want a partner who doesn't like going to parties or concerts or professional sporting events or any noisy venue? Loud noise physically *hurts* my ears, cigarette smoke and other random scents can make me nauseous, fluorescent lighting makes my eyes burn and seems to fog up my thinking. Sometimes, for no reason at all, my skin becomes a raw nerve, so that even a soft feminine hand on my arm can make me recoil.

In short, I'm a pain in the ass to anybody who wants to spend more than an hour or two with me. And there's not a thing that I or medical science can do about it, other than to narcotize me into Zombieland, an option I will not abide.

Over the years I have learned to conceal my more obvious reactions to unpleasant sensory stimuli, and to try to compensate for my aversion to public venues by being attentive and generous and affectionate. But there's only so much a woman can take.

My longest relationship, my marriage, lasted twenty-three years, but only because the only significant contact we had with each other was on the weekends. And even then I was usually able to escape at random times for some healing solitude.

What it all boils down to is the fact that, most of the time, I just want to be left alone. A few solitary hours in the woods might be all I need to recharge my batteries after human contact, or two weeks of no communication whatsoever, or any measure of time in between. Plus, I get restless easily. I have a very low tolerance for boredom. I am always in search of what is new, what is different, what is unique. And this need smashes head-on into my aversion to crowds.

I thank God for motorcycles and creative writing. Both allow me to be part of the larger society while keeping apart from it. I can participate with no physical contact and minimal interaction.

These tendencies of mine go a long way toward explaining not only why I live alone but also how I could get involved in such a convoluted fiasco as the one I am about to relate to you. Yes, I spend most of my time sitting at a desk, but I have also managed, long before the events of this narrative began, to put myself into several life-threatening situations.

I never realized how many times until that question was posed to me by my editor. During a book tour a few years back, my editor hosted a dinner for all her writers attending that particular conference. As we waited for our entrées to arrive at the big round table in a restaurant somewhere in North America—and with me struggling to conceal my discomfort—my editor deftly broke the awkward silence of three female mystery writers, two spouses, and me sitting there staring at our water glasses, and asked, "How many times have each of you come close to death?"

My editor is a very sweet, soft-spoken young woman, always very tactful in her editorial suggestions, so I was a bit startled, and delighted, to hear such a grim question from her.

I was seated on her right. She turned to the writer on her left and asked her to start us off. As it turned out, not one of the other writers or their spouses had ever had a true brush with death. *None?* There must have been nearly 250 cumulative years of living in that bunch, and none of them had ever come close to dying? I could hardly believe it.

It soon fell to me to speak. I said, "Off the top of my head, I can think of at least five."

Later that evening, alone in my hotel room, I recalled four more. Yep, this desk jockey has faced death at least nine times in his life. And that number doesn't include the time I stepped on a rattlesnake or the car or skiing accidents. The more dramatic incidents range from half drowning myself and my wife in class four whitewater rapids to putting an allegedly unspinnable aircraft into a deadly spinning nosedive to nearly going up in a ball of flames at sixty miles an hour on a motorcycle that had suddenly lost its gas tank cap and was splashing gasoline all over my legs and toward the searingly hot exhaust pipes. It stunned even me to realize how many times death had blown its hot breath down my neck.

Little did I know, back when I first counted up my nine escapes from the angel of death, that she wasn't yet done flirting with me.

4.

The place

My current address is in Mercer County, Pennsylvania, which sits two counties below Lake Erie with its western border hard up against Ohio. The town's most distinguishing feature is the county courthouse, whose lighted bell tower can be seen at night from every direction, lending the town a reassuring air of fairness and stability. Like nearly every town everywhere, the town of Mercer looks better from a distance than it does up close.

Just under half of the county's population aged sixteen and above are unemployed. Licensed firearm dealers in the county report approximately one million handgun and long gun transactions each year. Around twelve thousand violent crimes are committed annually with those guns and an undetermined number of unregistered weapons.

A majority of calls received by the police are for domestic violence; the same statistic holds true nationally, according to the National Institute of Justice. Over half of all deaths related to domestic violence involve guns. Most often, we shoot the ones we love.

This is small-town America. If you avoid certain neighborhoods, certain bars, avoid losing your head when an impatient driver cuts you off or tailgates or nearly T-bones you by ignoring traffic signs, if you keep to yourself and the people you know well, if you don't mind driving twenty or thirty miles for groceries or a decent restaurant, bookstore, or mall, a small town can be a peaceful place to live, and even more so if you live a few miles outside of that town. You will hear a siren maybe once a month, and it will almost always fade away into the distance. You can gaze up at a sky full of stars every clear night. You will seldom have to wait in line at the post office, can buy fresh fruit and vegetables and Amish doughnuts every summer at one of several roadside stands, and you can always find a parking space when you need to go to the bank. You will be surrounded by woods and fields and lakes and rivers, any one of which you can get to within minutes. You can enjoy a long hike or motorcycle ride or picnic without having to deal with heavy pedestrian or motorized traffic. You can, if you wish, live a fairly quiet, reclusive life without sacrificing the basic amenities.

Just never forget that the other side of the penny, the side that isn't so shiny, the dirty side, is also a part of every small town and its environs.

Contiguous to the southern border of Mercer County is Lawrence County, home of the village of Bell's Grove, which lies approximately five miles northeast of New Castle, the county seat, and approximately fourteen miles due south of my home. New Castle is famous for two things: the first Warner Brothers movie house, and the city's violent history as home of the Black Hand and subsequent Mafia groups.

Of Bell's Grove I knew almost nothing before my conversation with Kennaday. I had ridden through it many times on my motorcycle, but passing end to end takes hardly more than a minute and allows for no lasting impression other than the one that every small, economically depressed hamlet generates.

Nature's beauty and a soothing solitude by day, drugs and guns, booze and violence and despair by night. That's an oversimplified description of rural America, but not an erroneous one.

5.

The crimes

After my disconcerting lunch with Thomas Kennaday, an hour or so online not only confirmed what he had told me but also filled in a few of the missing details surrounding the murders in Bell's Grove. Lots of other details were left out of the news reports, as the police are wont to do, and this dearth of resolution had generated a fury of speculations and accusations on a couple of chat forums. The interest in the case was so intense outside of my home that again I had to marvel at my earlier lack of awareness of it. Apparently, camera crews as well as print and online reporters—every news source between Pittsburgh and Cleveland—had swarmed both crime scenes when the crimes were discovered, and hung around for days afterward hoping to pick up a crumb or two of uncirculated information, all while yours truly lived in blissful ignorance of all things happening outside his own head. By the time I finally got my ear to the ground, media interest had subsided, though the chat forums' fiery comments had changed from outrage that such a travesty could happen in their neighborhood to complaints about the inefficacy of law enforcement.

The facts, as stitched together from the verified information, follow here in summary form:

September 20: At approximately 3:30 in the afternoon, two unidentified teenagers, one male and one female, appeared at the home of retired GM chemical engineer Richard "Dick" Shaner, with an infant female they had found in the pine woods behind the outbuildings of the adjacent Walter Yoder farm. A 911 call was placed by Shaner. Police arrived at more or less the same time as the paramedics; Baby Doe, as she was named at the hospital, was determined to be approximately four to five months old and suffering from dehydration and a slight concussion; a stress fracture to her right tibia was confirmed by X-ray. Police have been unable to find a match for Baby Doe in local hospital birth records, and have identified no suspect among area women who recently gave birth. The beach towels in which Baby Doe was found were tested for DNA; a representative of the Pennsylvania State Police forensics lab explained, "We found plenty. But it's useless until we find somebody to compare it too." Baby Doe was held for observation in the hospital until the Lawrence County Children and Youth Services placed her with a temporary foster home. The identities of those foster parents are being withheld to preserve their and Baby Doe's privacy. The investigation into Baby Doe's identity and who might have abandoned her is ongoing.

September 22: At approximately 5:15 in the evening, three individuals entered the home of Dianne Burchette (thirty-two, Caucasian) and her two daughters, Michelle "Shelley" Jordan (seven, Caucasian) and LaShonda Burchette (nine, biracial). Also present in the house at that time were Burchette's boyfriend, Barry Faye (forty-one,

Black), who did not reside in the house, and a tenant, Phoebe Hudack (twenty-five, Caucasian). Hudack and the older daughter were in the girls' upstairs bedroom when the intruders let themselves in through the unlocked front door. Faye, Burchette, and Jordan were in the kitchen, relaxing after the family's dinner.

The intruders—identified as Justin Cirillo (twenty-two, Caucasian), Jolene Mrozek (forty-six, Caucasian), and Eddie Hudack (twenty, Caucasian, brother to the tenant)—allegedly proceeded to the kitchen area where they confronted Faye regarding some unknown matter. Phoebe Hudack later reported that she was able to recognize both Faye's and Cirillo's voices through the upstairs register, and that "they were both screaming at each other." The argument, she said, "lasted only a minute or so" before she and LaShonda Burchette, who were playing with the girl's dolls, were startled by four gunshots.

According to Hudack, LaShonda then "jumped up and started running for the stairs," with Hudack chasing after and calling for her to stop. Hudack caught up with the child midway down the stairs, at which time both saw Cirillo backing out of the kitchen with a shotgun in his hands. They froze on the steps, with Hudack holding on to the girl's arm. Cirillo turned and pointed the shotgun at them. Hudack yanked the girl up the stairs just as Cirillo fired again. Both females sustained buckshot wounds in the foot and ankle, with the child sustaining the most injuries. Hudack then locked the girl in the upstairs bathroom and hurriedly called 911 on her cell phone while at the same time retrieving a .38 Special revolver from her own bedroom. She then waited at the top of the stairs—"shaking like a leaf"—for Cirillo to come after her and the girl. When he showed himself at the bottom of the stairs, she fired two times. Both bullets missed him, but he did turn and run, apparently escaping out the front door with Mrozek and the male Hudack. At that time, Phoebe Hudack was unaware of the identity of Cirillo's two companions.

Burchette, Faye, and Jordan were all pronounced dead at the scene, each with a gunshot wound to the chest and neck area. Faye received an additional postmortem shot to his face.

That same night, Justin Cirillo was taken into custody while sitting in a booth at the New Castle Coney Island hot dog shop on Route 18 just north of New Castle. He was arrested without incident. The only information Cirillo would provide to the police was that "Jo (Mrozek) and Eddie (Hudack) didn't do none of it. They was just along for the ride." Cirillo was questioned, placed under arrest, and booked on three counts of first-degree criminal homicide, two counts of third-degree criminal homicide, and one count of criminal trespass. He is being held without bond at the Lawrence County Jail. The location(s) of Jolene Mrozek and Eddie Hudack remain unknown.

Phoebe Hudack told the police that the three deceased individuals and the surviving victims "all knew each other," and that Cirillo and the male Hudack were frequent visitors to the Burchette home. She described Cirillo and Faye's relationship as "not the best, I'd say. I could tell they didn't like each other much, but other than that, I don't know. They seemed to get along most of the time."

She and LaShonda Burchette were treated for their wounds and released. Both are expected to make a full recovery with no long-term damage, thanks to the distance from which the shot was fired. When questioned as to the ownership of the unregistered revolver with which she had defended herself and the girl, Phoebe Hudack told the police that she had found it a week or so earlier "up against a tree in Pearson Park, where I like to go walking on my days off." She said she decided to keep it because she "just had this funny feeling that I was going to need it someday." The police took possession of the revolver. No charges were filed against Phoebe Hudack.

As noted, those two events—the discovery of Baby Doe in the pine woods along a rural road in New Wilmington Township, and the three cold-blooded murders a few miles away in Bell's Grove—took place only two days apart. The facts surrounding the murders are known and clear-cut but for Cirillo's motive, which will come out eventually. Apparently the police have not associated the two events with each other, and have no reason yet to do so. However, Thomas Kennaday strongly insinuated to me that the events *are* related.

He also made, as I recalled, a statement that didn't jibe with the news reports. When he first broached the subject to me at Joy Buffet, he'd said that *four* people had been murdered. Had he misspoken? I doubted it. Everything he'd said to me seemed calculated and deliberate. So who was the fourth dead person? The Hudack boy? Jolene Mrozek? Baby Doe's mother or father? All four were currently missing and/or unknown. Which of them, if any, had been murdered, and by whom? And why?

———

I spent the rest of that evening investigating Kennaday himself, but I could find nothing suspicious about him online except for the most suspicious evidence of all, the fact that there was absolutely *nothing* about him online. No Facebook page, no Twitter account, no Instagram, Pinterest, address or phone number, no hint or sniff or clue or tease. A millennial with no online presence? It could only be deliberate. But why assume a pseudonym? What was he trying to hide?

Because there were no answers to these questions, I set myself the task of filling in the relevant events of those days between the discovery of the baby and the night of the murders, with the hope that by tracking the path of the homicide victims and perpetrators, I might also unearth pertinent information regarding Kennaday and why he had put me on the scent. The only mystery surrounding the murders was a question of why, and this was being vigorously investigated by professionals, but the mystery of who Kennaday is and why he chose me as his pawn was like a splinter digging ever deeper into my flesh. So yes, I was going to be his bloodhound, but only to satisfy my own need to prove myself invulnerable to his or anybody else's manipulation, self-contradicting as those actions might be. Besides, I was on the hunt again, nose to the ground, sniffing out a story. I hadn't been that excited for months.

6.

The baby

E d Phillips comes creaking back from the restroom with small, shuffling steps, holding on to the back of every booth he passes. After he lowers himself in beside Bryce Thompson again, he looks at me and says, "None of you writer fellas ever writes about going to the toilet, not that I've read anyway. I suppose it's because most people do it without hardly thinking about it. But for some of us it's a damn miracle it happens at all anymore. You should write about that."

Thompson says, "I haven't had a decent bowel movement since the morning after Jack Bigelow's funeral."

Dick Shaner says, "That was what, almost a dozen years ago."

"That's what I'm saying," Thompson answers. "They had that big pan of cabbage rolls at the dinner in the church basement afterward, you remember? All that rice and cabbage is what did it. Most satisfying BM I can remember."

"Maybe you should eat cabbage and rice for supper every day," Shaner says.

"You think I haven't tried that?"

"It's the prostate that's to blame," Phillips says.

"Tell me about it." Thompson looks at me to add, "Doctor says it's cancer, but no use operating at my age. Just let nature take its course. Easy for him to say, forty-some years old. Probably shits like an elephant."

The other two men do not react to this except with knowing smiles and nods. Together the three men have lived, by my guess, nearly two hundred sixty years. Thompson appears to be in the worst health of the three, but that doesn't mean he's the oldest. Dick Shaner wins that distinction at a vibrant eighty-nine. A former chemical engineer for GM, and a widower for the past six years, he is still a slender five seven, with rosy cheeks, an easy laugh, and a full head of white hair. His language is more formal and correct than that of the other two men, Thompson a retired machinist, Phillips a farmer who sold his herd and fields to his son for "thirty cents on the dollar."

Shaner had been mentioned frequently in the news clippings, so he was the man I called the day before this breakfast to ask what he could tell me about the baby girl discovered in the woods behind his home. Kennaday had told me that the location was in the pine woods behind an Amish farm, and it was, but the adjacent Shaner property had a dirt lane that had accommodated the law enforcement vehicles. Shaner promised to allow me access to the woods in exchange for breakfast for him and two buddies at the Roosevelt Diner next morning, 6:30 in the a.m.

By 6:45 the diner is packed, mostly with retirees, though there is one table with three young men in their early twenties. All three wear jeans and T-shirts and work boots, and are bent over their meals, not speaking, raising forks to their mouths as if the effort to do so is exhausting. I turn away from them to see Shaner smiling at me. "Looks like they indulged a little too much last night," I say.

"Look at what they're eating."

From my position there appears to be fried chicken on one plate, a hot meatloaf sandwich on the other. The third customer sits with his back to me. Shaner says, "They work the night shift at the forge. Come in dog-tired most every morning."

Phillips says, "I'd trade places with them in a minute."

"We all would," Thompson adds.

We are seated at a table that is usually positioned up against the wide front window but has been pulled out a couple of feet to accommodate a fourth chair. I feel the morning sun on my back, and the humming vibration of the glass when a large truck rumbles down the street. The wide, high-ceilinged room with its pounded tin ceiling and elaborate moldings hardly fits the definition of a diner. In the early 1900s it was a bank, and its imposing stone edifice still attests to that fact. Now the restaurant takes up the entire first floor, with a couple of small apartments on the second floor. According to rumor, the building, in the time between being a bank and becoming a restaurant, housed a "reading room" on the first floor, and, above it, five bedrooms that could be rented by the hour. The ladies at the Historical Society claim that no such thing ever happened, yet I couldn't help but notice the twenty-two-year gap between the closing of the bank and the opening of the diner.

After our eggs arrive, and I am the only one to thank the server— which brings her up short, and prompts from her a "Why, you're very welcome!"—Shaner gives me a wink across the table, then starts talking.

"So these two teenagers were out there in the woods having at it. The paper doesn't mention that. Must've been an hour or so after noon, maybe later. I don't bother looking at the clock much these days. Amish kids, a boy and a girl, both about sixteen, more or less."

"You must have been watching them pretty close, huh?" Phillips says with a grin. "Else how'd you know they were going at it?"

"Of course I was watching. Had the binoculars on them the whole time." Another wink. His eyes are clear and bright, and I make a mental note to inquire of his secret to such good health and equanimity.

He says, "It's a fairly regular place for the locals. By which I mean the Amish. We've got eight families of them within a mile of here. If I'm out on the porch swing, I can usually spot them crossing along the tree line behind Yoder's outbuildings."

"The young'uns don't even wait for rumspringa anymore," Thompson adds. "They're comin' into heat younger and younger these days."

Phillips snorts. "If that ain't the pot calling the kettle black, I don't know what is."

"They sneak along one at a time," Shaner continues. "First one, then ten minutes later the other one. Like nobody's gonna know what they're up to. There are no windows on the outbuildings, which is why those woods are such a popular place. Their folks are all busy inside, busy with the chores or reading their Bibles."

"Busy humping each other's wives," Phillips says.

"Or else the sheep," says Thompson.

Shaner rolls his eyes at me. "You just sorta have to ignore these two. They fancy themselves to be a comedy team."

"Like we were pure as the driven snow when we were kids," Phillips says.

Thompson is quick with a rejoinder. "Yeah, but Dick and me only fooled around with two-legged girls. You preferred the four-legged ones, as I recall."

Phillips takes it good-naturedly. Says, "As *I* recall it, you had a special fondness for the Guernsey I called Bambi."

"A fine, fine specimen," Thompson says.

They're having fun with me, trying to shock me, I suspect. But Shaner's narrative, with constant asides from Thompson and Phillips, promises to take all morning. To Shaner, I say, "According to the news reports, the kids brought the baby to you. The Yoder house is closer, right?"

"Yoder's an elder in their church," Thompson explains. "They're not going to go to him or else he'll know what they've been up to."

"Aha," I answer.

Shaner says, "I promised them I wouldn't give out their names. The cops were good about keeping them out of it. The girl was a mess already. It was all I could do to get her to quit bawling."

"What kind of condition was the baby in?" I ask.

"Pretty good, considering. I saw the bump on its head, smelled the dirty diaper, of course, but you can't see a stress fracture. She looked to me like she couldn't have been out there very long."

Upon being presented with the infant, Shaner recognized its scent and laid the infant on the kitchen counter to delicately unwrap what he referred to as "a couple of old beach towels. She just laid there looking at me, never a whimper out of her. But I could tell by her little eyes that she was hurting." He and the female teenager then cleaned the baby in the sink and examined her for injuries.

"The kids were scared to death. They wanted to skedaddle," he says. "But I told them if they did, I was going to let the police know where to find them. They stayed."

Upon examination of the child, Shaner discovered two sources of inflammation, one on the infant's right leg just below the knee, the other on the back of her skull. Paramedics arrived and confirmed a possible stress fracture on the tibia, and a probable concussion that might have resulted from either a fall or a deliberate blow.

Both teenagers were questioned by the police, then were allowed to hurry home with a stern warning about their behavior, plus a promise that their identities would not be revealed. Police also interviewed Shaner that day, as well as the entire Walter Yoder family, none of whom had any further information to provide. "Those woods," Shaner says, "are wide-open to anybody who wants to go in there. It wouldn't be hard to come and go from there sight unseen from any of three directions."

"And the police still have no idea who she is?"

"If they do," Phillips says, "they're keeping it to themselves."

Every state plus the District of Columbia has some form of the Safe Haven program, which allows parents and guardians to safely abandon an infant; states can specify different places that represent Safe Haven, and different maximum ages for the children. Pennsylvania allows for an infant up to twenty-eight days old to be legally surrendered to a hospital or placed in the custody of a police officer. Most states report more illegal abandonments than safe surrenders. No state includes abandonment in the woods as a safe surrender.

Kennaday had told me that Phoebe Hudack, the tenant in the house where three murders had taken place, "knows everything." Would that include information about the abandoned baby and the fourth murder? I was determined to do whatever I could to find out. But first I wanted to see those woods.

———

Red pines tend to lose their lower branches as they grow, which allows for more pleasant walking. The piney scent, too, is a draw for me, an incense that adds to a sense of sanctification when one enters the trees' dimness. As a boy I often spent afternoons lying on a bed of dry needles, looking up through the branches at the way sunlight splinters on its way down. Sometimes I would fall asleep, then awaken an hour or two later with the sun coming in from the side, pink or orange now instead of golden, as if it had slipped along the curvature of the firmament to make for me a softer day through which I could now return home.

The pines I entered from Dick Shaner's dirt lane took me back to those days, though no golden sunlight accompanied me that morning. The sky was dark and low, the wind mournful through the creaking trees. I could hear a cello in the sound the wind made, uilleann pipes in the scraping and screeching branches and the thin, protesting trunks.

I wished I could ask the trees what they had seen and heard.

There was, of course, no visible evidence regarding the brutal act that had happened beneath those pines, though evidence of numerous visitors had not been smoothed over. Law enforcement and others had left paths and piles of disturbed needles, so it was easy to identify the general area where the baby had been found. And that was all the reason I had for coming there, just to absorb the ambiance and perhaps to glean from it a glimmer of what the baby and her abandoner might have felt.

I lay in the center of the irregular circle of disturbed needles and gazed upward. Patches of gray sky could be seen, as could thick, heavy clouds with their underbellies dark. The air was dense with humidity that day, yet fragrant with the incense of pine. Despite the likelihood of getting wet I was not eager to hurry home to the tiny suburban enclave I had come to resent. At least one of my neighbors would be using his lawn tractor to suck up leaves as they fell to earth, chasing them from tree to tree, and the three noisy dogs on the other side of my house would be continuing their daily chorale of barking at nothing. So I contented myself with lying quiet and still, the coolness of the ground seeping into my shoulders and the backs of my legs, just as I had done so frequently as a boy, hoping then for something extraordinary to happen, some miracle of divine intervention that would obviate my ignorance, my shyness and timidity, my insignificance. As a boy I would imagine that a cloud sailing above the treetops was an angel coming to my rescue, and that soon she would scoop me into her arms and carry me off to a happier place.

Despite a few sporadic incidents since boyhood of what I can only explain as divine intervention, I remain uncertain as to whether or not angels exist. But I did take some comfort that day in squinting through the branches, imagining the way an angel might have hovered over Baby Doe, keeping her warm and safe and loved until two Amish teenagers, startled out of their amorous embraces, were moved to search her out and save her.

7.

The tenant, first interview

The next morning, I read through my notes again, did more research online, and compiled the summary of events that appears in the previous chapter. All morning the sky remained a uniform gray, not dark but more of a dirty white. There had been a gusting wind the previous night but I'd heard no rain. Wet leaves, most of them yellow or brown, now lay stuck to the boards of my back deck.

This year the weather had been fickle since February, with temperatures dropping and rising crazily, the skies usually thick with slowly diffusing chemtrails and weird, unlikely cloud formations.

So imagine my surprise when I rose from my desk just before noon and glanced outside again. It was as if some magician had whipped the gray sheet off the sky. Not a single wisp of cloud remained. The sky was now robin-egg blue, every treetop glowing, the reflections on the lake as vivid as a Matisse landscape. And the temperature had already hit sixty-nine. I couldn't help it; I giggled like a schoolgirl: *Riding time!*

I decided to make first contact with Phoebe Hudack in person rather than by phone; I found a listing for D. Burchette in Bell's Grove, but it didn't seem appropriate for me to call Phoebe on a dead woman's line. Besides, most people have a harder time saying no to a real face than to a disembodied voice. And certain women, I had learned over the years, find a man on a motorcycle irresistible. With luck I would be able to park my bike in such a position that when Phoebe opened her door to me in Bell's Grove, she would see Candy—my sexy candy-apple-red cruiser—parked at the curb, and a scruffy-bearded biker smiling from her doorstep. Anyway, it was worth a shot, and it gave me a good excuse for riding.

I counted thirty-one modest homes lining the half-mile-long Main Street. There is also a Church of the Brethren, another church that has been converted into a community center, a bar, several boarded-up buildings, and, on the southern end of town, a low-income apartment complex. Surrounded by woods, and approachable by way of two winding blacktop roads serviced by the township, Bell's Grove, like many small towns in the area, conveys an air of weary resignation to its inevitable decline.

The ugly green Burchette house in Bell's Grove was, as Kennaday promised, impossible to miss. Phoebe Hudack responded to my knock promptly and invited me in. More about that first interview will follow shortly, but first I will provide an introduction to Phoebe based on information plucked in bits and pieces from my research and the four conversations I had with her.

As it turned out, Ms. Hudack is a young woman who knows both sides of small-town life. She was a popular girl in high school, pretty in an average sort of way, a solid B- student. She worked hard for her grades, and if not for the science and math classes, she would have been an honors student. Any class that required memorization was difficult for her. "I was good at art and music and anything creative. But trying to remember stuff... I don't know if there was something wrong with my brain or what. I just couldn't do it."

She was a willowy five five back then, careful about what she ate, usually a quiet girl who sought no attention for herself, though she could be funny and loud around her friends, most of whom were art and music nerds like her. She attended all of the school's sporting events, sang alto in the choir, always had a date for the dances, and was even nominated for the prom court her sophomore year.

It was in the middle of her senior year that she stumbled onto a downhill path. Mid-December. An old boyfriend home from college on semester break introduced her to cocaine. She had already decided that she didn't care for the taste of alcohol and didn't like weed because it made her paranoid. Cocaine, on the other hand... oh, wow, cocaine.

Before the old boyfriend headed back to Penn State, at a party on New Year's Eve, he asked, "Ever smoke meth?" and fired up a pipe. And meth... *Oh my god.* She had never felt so awake. So capable and smart and confident. And the sex! "Unbelievable. Just... the best there ever was."

The next day, the boyfriend was gone. Back to college two and a half hours away. One hundred forty-six miles. And her without a car. No matter; he had introduced Phoebe to Davy Moore, who, though not half as handsome or sweet as his predecessor, was more than willing to hook her up with whatever she desired. No charge for somebody as pretty as her. No monetary payment, that is. Not in the beginning anyway.

For a while, she smoked only on Saturday nights. Problem was, the rest of the week was a drag. Friends, poetry, indie music, drawing, even her cockapoo Miss Bitch—all the things she used to adore—were now boring with a capital B. Her grades dropped, her friends fell away, and in May she skipped graduation to get high with Davy and his buds. That was the first time she pulled a train. She hated herself afterward, but what else was a girl supposed to do? Besides, she wasn't even in her body at the time, but was floating in the ether somewhere, conscious of only the distant throbbing music that flowed through her like smoke.

Where were her parents all those months? Good question, usual answer. Phoebe's variation on the neglectful parents theme was a father whose whereabouts were unknown, a mother who worked three minimum-wage part-time jobs six days a week, treated herself to a night out every Saturday, slept off the hangover most of every Sunday. When Phoebe packed up her things that summer and told her mother she had a job with a cleaning service, her mother was happy, said, "All you need now is a good man." For both of them, the next six years passed in a blur.

By the time Thomas Kennaday met Phoebe Hudack, she was twenty-five years old, had been sent to the hospital twice for overdoses that nearly killed her, had called the police three times to report being beaten up by whatever man she was with at the time, had sobered up and backslid a half dozen times, and was now trying her best to stay away from bad company and every drug harder than weed, which no longer made her paranoid. Life made her paranoid.

Despite a wariness toward others engendered by her troubled years, she was now working thirty-five hours per week at the New Castle Walmart and taking courses online for an associate's degree in medical billing and coding. Ten months prior to the murders, she became a boarder in Dianne Burchette's big clapboard home in Bell's Grove.

Living in an economically depressed neighborhood only a few miles from one of the nation's most dangerous cities means keeping your eyes and ears open and your head down. Phoebe Hudack has been doing both since getting sober. A considerate and unobtrusive tenant, she didn't mind pitching in with the housecleaning and babysitting. Burchette, who had her own share of problems when young, proved to be an empathetic big

sister for Phoebe, and it was her landlady's friendship and kindness, coupled with the love Phoebe received from Shelley Jordan
and LaShonda Burchette, Dianne Burchette's two prepubescent
daughters, that reignited in her a childlike belief in the possibility of a good and positive future. "And having Barry Faye here
most of the time, it just made us all feel a little bit safer. He was
a big man but always very gentle. If not for him we'd have been
a household of all girls."

All of the previous information concerning Phoebe Hudack is,
to my mind, wholly credible, though based by necessity on my
memory and scribbled notes. Not so for the revelations she imparted
to me. I will start again at the beginning of my acquaintance with
Ms. Hudack, which began the day after my visit to the pine woods,
but will compress our conversation to the relevant points. In this
and the three additional interview transcripts, **P** stands for Phoebe,
S for Silvis.

She opens the door to my knock, and I tell her my name, that I am
a writer and that a mutual acquaintance named Thomas Kennaday
suggested that she might be able to fill me in on some of the details
of the triple homicide committed in that house weeks earlier. Her
eyes go wide at the mention of his name, and she smiles so ingenu-
ously, like a child receiving a gift.

P: So that's who you are! He didn't tell me your name.

She escorts me into the living room and waves a hand toward a battered green wing chair adjacent to an equally worn brocaded sofa.

S: [*sits*] So he told you I might show up?

Phoebe wedges herself into the corner of the sofa, crosses both arms over her belly and leans toward me.

P: How is Thomas? How is he doing?

S: He's fine, I guess. I met him yesterday for about an hour or so. You must have talked by phone since then? You and Thomas?

P: No, it's been a while. A few days before all the stuff happened. Did he say anything about where he's living now? Or about coming to see me again? [*Tears pool in her eyes.*]

Have I misheard, or did she misstate the chronology of events? It sounds as if Kennaday had mentioned or at least alluded to my visit long before I met him.

S: Let's start with *you*, okay? Are you from Bell's Grove originally?

P: No, but I grew up not far from here. The south side of New Castle. [*She talks freely about herself for several minutes.*] And I guess that's it, that's all there is to know about me. I've never done anything very interesting in my life.

S: How did you come to meet Thomas Kennaday?

He came into her life out of nowhere. She was working the express checkout line at the Walmart on the western edge of New Castle when Kennaday placed a small plastic container of General Tso's chicken and a bottle of vitaminwater on the belt. September 9, a Wednesday.

P: He was like, I don't know, like the boys I first dated in junior high. So clean-cut. A real straight-edge kind of guy. I could never figure out why he liked me. [*A couple of beats pass.*] I got dizzy just looking at him. Those eyes and that smile, I couldn't think straight. I bagged his chicken and water without even ringing them up.

He pointed out her error and they both laughed, then he invited her to share his lunch.

P: Just like that. I've said maybe ten words to him and he's asking me to have a picnic with him!

She wasn't due for a break for another thirty minutes but he didn't mind waiting. She agreed to meet him outside the garden center's rear entrance at a grassy area at one end of the parking lot. That same night she met him again at "a really nice house" near the center of New Castle, a place he was caretaking for the month "for friends." Over the next ten days she spent several afternoons or evenings with Kennaday in that house.

P: It wasn't all sex either. We talked a lot. He had a way of getting me to open up. I told him practically my whole life story, more or less right up to the minute we met. He told me a lot of stuff about him too. Stuff that, you know, I found hard to believe at first.
S: Such as?
P: I'm not supposed to tell you that yet.
S: Why not?
P: Because it will get confusing and you won't remember it.

I pull my cell phone out of my side pocket.

P: No, I'm sorry, you can't use that.

S: No one else will hear any of it. This is how I take my notes
sometimes.

P: I'm sorry, you can't. He said to tell you that you can't record or
write anything down.

S: Thomas told you that?

P: [*nods*] He said there are rules. We have to follow the rules or we
can't play the game.

S: I don't consider this a game. Do you?

P: It's just the way he talked. I'm not supposed to tell you anything
unless you agree with the rules.

S: Are there any other rules?

P: I'm not allowed to mention him to anyone but you.

S: When did he tell you all this?

P: The last time I saw him. Like I said, three days before we lost
Diney and Barry and Shell.

A swirl of disorientation overtakes me. Kennaday mentioned me
to her three days before the murders, two days before the discovery
of Baby Doe, and *weeks* before he met me?

I look around the room, everything clean and orderly but mis-
matched, old and well worn. A hodgepodge of tastes and eras. Then
I spot the speckling of small white circles on the far wall, dozens
of them above the stairs, and again, in lesser number, on the side
of the stairs. Buckshot. The holes have been spackled and filled.

P: [*follows my eyes*] They didn't get shot in here. It was out in the
kitchen it happened. Over at the stairs is where he shot at me
and Shonnie.

I can't seem to take my eyes off those little white circles on the pale blue wall, each hole meticulously spackled, a wide cluster of tiny white orbs on a summer sky.

P: It's a relief to be able to talk about him to somebody. It's been so hard to keep quiet, what with all the questions I've been asked.

My train of thought has been derailed. I struggle to get it back on the tracks.

S: You've told all this to the police, right?

P: Everything I could. I was upstairs with the girls, so we didn't even know that Eddie and Justin and Jo had come in down here. Not until I heard Justin and Barry yelling at each other. And then the gun went off. Four times. Shonnie and me, we just froze. Till Shon went racing for the stairs and I had to go after her.

Her cheeks are wet now, eyes full of mourning.

P: I pulled her back up the stairs just in time, or else we'd have been in the obituaries too.

S: Both of you were wounded?

P: [*leans forward to touch her foot*] Just once, here on the heel. Shonnie got hit three times on the ankle and foot. The deputy told me there were thirty-six little balls in the shell, so we were lucky to be the whole way across the room from him.

I say nothing for a few moments and imagine what her nights must be like now, what monstrous thoughts go creeping through her dreams. Yet I am troubled by the incongruity of dates she mentioned earlier. Obviously, she is grieving, and probably also confusing dates. Grief has a way of scrambling memories and shuffling events.

S: But you've told the police nothing about Thomas?

P: He told me I couldn't, and I didn't. I've never mentioned him to anyone but you.

S: And why me?

P: He said a writer would come. He didn't tell me your name. And he didn't say when. He didn't say it would be today. He just told me to be ready.

S: [*confused*] Let me get this straight. It's been over a month since you last saw or spoke to Thomas Kennaday. That's when he told you that you should keep quiet until...until what? Until a writer showed up?

P: [*nods*] He said I should tell the police the facts about the shooting but nothing about him. That I should pretend like there never was a him, you know? Until a writer showed up and asked to talk to me. And not somebody from a newspaper. A real writer. The kind who writes books. Then I could talk about Thomas but only according to the rules.

S: But the only time I ever spoke with him was *two days ago.*

Phoebe shrugs, as if the incongruity is of no importance.

S: But doesn't that strike you as strange?

P: [*smiles*] It's all been very strange.

S: [*tries to refocus*] How much do you know about him?

P: That's just it. You can't imagine someone like him with me, can you? I couldn't either. I still can't. That's the other reason why I won't tell anybody else about us; nobody will believe me saying I spent time with a guy like him. I kept wanting to take a photo of him, but he wouldn't let me do that either. That's how I knew he was going to dump me sooner or later. I knew what I was to him. Anyway, I thought I did. Right up until he gave me the gun and told me what I needed to do with it.

I don't even have time to ask *what gun, do what,* before a look of panic lights up her eyes.

P: Wait, wait, I wasn't supposed to tell you that yet. Forget that I told you that, okay?

S: Are you talking about the .38 Special the police confiscated?

P: I can't tell you yet. Just forget I even mentioned it, okay?

S: How can I forget it?

P: Well, we just won't talk about it now. We can't. Later I will. There's a lot more I'm allowed to tell you but not today.

Something about this interview feels very wrong.

S: Why are you allowed to tell *me* things, but not the police?

P: I asked him the same thing! And he said it was because we needed you for the twelve. And I said the twelve what? And he said the divine twelve, the three doorways from each side, north, south, east, and west. And I said "Thomas, I don't know what any of that means." And he said, "Never mind. Don't worry about it, okay? We're not all assembled yet. That's all you need to know right now. I'll fill you in on everything at the appropriate time." And that's what I'm supposed to do with you too. You see? Everything at the appropriate time.

She smiles, then looks past me, a quick glance at the clock on the cable box.

P: I have to get ready for work now anyway. I want to spend the weekend with Shonnie doing something fun for her, but you can come back Sunday if you want to. He said you will. Four sessions, he said. Counting today. And then you can do whatever you want with the information.

S: Why four sessions? Why not one or two longer sessions?
P: Because the number four is important, he said.
S: In what way?
P: [*smiles*] He said you would want to know that.

My confusion is quickly turning to anger. I have always been a
very private person, willing to open up to only a very few special
people in my life. A common nightmare among introverts is to
appear naked or wearing no pants in the midst of a crowd, a meta-
phor for having their privacy exposed. And I am now beginning to
feel very exposed indeed.

P: Four reasons.

Her gaze goes into the distance, as if she is calling up a memory.

P: Four is the number for order and the completion of justice. That's
    one reason. It's also the number that connects a person's body,
    spirit, and soul to the physical world. And it's the fourth astrologi-
    cal sign, Cancer.

I am a Cancer. Probably not a difficult fact for Kennaday to
uncover online. But here is his mouthpiece, an uneducated young
woman who has so far evinced no apparent interest in spirituality
or mysticism, speaking of the tripartite nature of man?

S: That's only three reasons.
P: The four Gospels. Matthew was speaking to the Jews, Mark to
    the Romans, Luke to the Greeks, and John to the Christians. I
    really don't understand what that's supposed to mean, but he
    said that you will.

What I know is that the Gospel of Matthew depicts Jesus as the King, Mark depicts him as the servant of God, Luke as the Son of Man, and John as the Son of God. How any of that corresponds with the murders in the Burchette home, I have no idea. Ditto the reference to the number twelve—the divine twelve, as some call it. I know just enough about the divine twelve to make me twelve times more confused: twelve months in a year, twelve signs of the zodiac, twelve hours in a day, twelve in a night, twelve notes in an octave, twelve eggs in a dozen, twelve jurors in a jury, and so forth. The Masons allegedly had twelve hand signs or gestures with which they secretly communicated with each other. Christ had twelve disciples and there were twelve tribes of Israel. Twelve is the most frequently repeated number in the Bible. In numerology the number symbolizes universal harmony and completion.

As for Thomas's statement to Phoebe about the twelve divided into four sets of three doorways, that was an echo of Ezekiel's trip to Heaven, when he was shown the Holy Temple of the New Jerusalem, on which each of the four exterior walls had three doors.

But what does *any* of it have to do with *me*? I am supposed to be part of some divine group of twelve? *Me?* It makes zero sense. Negative sense. Anti-sense.

P: I'm sorry, but I have to get ready for work now or I'm going to be late.

S: All right. All right. But I really need to know who this Kennaday guy is and what you two are up to.

P: [*smiles, then stands*] Come back at the same time on Sunday and I'll tell you more.

S: Wait, please. Just another minute or two? I apologize for my impatience. Just a couple more questions will help me to get my head straight.

P: I can't, I'm sorry. He said a half hour the first time and no more. The other interviews will be longer.

I resent my confusion, but more than that I resent the feeling of being manipulated, whether the strings are being pulled by Phoebe Hudack or Thomas Kennaday. Who the hell is he anyway?

S: I don't like rules, Phoebe. Maybe I'll just walk away from this and forget all about it.

P: [*still smiling, eyes going soft and sympathetic*] He said you won't.

8.

The victims

B arry Faye was the first and the last to be shot.

A third-year employee of the B&D Metals Recycling center just west of the New Castle corporate line, Faye earned fourteen dollars an hour for inspecting, sorting, and processing scrap metal when it first arrived at the center. It was dirty, rusty, laborious work. Sometimes he had to use a hand tool to separate the metal from nonmetal or to grind off a jagged edge that could puncture a man's hand. The rest of the day was spent lugging and dragging and hefting pieces into their proper bins or onto a forklift.

"He was a good worker," his foreman said. "That's about all we expect of anybody here. I can't tell you a thing about his personal life because I don't know nothing. He came to work on time, got along, did his job, and went home. That made him a pretty solid guy in my book."

No illegal drugs were found on or in his body at the time of death. In his jeans pocket he was carrying two tabs of the prescription painkiller Percodan, a combination of aspirin and oxycodone, with the latter ingredient being an opioid. The usual dosage for moderate to severe pain is one tab every six hours. A sheriff's department detective, I'm calling him Detective Smathers, reported that none of the local pharmacies had a record of Percodan being prescribed to Barry Faye, but that he was known to have suffered whiplash in a drunken driving crash four years earlier.

According to an individual with the online handle of Poncey, commenting on a chat forum, the medical examiner had explained to him or to somebody he knew or to somebody he knew who knew somebody—it was never clear where Poncey got his information, despite my repeated inquiries via the forum—that the four shots Cirillo fired in the kitchen had come in such rapid succession as to make any certainty about the order impossible for all but the last shot, but that the blood spatters and the final position of the bodies suggested a likely scenario: Faye, standing with his back to the sink until he turned to see the intruders and engage in an argument with Justin Cirillo, was shot in the chest and went down. Cirillo then turned the twenty-gauge pump-action Winchester Defender on Dianne Burchette, standing a couple of feet to the left of Faye while partially concealed behind an open refrigerator door; she took most of the T-rated buckshot in her upper shoulder and neck. The little girl, seven-year-old Michelle Jordan, the victim closest to the shooter, was shot in the upper chest while sitting at the kitchen table, an open coloring book in front of her.

Because of the unreliable provenance of that information, a call to the office of the Lawrence County medical examiner and coroner was warranted. An assistant in that office first suggested that I put in a claim for the autopsy reports, but he eventually did confirm the scenario suggested on the chat forum. "Yep, sounds about right," he said. "The shooter unloaded one in Faye's face before leaving the kitchen, but the man was already dead."

He would offer no opinion as to the nature of Cirillo's gripe with Faye and Burchette, no clue as to the motive. "There's only one person who can answer that," he said. "And so far, all he's been willing to say is 'I don't remember.'"

"Was the shotgun registered?"

"Not to him it wasn't. Sheriff's office tracked it to a home break-in. The owner used it for turkey hunting, he said. A dentist over around Harlansburg. Reported it missing thirteen months ago."

———

Dianne Alecia Burchette, called Diney by her friends, had been married once, at the age of seventeen. The marriage lasted one month short of two years and produced no children. She then reassumed her maiden name, which was also allocated a year later to her first born, LaShonda. A later affair produced another daughter, Shelley Jordan. The girl's father was not known to have ever had steady employment or place of residence; he could not be reached to be informed of his daughter's death, nor did he attend her memorial service. Initially I could find no information pertaining to LaShonda Burchette's biological father, last name Christy, but was later informed by Phoebe Hudack that, according to Dianne Burchette, LaShonda's father had enlisted in the army shortly after the end of his brief affair with Dianne and was now finishing out his military career as a recruiter at the Kahului, Hawaii, station; although married and with four children from that marriage, he visited LaShonda at least once a year, returning for a week each summer to take both girls to Kennywood, Splash Lagoon, and wherever else they wished to go. Sergeant Christy had also called his daughter every few months and congratulated her on every elementary school achievement. It was understood by Phoebe Hudack that Dianne Burchette had kept Christy informed as to his daughter's development.

LaShonda, Phoebe told me, spoke often about moving to Kahului to attend high school and live with her "other family." Now that her mother and sister were gone, she "plans to go there as soon as her dad can get here and take her." Phoebe did not know for certain, but felt that Christy had implied to her during their most recent phone conversation that "his wife isn't happy about the idea."

LaShonda's father, but not Jordan's, paid child support as ordered by the court. That monthly check along with a monthly welfare stipend for Burchette and her children, food stamps and WIC vouchers, brought Burchette's official total monthly income to approximately $2200. That sum put her just under the HUD eligibility threshold for a housing subsidy, so she did not include on her update reports the $350 paid to her by Phoebe Hudack every month.

No notable achievements or triumphs marked Dianne Burchette's life. She probably grew up expecting none. We all come into life with genetic blueprints for how we will confront the world, but our environments exert a powerful influence on those blueprints. An environment of poverty and violence will generally produce one of two results—either a steely resolve to rise above the degradation of such a milieu, or a surrender to it. Burchette, according to a couple of her neighbors, managed to pull herself only a rung or two above the life her parents gave her. She did what she needed to do to get by. Yet by all accounts she was a devoted mother who wanted far more for her daughters than she thought herself capable of. She supervised their homework, made certain they had healthy diets and clean if secondhand clothing, and routinely exhorted them to excel as students, with an expectation that both would one day attend a good college. She did not squander the little money that came her way but routinely deposited five or ten dollars into college bank accounts in her children's names. She was the epitome of kindness to elderly neighbors and often cleaned and ran errands for them.

"She was a very thoughtful person," Phoebe Hudack said. "And a great landlady. Until I met Thomas, she was my only real friend."

———

Michelle Jordan, always referred to as Shelley or Shell, was "a bit of a drama queen," according to Hudack. But everybody "just loved her to death." Like many second or third children, she sometimes fell victim to sibling jealousy, yet often crawled into her sister's bed at night instead of sleeping in her own. Her favorite activities were coloring and drawing, and her most recent artwork, like her sister's report cards, always remained posted on the refrigerator until a new one was completed.

"Personally," Hudack said during one of our interviews, "I think she was probably smarter than all of us, including Shonnie, and that's saying something. She was always flitting around like a butterfly, pretending that the floor was an ocean and the rugs were little islands full of flowers, stuff like that. Just out of nowhere she could come up with some remark that made her sound like a little professor or something. I don't know where she got them. She was only in first grade for a couple of months, but boy, she was sharp as a tack. I cry every time I think about her being gone, which is still almost all the time."

Shelley Jordan's tombstone, paid for by her classmates and teacher, is of polished black granite in the shape of a box two inches thick. The white laser engravings depict a child angel on her knees, praying; three butterflies are frozen in midflutter above her name, the dates of her birth and death, and the words in script, *God's garden has need of little flowers. You will always be remembered and loved.*

———

LaShonda Burchette—"Call me Shon or Shonnie, okay? I know it sounds like a boy's name but I like that about it. Not that I want to be a boy or anything, but boys are supposed to be tougher than girls and they're not"—is small for nine, only a couple of inches taller than her little sister was. "We could almost wear the same clothes," she told me. "The only real difference is my feet are bigger. Mom says that means I'm going to be tall one day."

It is impossible to know if she uses the present tense out of denial or simply youthful error, but the nine-year-old wears the face and posture of abject sorrow. She all but buries her face in Phoebe Hudack's side as the two sit huddled together on the living room sofa. This brief encounter takes place during my second visit to the Bell's Grove home. Phoebe agreed to allow me to speak with the girl only after I promised to "go easy," which to Phoebe meant not referring to death or loss or murder. I readily agreed. "I need you to promise," she said. I promised again.

The girl's features are striking, angular yet delicate. Her eyes are the darkest shade of brown I have ever seen, her complexion a tawny beige. She wears her caramel-colored hair, which is only a shade or two darker than her skin, in thick dreadlocks bundled into two ponytails. She sits with both legs up on the sofa, feet bare, and keeps flexing her toes or rubbing her feet together as we talk. On the outside of her right foot are two pink circles of freshly scarred skin, each the diameter of a number two pencil, with another one just above the ankle bone. For the most part she holds her head lowered, and when she looks at me it is only a quick peek before averting her gaze again.

"So what's your favorite subject in school?" I ask.

"Gym class," she says. "Especially the climbing rope. I can do it faster than *anybody*." A note of aggression is discernible in her last statement—a petulance that, if allowed to mature into a dogged determination to not just survive but excel, will serve her well as she navigates the difficult days ahead.

"You're in third grade now?"

"*Fourth* grade."

"Fourth grade, sorry. So what's your second favorite subject?"

"Mmm, I don't know really. Maybe lunch." She giggles at this, then looks up at Phoebe for approval.

Phoebe, with one arm around the girl, smiles and kisses the side of her head. "She's good at everything. She's at the top of her class in every subject."

It is difficult to know where to take this conversation when forbidden to mention the wounds on her feet, her mother's and sister's deaths. Can I ask her impressions of Cirillo, Mrozek, and Phoebe's brother Eddie? No. Nor would it do any good; no doubt both she and Phoebe are inflamed with anger against them. And the child is obviously uncomfortable in my presence.

"Well, I can see that you're a very strong and beautiful young woman. Thank you for letting me get to know you better."

"It's okay," she says, though it comes out in a whisper.

A little nod from me to Phoebe ends the conversation. She kisses Shonnie's head again and gently suggests that the girl should go upstairs.

Shonnie holds tight to Phoebe for several seconds, then pulls away, stands, mutters "Bye" to me, and races up the stairs.

My second conversation with Phoebe Hudack will follow in a future chapter.

9.

The perps

Eddie Hudack, Phoebe's younger brother by five years, is still at large as I write this; his sister is my principal source of this information. "Personally, I think it was fetal alcohol syndrome," she said after mentioning his learning disabilities. "Our mom was into a lot of stuff back then. I remember the rage she went into in the doctor's office when he told her she was pregnant. She must've been four or five months by then, because that happened in winter. I remember how the windows outside the clinic were all frosty and frozen looking, and the snow sticking to it along the sills and stuff. Then Eddie was born in April. April Fool's Day, in fact."

She shook her head, eyes lowered. "She joked about it, which I just hated. Called him her April fool."

Now she looked up at me, her eyes glimmering with either pain or anger, and probably both. "I loved him enough for both of us, though. I always told him that we didn't need her, we could take care of ourselves. And we did. I was seventeen when she died from an overdose, so he was twelve. He cried for days afterward, like he'd lost something really important in his life. I felt just the opposite."

The grandmother on her father's side moved into the Hudack home until Phoebe reached the age of majority, then for the next few years served as young Eddie's principal babysitter. "She had a hard time dealing with him," Phoebe said. "She wasn't all that big herself, so he was already taller than her when she moved in. I'm just grateful that somebody stepped up to the plate for us. That was just about the time I lost it myself, getting into the drugs and stuff. I knew I was turning into my mother, and I hated it. But not enough, I guess. That didn't come till later."

Because of his learning disabilities, Eddie Hudack was involved in a scuffle nearly every school day. "Most of them he started himself," Phoebe said. "I can't remember a single one of them he actually won."

She didn't know exactly when Eddie met Justin Cirillo, only that she came home from work one day and he was sitting on the sofa beside Eddie, six empty cans of beer on the coffee table. Cirillo turned as she came through the door, said, "Hey, I'm Justin. Any chance you could run out and get us another six-pack?"

Despite that first impression, a few months later she had a brief affair with him. "I was just lonely, I guess. Thank God it didn't last long."

Why did it end?

She hesitated.

I said, "You're supposed to tell me everything, right?"

"No," she said with not the slightest hesitation. "I told you that already. There are rules."

"Okay. Sorry. But can you tell me why you stopped dating Justin?"

She seemed to be holding her breath. Then inhaled, blew it out, and said, "He was too rough. I don't like angry sex. So I told him I was done with him."

Not long after that, Cirillo took an apartment at Creekside Apartments, a low-income complex on the southern end of Bell's Grove. "Eddie moved in with him to split the rent. I said, how are you going to pay rent when you don't have any income? But I guess he found some way to pay his share. I don't even want to think about what it was."

That same year, Phoebe decided to further her education, and cut her own expenses by moving out of the rented house she had grown up in and into one of Burchette's second-floor bedrooms. "They started coming by there every week or so," she said, meaning to Burchette's house. "Before I knew it, Justin was banging *her*. She was lonely too, I guess. She apparently liked it more than I did. Especially when they got to drinking together."

Eddie served as a kind of Pancho to Cirillo's Don Quixote, except that there was no nobility to Cirillo's schemes and no resistance from his Pancho. "I told him again and again he was selling his soul to the devil, and they were going to get caught sooner or later. Thing is, they never did get caught. Anytime they'd run short of cash they'd break into another house somewhere. Usually it was up north in one of the little towns. He used to laugh about how careless they were up there, not using security systems or anything. He and Eddie would come back with a duffel bag full of stuff, most of it discount store jewelry and stuff like that, and Justin would sell it off piece by piece."

Was Dianne Burchette aware of all this?

Phoebe's smile was crooked with disapproval. "She had some of the jewelry on when he shot her."

As for where her brother and the other fugitive, Jolene Mrozek, might be: "All I know is that Eddie's either with her or he's already dead. He's just not equipped to be making his own decisions. Never was."

Had she met Mrozek previously? "Justin brought her over a couple of times. Thing is, anytime he was there I'd go upstairs with the girls. So I have no idea how she and Diney got along. For the most part, Diney liked everybody, took them just as they are. Especially when they came with something to drink."

Were Mrozek and Cirillo having an affair? "Probably. I wasn't interested enough to ask."

Was Cirillo still having an affair with Burchette? "I'm pretty sure that ended when Barry started coming here."

How did Barry Faye and Cirillo and Eddie get along?

"Like I said, I seldom stayed in the same room with them long enough to know. There were times we could hear them all laughing, though, me and the girls, so they must've been enjoying each other's company."

"Until that last meeting."

"Yeah," she said, her eyes on the wall. "Up until then."

I assumed that the conversation was over, but she had more to say. "I often wonder what would have happened if I'd said something to Diney. If maybe I'd warned her off Justin or something." She looked at me, her mouth frowning, and shook her head. "If it wasn't for Thomas telling me that it was all out of my hands, that I couldn't do anything to change it, I'd probably drive myself crazy feeling guilty."

When had he told her this?

"The last time I saw him. He said things are going to happen soon, bad things, but what I needed to know was that none of it was my fault. Not what had already happened or what was going to. He said there wasn't anything anybody could do to stop it."

And now her eyes crinkled and her head cocked to the side. "I don't think he lied to me about it either. He knew so much. I really don't think he would."

Jolene Mrozek remains, at the very least, a partial mystery, though local journalists and neighbors have done a fairly good job of filling in her personal history. Like Cirillo and Eddie Hudack, she was a resident of the Creekside Apartments in Bell's Grove. She lived alone but was known to have "a slew" of male visitors, most of whom came and went from her third-floor apartment after only a few minutes.

A chat forum for residents of the Creekside Apartments includes effusive comments from tenants who praise the friendliness and helpfulness of their neighbors to those who rail against "all the dope heads and old farts that stink up the place" and the "noise that never stops" and "the filth some of these people live in."

Neighbors who live on the same floor as Jolene Mrozek did describe her with a similar range of sentiments. She was "nice, I guess, though we never talked much, just to say hello and stuff," or the cause of all the "mud and dirt in that part of the hallway because of the people coming and going. It was like Grand Central Station or something when she was here." The property manager, who smelled strongly of marijuana smoke, called her "one of the better tenants, I'd say. Pretty quiet and all. Paid her rent on time and didn't complain. What more could you ask for?"

Phoebe Hudack had to be coaxed to express an opinion on Mrozek. "Let's just say we didn't have much time for each other."

And why was that?

"I didn't think a woman her age had any business with guys like Justin and Eddie. And I especially didn't like the idea of Eddie fooling around with that woman."

Fooling around in what way?

"As far as I could tell, she was doing them both, and probably a hundred other guys. She spent way too much time with them, that's all I know."

When Phoebe was asked to provide a physical description, she said, "She claimed to be thirty-nine, but she looked sixty to me. She looked *hard*, you know? The way lots of women around here look. Their faces get old and wrinkled and brown even if their bodies hold up pretty good. I just always got a bad vibe from her. And Thomas told me to stay clear of her. He said not to tangle with her cause she was a psychic vampire."

A psychic vampire?

"They're people who can suck the life force out of you. Or who can drag you down into all kinds of trouble and misery."

And how would Thomas Kennaday know that about her?

"I can't get into that. But I will tell you this. Eddie changed after he started hanging around with those two, Justin and her. He could lose his temper, yes, but he was never mean unless you hurt him first. Mean to himself, okay, yeah. But after those two? I don't know. He just wasn't like my little brother anymore. I practically raised him, and I sure didn't raise him to act that way."

––––––

If such a group of misfits and underachievers could be said to have a mastermind, that would be Justin Cirillo. His senior photo from the 2016 *Wilarean*, the New Wilmington, Pennsylvania, high school yearbook, shows a round-faced boy with a wing of black hair hanging over one eye as he smirks at the camera. His eyes are green flecked with brown, and narrow set, his olive complexion evidence of his Greek ancestry. His nose shows a small nasal bump that might bespeak an earlier break, though this feature is common to Greeks too. His mouth is small, lips thin. Altogether his features insinuate a mendacious, even predatory nature (though that perception might be influenced by Phoebe Hudack's earlier mention of Cirillo's proclivity for rough sex). The lack of any other photos of him in the yearbook suggest that he was not a joiner, not an athlete, not a participant in any of the school's extracurricular activities. Graduation from high school seems to be his only accomplishment—that and his facility for breaking into homes without getting caught.

He is no doubt a narcissist and more than a little sociopathic. He probably holds a grudge against a former authority figure, an abusive or negligent parent, which has expanded to encompass all of society. Such individuals tend to keep to themselves, though they might also incorporate weaker, subservient others into their circle. By all descriptions, this is a viable assumption. Cirillo carried the shotgun. Cirillo committed the murders. Mrozek and Hudack were there to provide backup or simply to observe so as to further solidify Cirillo's hold on them. The very weak will either hide from life or hitch themselves to someone more confident and aggressive than they.

This and the fact that Barry Faye was the only victim to be shot twice, and that he was dead prior to the finishing shot, strongly suggests that Cirillo's animus was focused on him and did not necessarily extend to the other two victims, whom Cirillo would have viewed as witnesses to his crime. The first shot in Faye's chest was to take him down. He outweighed Cirillo by at least fifty pounds and stood five inches taller than Cirillo's five feet eight inches. The second shot, point-blank in Faye's face, was to show Cirillo's contempt. His superiority. His sick need for control.

He is now exercising that control from his jail cell. So far he has refused to answer a single question, whether posed by law enforcement or his lawyer, other than to say "up yours," "go fuck yourself," or some similar response.

When first approached by two law enforcement officers shortly after the crimes, Cirillo had ignored their questions and continued to eat his chili dog, fries, and root beer float until he was yanked to his feet and handcuffed. At his hearing, when asked to enter a plea, he stood in his orange jumpsuit, hands cuffed and legs shackled, glared at the judge, and said loudly enough to make the gallery gasp, "All you motherfuckers can eat my shit."

As of this writing, now four weeks after the murders, the trial is set for mid-January. In the meantime, Cirillo is enjoying the hospitality of the Lawrence County Jail in New Castle.

10.

The tenant, second interview

Sunday was a pleasant day in the low sixties, with rain unlikely. The sun played hide-and-seek behind a slow parade of gray-bellied clouds. So I donned my heaviest leather jacket, leather gloves and a black ski cap, packed a couple of things in the trunk and, just in case of rain, a helmet in one of the saddlebags, then climbed onto Candy and headed for Bell's Grove.

The Burchette house seemed inordinately quiet when I was granted entry twenty minutes later, but it was more than the stillness that flashed across my radar. The house felt positively empty even with me and Phoebe in it. And a vaguely familiar scent seemed to be hanging in the air.

———

As I take my seat in the wing chair, I look around the room. No soft music playing upstairs. No footsteps shuffling across the floor.

S: What's different here? Shonnie isn't home, is she?

P: She'll be back soon, she's at a friends' house. But that isn't what you feel. I had the house cleansed.

Cleansed, she said. Not cleaned. The scent I detect is of the smoke from a stick of smoldering white sage. I have saged my own house a couple of times in the past, and at those times the smoke smelled like a mix of pot smoke and something floral, but after the smoke dissipated, a faint oniony smell lingered in the air.

Phoebe sits there smiling at me, waiting for my reaction. Something is different about her too; she is calmer, not the jittery, anxious young woman I first met.

S: [*nods*] I had someone in my place a while back. It felt to me like an old man. Cara, my girlfriend, felt him more strongly than I did. She said he had crawled into bed with us once. I don't mind harmless spirits hanging around, but when they start getting frisky with my girlfriend... I saged the house and sent him on his way.

P: Shonnie didn't want me to do it. She didn't want her mother and Shelley to go. But there were too many other ones coming in, especially after Thomas left the last time. He gave me the sage and told me how to use it. I finally got around to doing so yesterday.

He gave her the sage to rid the house of spirits *before* the spirits arrived? Who is this guy—Nostradamus?

S: So the spirits of Dianne and Barry and Shelley were all here?

P: Oh yeah. They never left. But they were here too long, so they had to go too. The other ones...they were never welcome. But, you know, violence opens up a hole for them. For the bad ones especially.

S: I have to admit it feels a whole lot different in here now.

P: I know, right? And no nightmares last night, not for either me or Shonnie. That's the first time since it happened.

S: No nightmares is a good thing.

So Kennaday not only gave Phoebe a gun and predicted that she would have to use it, but he also gave her a stick of white sage for removing negative energy from the house. All well before the murders happened. He is either a psychic or he played some role in orchestrating the murders.

I have met maybe twenty people throughout my life who claimed to be psychic; I believed only three of them. Predicting the future, like mediumship (talking to the dead) is one of those vocations that requires no credentials, and the exercise of which produces no concrete results. Consequently, the world of paranormal theorists and practitioners is rife with charlatans. Yet a few come across as genuine.

And there in Bell's Grove, at the site of three ghastly murders, I receive more corroboration that intuition is real. The house *has* been cleansed. I feel it upon first entering the house that day, an increased lightness that is both visual and barometric. The only negativity, for the moment, comes from what I brought in with me. My confusion, my resentment, my perhaps overly insistent determination to figure out Thomas Kennaday's true identity and what it has to do with me.

Phoebe, however, is in a pensive mood.

P: You're an educated man, Randall. What do you think it is that brings two people together and keeps them together?

Her question, non sequitur that it is, throws me.

S: Are you referring to you and Thomas?
P: No, not really. I knew from the beginning that that would be temporary. I was thinking more of other relationships. Like Diney and Barry. My parents. Just people in general.

S: I really don't know. I guess there could be a number of different
reasons.

P: Diney asked me that question once, just a few days before she
died. I said love, and she shook her head no. Loneliness, she
said. People are scared to death to be alone. What do you think?
Is it love or loneliness?

S: Well, I wouldn't want to rule out love altogether. But I do think
a lot of people stay together because they're afraid of being
alone. On the other hand, maybe love is a response to no longer
being alone, an expression of gratitude.

P: Hmm. But you're not afraid of being alone, are you?

I cock my head.

P: Thomas said that's one of your strengths. You don't need anybody else.

Involuntarily, my eyes narrow. Who *is* this guy, this stranger
who claims to know me so well? I don't want to move too aggres-
sively with my interview, though, or to otherwise show my hand.

S: My girlfriend certainly doesn't think of it as a strength.

Smiling, Phoebe turns her body sideways to mine and looks
toward the kitchen.

P: Do you remember how I told you about sex with him and how
amazing it was?

I nod.

P: He said it was because sex between two people whose spirits are connected is a sacred act. And that the orgasm is a gift to remind us that we are part of the divine. He said you understand that too.

A shiver races up my spine. This is too much. Every mention of him and what he knows of me feels like another violation of my deepest privacy.

S: How much do you know about Thomas Kennaday, Phoebe?
P: I know everything he told me. And he told me a lot.

Did I just now see a crack in her story?

S: For somebody who had difficulty memorizing things in high school, you seem to have a near-photographic memory now.
P: He hypnotized me.
S: Excuse me?
P: So that I would remember my instructions. He said it was very important that I remember every word of it so that I could repeat it to you in the same order he gave it.

Her story is getting harder and harder to swallow.

S: All right, good. Let's have it.
P: You don't believe me, do you? He told me you would—
S: [*holds up a hand*] Don't. Please stop telling me that he knew in advance what I would say or do.
P: I don't mean to offend you.
S: Honestly, I'm beginning to find this whole situation offensive. I need to know every single thing you know about the person who calls himself Thomas Kennaday.

She holds herself very still for a moment, then looks to the front door.

P: Shonnie's home.

Three seconds later the door swings open and the young girl strides in, a pink-and-gray backpack strapped to her shoulders. She looked taller when sitting beside Phoebe on my previous visit. Now I see that she can't be taller than four feet and a couple of inches. But yes, her feet in their pink Nikes look huge on her. She will likely have a growth spurt one of these days.

Shonnie flops down beside Phoebe and hugs her. Afterward, the girl turns to me shyly.

Shonnie: Hey.
S: Hey yourself.

I inquire if I might ask a question or two of her; both she and Phoebe agree. The useful information gleaned from those questions has been presented earlier. We talk for maybe five minutes max, then Phoebe pulls Shonnie close and kisses her head.

P: Why don't you go grab yourself a snack, sweetie, then go on upstairs for a while. I'll be up soon, and then you can tell me how your day went.

Neither of us speaks while the girl goes into the kitchen, then returns through the living room with two long meat sticks in her left hand, a bottle of water in her right. She flashes me a smile in passing.

Shonnie: See ya.

S: Later, gator.

She ascends the stairs quickly, and I cannot help but envision her on the day of the shooting, as she had hurried down those stairs only to be yanked away by Phoebe just as the fifth shot rang out. The spackled buckshot holes are still clearly visible.

But this time she runs upstairs safely. A few seconds later, an upstairs door thuds shut.

Phoebe turns to face me more directly.

P: Do you know who Dan Aykroyd is?

S: Of course. *Saturday Night Live. Ghostbusters.*

P: Thomas knows him.

S: Oh?

P: Several years ago, Aykroyd was taping a new show in New York. It was called *Out There* and had already been sold to the Sci-Fi channel. He was taping the final installment, having already interviewed the most prominent people in the fields of UFOs, abductions, crop circles, interplanetary intervention, and so forth.

She is speaking more quickly than usual and staring at a point over my shoulder, as if she is reciting from memory.

P: Between his interviews with Stephen Bassett and Dr. Steven Greer, Aykroyd stepped outside to smoke. His cell phone rang, and it was Britney Spears. She wanted him to appear with her on *Saturday Night Live.* He said sure, he'd be happy to. And while they were talking, a black Ford sedan pulled up on the street. It was at the corner of Forty-Second Street and Eighth Avenue.

Aykroyd had a funny feeling about the car, so he tried to see the license plate, but he couldn't read it. It was fuzzy, he said. But he had a definite impression that it was an undercover police car. Then two guys climbed out—one from the front seat and one from the back. The one in the back was a big, tall guy, he said. With a really pale face. That guy looked straight at Aykroyd, and it wasn't a pleasant look. "It was a real dirty look," Aykroyd said. He looked away for just a moment, turned back, and the car was gone. It happened so quickly that he would have seen if the men climbed back into the car and drove away, but it was completely gone. Not a sign of it anywhere on the street. "That car *vanished*," he said. And he had a feeling that it had been some kind of warning for him. Maybe to stop investigating what he was investigating for the show he was taping. He finished the call and went back inside. Two hours later he was informed that the show was cancelled and that none of the episodes already taped would air.

She stops, blinks, takes a breath, and smiles at me.

S: What the hell?

She blinks again.

P: That's all the time I have today. You can come back on Tuesday.
S: Whoa, whoa, whoa. What does that story have to do with anything?
P: Thomas didn't tell me that.
S: Men in black? I'm supposed to understand what that means?
P: [*stands*] I'll see you Tuesday. The same time is good.
S: Why not today? I've been here only a few minutes.
P: He said you will need time to consider it all. To assimilate, he said.
S: I'm getting pretty darn tired of hearing you say *he said*.

She flinches. Her cheeks flush red and her eyes grow damp.

S: [*stands*] Wait, I'm sorry. I don't mean to take it out on you. But this game he's playing with me is infuriating.

Phoebe sniffs and blinks back the tears before speaking.

P: Thomas drove a dark-blue Trailblazer. The house where I'd meet him is on East Wallace Avenue in New Castle. House number 414. That's all I'm allowed to tell you today.

S: [*surprised*] Okay, great. I, uh...I mean thanks. It's better than nothing. Any chance you happened to see the license plate?

Another surprise: she rattles off the number.

S: That's fantastic, Phoebe. Thank you!

As I quickly repeat the number to myself a couple of times, she turns and crosses to the door and holds it open for me.

P: [*smiles*] Tuesday.

I agree, then step out into the dirty light.

I am almost giddy as I dig into Candy's fiberglass trunk, pull out my notebook, and write down the information. Even if the Trailblazer was a rental, I can still gain some useful information, though I will have to go through one of my law enforcement contacts to do so. The location of the house where Kennaday and Phoebe had their liaisons, however—it is only a few miles away. The solution to the mystery of Thomas Kennaday is finally within reach.

11.

Pardon my rumination

I settled onto Candy's seat and slipped the ignition key into place. But my thumb on the ignition switch didn't depress. With my thoughts racing, I was in no state of mind to be riding very far. And what did I plan to do when I found the house on East Wallace Avenue? I would knock on the door, to be sure. But if nobody answered, then what? Just how far was I willing to go to investigate Kennaday?

As a writer I have always found that getting a feel for a place—the *spiritus loci*, as Lawrence Durrell called it, the true spirt of a place—contributes to a more authentic depiction of it within the pages, and I have never hesitated to pile up the miles in pursuit of that depiction, whether the place was an hour's drive away or in Mexico or Europe or Labrador. Sometimes I am forced to bend the rules in order to get close to a particular building or historical site, as happened the first time I visited Stonehenge, way back in 1977. I made sure to arrive there at first light, with the mist of dawn still clinging to the grass, the visitor's center still locked and dark, and was able for a good hour or more to wander freely between the mysterious stones, soaking up their vibrations. But I was younger then and more agile and knew that I could outrun the angry shouts of any guards who might pop up. These days the knees not quite so cooperative, yet I will still test doors and sometimes windows, and, if one of them happens to be unlocked, well, that is an invitation to enter, isn't it? I have never literally broken into a place—at least not since my thirties. Was I willing to do so again if necessary at the house on East Wallace?

I needed to figure this out, as well as a few other things. Before I did anything as rash as breaking into a man's home, I needed to decompress somewhere and empty my head out onto a legal pad. Like many writers, I think more clearly when I write things out. For that reason, I always pack a yellow legal pad and several blue gel pens to record the ideas when they start to drip out.

Since moving to my current home, one of my favorite places for catching that drippage has been the Coney Island hot dog shop on Route 18 north of New Castle—the very same place where Justin Cirillo had been apprehended by the police after he slaughtered three people.

The irony of that appealed to me; maybe I would even sit in the same booth Cirillo had before being yanked to his feet and handcuffed. His last meal in freedom had consisted of two chili dogs with onions, French fries with chili, and a root beer float. I usually ordered only three chili dogs and a glass of water, but maybe this time I would make an exception.

I started the bike and rolled away. No way was I going to give up my love of unhealthy food just because a murderer shared my tastes. Our similarities didn't make *me* a bad man too, except to my stomach.

Between bites at the Coney, I managed to scribble down a full page of notes and questions to myself. I was particularly bothered by two things Phoebe had told me that day: the divinity of the orgasm, and her hypnotism.

More than a few times in my writing—in fact, in one of the DeMarco novels—I had espoused a belief that the orgasm is a shuddering reminder of the blissful connection we share with the Source, and that when a couple shares the kind of love and respect DeMarco and Jayme do, lovemaking can be a holy act. Remembering that brought a measure of relief; Kennaday hadn't read my mind, he had read my books! Had he repeated my belief to Phoebe then instructed her to repeat it to me precisely because he knew I would recognize it? So it seemed. But why? What did he hope to gain from it? And how could he have told her about my belief, and known that I would eventually talk to her, *before* he and I ever met? Or was she lying about when she last spoke to him?

As for Phoebe's alleged hypnotism, had it really happened? Had it actually *worked*? I already knew that Kennaday was manipulative. Was he also a Svengali? Was I, God forbid, also under his spell? Or was this some kind of elaborate prank Kennaday and Phoebe were playing on me? Kennaday knew my work, and he wouldn't be the first demented fan to try to insinuate himself into my life. Though no others had been so devious or—I had to admit—so clever about it.

For the moment, I had no way of knowing the answers to those questions. And that really ticked me off. I climbed back onto Candy with the intent of unearthing, once and for all, the true identity of that well-groomed worm, for that was how I was starting to think of him. I knew the make of his car now and the license plate number and the location of the house where he and Phoebe had held their liaisons. That house would contain clues that should at least hint at who he really was. One way or the other, I had to get a look at them.

12.

The funkdafication grows

The house on East Wallace Avenue was a large five-bedroom home made of yellow brick, built in 1918. To my surprise it showed up on Zillow, was listed as "currently not for sale," and had been added to the National Register of Historic Places back in 1998. Interior details included a "grand foyer with arched nook" and a butler's pantry. An unusual choice, I thought, for a single young man's temporary home.

The only time I had ever tested the popular movie idea that a credit card could be used to unlock a door was a few summers ago when I went out for a bike ride without remembering to take my house key, got caught in a thunderstorm, and returned home soaking wet and shivering to a power outage, which meant that I couldn't open my garage door from the exterior code panel. Opening the front door took me a while and chewed up the edge of the credit card as if a mouse had been nibbling on it, but eventually the lock clicked open.

After knocking on the front and back doors of the East Wallace house and getting no response, I gave the rear doorknob several hard shakes. Then a couple of harder yanks. I have to admit that I was more pleased than frustrated to find ingress not easy to obtain. Truth be told, I would probably have sought illicit entry into the house even if Kennaday hadn't violated my privacy. Some people like fences; I like jumping over them. Borders and boundaries, fences and locks and obstructions of every kind entice me with their challenge: what's the best way to get past this thing—over, under, around, or through?

The large lot was surrounded on three sides by a privet hedge at least eight feet high, so I felt relatively invisible as I huddled close to the door and worked my previously nibbled card back and forth between the door and its frame, both of which had seen stronger, firmer days. The lock, already halfway out of the box and strike plate because of their advanced age, yielded as easily as a black tooth floating in an old man's gums.

The door opened onto an eight-by-ten room off the kitchen, a small multipurpose room my parents would have called a pantry but was now called a mudroom, with metal cabinets for canned food, a washer and dryer, and an old American Empire–style armoire that had probably once stood in a dining room. The metal cabinets and armoire were empty.

Before leaving the little room, I locked the back door again, not wanting to be caught off guard by a nosy neighbor, and was surprised to see that the door was also equipped with two dead-bolt locks, neither of which had been employed. This struck me as odd, now that I knew Kennaday a little better, and also because this neighborhood wasn't a particularly affluent one. The house, all three thousand square feet of it, spoke of a former affluence—the elaborate moldings, the dark hardwood floors, even the enameled cast-iron sink and four-burner stove could have been ripped out and sold for a pretty penny to vintage-hungry millennials. And if an amateur like me could get into it with so little effort, how could it remain unviolated? Other houses on the street had not fared so well. Had I possibly tripped a silent alarm that would soon bring a couple of police officers to the door? I had to move quickly.

There was nothing to see on the first floor. The kitchen held a large black refrigerator, unplugged and with its door standing open, the big gas range and oven, a Mr. Coffee and microwave on the counter beside the sink. The cabinets held a minimum of dishware. Each of the other spacious rooms was sparsely furnished with Victorian furniture—a settee here, a sofa and dark leather chair there, a plastic potted ficus in the corner, a white brick fireplace with a heavy wrought-iron screen. The oak floors were bare, the window curtains drawn. Overall, the only evidence of recent habitation on that floor was the fact that the lights worked and a small vacuum cleaner stood against the powder room wall.

Upstairs it was the same. Another Victorian sofa sat against the front street windows in the room at the top of the landing. Surprisingly, each of the five bedrooms was painted a different—and to my eye, offensive—color: one fuchsia, one bright blue, one orange, one red, and one lime green. The green bedroom held two twin beds with matching brown comforters and pillowcases and a tall IKEA dresser; the blue room, which I took to be the master, held a queen bed with a flowered comforter and a heavy cherrywood dresser with a mirror. The drawers in both dressers were empty, the first with its top bare, the one in the master holding nothing but a folded newspaper, yellow and brittle with age. The only furnishings in the two bathrooms were the toilet brushes in their plastic holders. No soap in the soap dishes, no damp towels hanging from their racks. Each of the closets contained a dozen or so black wire hangers and nothing more.

I was having another WTF moment when the old newspaper on the dresser caught my eye a second time, probably by virtue of being something of an anomaly. Maybe Kennaday had left it behind. But no; it was years old, section B from the *Post-Gazette*. Pittsburgh's last printed newspaper, the P-G has been decreasing the number of daily printings since 2018, with plans to go digital-only soon.

I stood there looking down at the paper, not really looking at it but wondering about the truth of Kennaday's stay in this all-but-denuded house, when the face in the paper's photo registered on me. I had seen it before. Delicately I unfolded the brittle paper. Ray Gricar, the caption told me. *Missing*, said the caption, *since 2005*.

I remembered the circumstances, particularly because of my fondness for Joe Paterno and Penn State football. Ray Gricar had been the Centre County district attorney who had declined to prosecute Jerry Sandusky, an assistant coach for the Lions, for allegations of sex crimes against young boys. Six years after Gricar's disappearance, Sandusky was finally indicted on fifty-two counts of child sexual abuse. Eight months later he was found guilty on forty-five of those counts and was sentenced to thirty to sixty years in prison.

The *Post-Gazette* I now held in my hands was dated November 2011, the same month Sandusky was indicted. The Penn State scandal had rocked the entire nation, especially since the university's revered football coach and others on his staff had allegedly known about Sandusky's activities as early as 1998 but had failed to report them. As a result of that failure, the football program was hit with the most severe sanctions ever imposed on an NCAA member, and the reputation of the entire university suffered a severe blow from which it has not yet fully recovered, and perhaps never will.

And that, for the moment, was my only response to the anomalous newspaper. I had already been in the house too long, so I made a quick exit, relieved to hear no sirens in the distance, no police cars parked at the curb. My relief, as it turned out, was premature.

I hurried back to the corner where I had parked Candy. As I rushed to recover my leather coat and gloves from the trunk, a vehicle pulled up behind me. From the sound of its idling engine, it was only a few yards away. What to do? Ignore it, climb on my bike and ride off as if I'd never heard it? Or turn and face the music?

My father, an ex-Marine and steelworker, had imbued me with two related disciplines: be your own man and live however you wish to live, but be prepared to own up to any mistakes you make along the way.

So I turned, smiling, fully prepared to claim that I had come to visit a recent acquaintance and found the back door unlocked but the house empty.

The vehicle was a black SUV, no police or other markings, its windows tinted. I held my smile, though it twitched a little of its own volition. Then the passenger door sprung open. Out stepped a man in a dark-blue suit and sunglasses. He was of average height, neither well tanned nor unusually pale. His pants were too short by a couple of inches, and that struck me as peculiar, for otherwise it was a nice-looking and probably expensive suit. He stood alongside the outer edge of the door, as mute and still as a statue. I found that stillness unnerving. Arms at his sides, palms against his outer thighs, he made not the slightest of movements. Yet I got the very uneasy feeling that under those sunglasses he was glaring at me with murderous eyes.

I took a step toward him. Immediately he ducked back into the SUV, slammed the door, and the vehicle roared away. I stepped out into the street as it zoomed past and squinted to read the license plate. It was a wasted effort, seeing as how there was no license plate at all.

And I had my third WTF moment of the day.

13.

The puzzle proliferates

The next morning, I spent some time transcribing my most recent conversation with Phoebe, then shuffling and rearranging the puzzle pieces it had dropped onto my lap. None of them fit together, not with each other nor with any of the earlier pieces. Could it have been a mere coincidence that I had an encounter with what some might call a man in black less than an hour after Phoebe had told me—out of the blue, by the way—of Dan Aykroyd's encounter? I didn't think so.

And what was I to make of the ten-year-old newspaper left behind in the East Wallace house? What were the chances that it had been left there by accident, when the rest of the building seemed positively scrubbed of all evidence of habitation?

I'd had a vague knowledge of the Ray Gricar story before seeing that paper, but at the time of his disappearance I was managing a restaurant for a business partner who would turn out to be a liar and chiseler, plus my marriage was on the brink of collapse, *and* I was trying to maintain a career as a writer while spending as much time as possible with my sons, one of whom was in college a county away. My life was full if not fulfilling, and I had time for few other concerns. As far as I could recall, Ray Gricar's disappearance would not be associated with the Penn State sex scandal until years later.

But an afternoon of research suggested that my glimpse of the old newspaper might not have been an accident. I composed a summary of the Gricar/Sandusky story:

1998: Ray Gricar declines to prosecute Jerry Sandusky for sex crimes. Gricar never fully explains why he failed to prosecute, but the common supposition is that he lacked sufficient evidence to make a case.

April 15, 2005: Gricar disappears. The next day, Gricar's red-and-white 2004 Mini Cooper is found locked in a Lewisburg, Pennsylvania, parking lot, not far from the Susquehanna River. A search of the vehicle shows no signs of foul play, though a small amount of cigarette ash is discovered in the car. Gricar did not smoke, nor, according to his family, did he ever allow anyone to smoke in his car. His cell phone, its contents locked, is also found in the vehicle, but no other personal effects are. Over the next few days, local store owners are questioned, and at least one feels certain that the district attorney visited the shop on the day of his disappearance. A second witness claims to have seen him speaking with a dark-haired woman. In Gricar's home, nothing is found to be missing but for his work laptop. Because Roy J. Gricar—Ray Gricar's brother, who was said to suffer from bipolar disorder—had disappeared in Dayton, Ohio, back in 1996, only to have his body turn up in the Great Miami River a few days later, his death ruled a suicide by drowning, authorities fear that Ray Gricar might have taken his own life too, so they conduct an extensive search of the Susquehanna River but are unable to locate any sign of the district attorney.

July 2005: Ray Gricar's missing laptop washes up under a bridge. The laptop, while obviously damaged by exposure to the water, is complete but for the hard drive. A couple of months later, the hard drive is found near a railroad bridge not far from where Gricar's Mini Cooper had been abandoned. No information is retrieved from the hard drive. The case grows cold. Sporadic sightings of Gricar are reported in various states, but none of the tips pay off. No suspects or people of interest are named. In the months and years to follow, numerous conspiracy theories develop around the case.

April 2009: Evidence from Ray Gricar's home computer shows that somebody, in the weeks prior to Gricar's disappearance, used that computer to research ways of destroying a hard drive.

November 2011: Jerry Sandusky is indicted for sex crimes against young boys, is consequently found guilty and sent to prison. That same year, Ray Gricar is declared dead.

2013: A former Hells Angel turned FBI informant tells police that Gricar's throat was slit and his body tossed into a mine shaft by another Angel as retribution for him getting a long prison sentence. Police follow up on that and similar leads, but Gricar's body is never found. The most popular theories regarding Ray Gricar's disappearance remain homicide (because he knew too much about the Sandusky scandal, or he made too many enemies as a DA) and suicide (because he was bipolar, or just too tired of his life to continue). Social media being what it is, however, other less credible theories popped up like fungi. One is that he simply chose to leave his old life behind and start over again with a new identity; a witness early in the case claimed to see him on the streets of Lewisburg with a dark-haired woman, and despite reports that Gricar was devoted to his live-in girlfriend and his daughter, he wouldn't be the first man to abandon his family for a love interest. Another theory proposes that the facts surrounding Gricar's disappearance mimic those of a sci-fi mystery novel about time-traveling cops; Gricar had earlier helped that novel's author, Pamela West, research the murder of a Penn State student, and West later modeled her fictional setting in *20/20 Vision* on the town of State College. There are also some eerie similarities to another disappearance Gricar was reportedly very interested in—that of a chief of police in a township near Cleveland, who, as a former Centre County assistant DA observed, disappeared in 1985 "under near-identical circumstances to those surrounding Ray's disappearance."

What could it all mean? Men in black, Dan Aykroyd, UFOs, time-traveling cops, Hells Angels, child sexual abuse, disappearing police and prosecutors? Now tie all that to the Burchette murders and Baby Doe. What is the only thing to link them together? The mysterious Thomas Kennaday, he who could hypnotize Phoebe Hudack to remember everything he told her; he who promised her, before I ever met him, that a writer would come to inquire about the case; he who supplied her with a .38 Special for a then-unknown purpose; he who successfully forecasted several of my reactions and responses during my interviews with Phoebe; and he who had quite possibly left a ten-year-old newspaper in plain sight for me to read—which meant that he also seemed to know that I would break into his rented house.

By noon the sky had lightened to a bluish Confederate gray, but with only a thirty-watt bulb shining behind it, which kept the world below in a state of adumbrated stillness. By four the drizzle began and continued through the night, just enough dampness in the air that if you were to walk from your car to your front door, you would feel the icy drops sliding from your hair and down the back of your neck—an insidious kind of dampness in that you don't notice it until you do, and then you feel it with every breath and in the soreness deep in your bones.

And that was how I passed the night. The recognition that I was being gaslighted, observed, or otherwise manipulated by Thomas Kennaday sickened me with dread and nearly paralyzed me with fear.

14.

Stranger connections

Lucky for me, fear doesn't survive long in its native form inside my body. I was a timid boy growing up, but it didn't take more than a few years of life in a milieu rife with violence, and with a generally gentle ex-Marine father as an exemplar of self-reliance, to realize that anger can convert fear to action. *The best defense is a strong offense* was my old man's mantra, and it became mine as well.

I woke up on Tuesday morning, the twentieth of October, convinced that Kennaday was nothing but a hoaxer, and I set out to prove it. His story about Dan Aykroyd, an actor whose work I had enjoyed since the first episodes of *Saturday Night Live* back in the late seventies, should be easy to debunk. Until Phoebe mentioned it, I'd had no notion that Aykroyd was interested in the UFO phenomenon, so I started my research on him by assuming that Kennaday's anecdote, delivered through Phoebe, was a fairy tale of his own making.

I was wrong. Aykroyd's history with UFOs and the paranormal was, to my surprise, well documented. Not only has he had multiple sightings of UFOs, but he expounded his beliefs on the subject in the 2005 documentary *Dan Aykroyd Unplugged on UFOs*, and in many other sources.

The ease with which I found Aykroyd's story about his encounter with two men in black suggested that Kennaday could have found it just as easily, only to insert into it a fallacious friendship with the actor, then feeding the story to a gullible Phoebe. I chalked that up as a point for me in my quest to prove Kennaday a fraud.

But why would Kennaday want me to read about Ray Gricar's disappearance?

According to NamUs, the National Missing and Unidentified Persons System, a project of the Department of Justice and the National Forensic Science Technology Center, some six hundred thousand people go missing every year in the United States. Many of these individuals are quickly found, alive or dead, but some never are. Of those twenty thousand or so currently missing, approximately 60 percent are male, the rest female. The average age is thirty-four. Alaska, as one might guess, has the highest number of missing per capita, with 41.8 per 100,000 residents. California, with a total number of 2,133, has the highest number of individuals missing. Pennsylvania, the state where Gricar went missing, currently ranks as ninth among the ten states with the highest number of missing persons. The Department of Justice calls these disappearances "the nation's silent mass disaster."

Investigator David Paulides, a former cop and author of nine books on the subject of missing persons, has found that mountainous areas, and national parks in particular, account for the setting of many if not most of these disappearances. Although Lewisburg, Pennsylvania, where Gricar disappeared, rests in the Susquehanna River Valley, a short drive east would have taken him to the Pocono Mountains. His own car was recovered in Lewisburg, but perhaps he traveled east with the "dark-haired woman" in whose company he was allegedly last sighted.

But I could find no link between Gricar's disappearance and the Burchette murders or the abandonment of Baby Doe—*unless* pedophilia was factored in. Were Kennaday's puzzle pieces intended to insinuate that Gricar's death *did* have something to do with Jerry Sandusky's pedophilia? Or was he merely suggesting that pedophilia was somehow related to Baby Doe, who in turn was related to the Burchette murders?

If so, why be so elliptical about it? And why involve me? Why couldn't Kennaday simply turn over his information—if it *was* information and not simply speculation run amok—to the police? Perhaps it truly was nothing more than speculation, and Kennaday hoped that I would prove it factual. And perhaps he, through his relationship with Phoebe, had played a role in the tragedies, and therefore could not go to the police without risking arrest.

Hmm. The Centre County police had all but ruled out any connection between Gricar's disappearance and the Penn State sex scandal. But wait a minute. There was also Gricar's earlier involvement with the Penn State novelist to factor in.

Used copies of West's 1990 novel are still available on Amazon. Interestingly, further research into the novel led to a 2012 article in the *American Free Press* about Ray Gricar's disappearance. The author of that article, Victor Thorn, quotes an unidentified source as saying this:

There is no physical evidence of Gricar's visit to Lewisburg. Granted, people did see him, but none of them personally knew Gricar. Plus, nothing can be concretely confirmed because there were no photographs, surveillance videos, credit card receipts or a money trail. Further, the mystery woman in his presence remains unidentified and has never stepped forward, even though this was the area's highest profile case in recent memory.

And this:

> When search dogs were brought in on April 17, they couldn't locate Gricar's scent at the Street of Shops or around the river. Then, only two days after he went missing, Gricar's Mini Cooper was returned to his girlfriend instead of being held as evidence. This point is important because Gricar's car withheld a secret compartment that had not been searched.

A secret compartment? Were the police later informed of its existence? Was it searched? What did it hold? None of this information is provided in the article. Why not? The article goes on to say this:

> In the late 1990s a woman named Pamela West approached Gricar with information relating to the infamous 1969 murder of Penn State student Betsy Aardsma in the university's campus library. With Gricar's encouragement, West proceeded to write a fictionalized science-fiction novel entitled *20/20 Vision*... Gricar and West's main character both disappeared on nearly the same dates of April 14 and April 15. The setting for each was State College, Pa. Both Gricar and her (fictional) detective drove sporty cars with personalized license plates. Both Gricar and West's protagonist were soon about to retire, and ashes were found in both vehicles. Lastly, West's detective proceeded to fake his own death. The way I see it, there are no coincidences. What are the chances that so many things lined up in this way?... After Gricar vanished, Pamela West came forward and said that Gricar knew about her book. A state police trooper confirmed that Gricar had read it. West was startled by how closely Gricar's case mimicked details in her novel. On top of that, West theorized

that a policeman or an influential member of the Penn State community had murdered Aardsma. So, Gricar told her to write the book, but suggested that she fictionalize it and not name any names.

Despite the questionable veracity of the unnamed source, all of this is intriguing in a confounding kind of way, especially in regard to having some link to the Burchette case. Nothing in the article mentions pedophilia; the murdered Penn State student was a twenty-two-year-old graduate student in 1969 when she was stabbed through the left breast in Penn State's Pattee Library.

Two books about the murder later theorized that a Penn State doctoral student in geology, Rick Haefner, was responsible for the murder. One of those authors, a former investigative reporter for the Harrisburg *Patriot-News*, stated in a *Lancaster Online* piece in 2011 that Haefner was "a molester of boys, again and again throughout his life. He harbored a violent rage against women that could erupt without warning." In 1975 Haefner was arrested for molesting *two boys*, but the trial ended in a hung jury, though he would spend a month in prison on a contempt of court charge. In 2002 Haefner died of a heart attack in the Mojave Desert.

Aha, there it was, the pedophilia connection. The assumed murderer of Penn State student Betsy Aardsma was a woman hater and a pedophile. Ray Gricar had been a consultant for Pamela West's novel about a fictionalized Penn State murder, and, according to the *American Free Press* article, had encouraged "her to write the book, but suggested that she fictionalize it and not name any names."

But why suggest that she name no names? Aardsma's murder took place almost thirty years before Jerry Sandusky's crimes became known to Gricar. Or did it? Was there something going on at Penn

State or nearby long before Sandusky's behavior was brought to light? Just how extensive *is* the problem of pedophilia?

In 2019, a CNN online article revealed Interpol's "Operation Blackwrist," which was launched after discovering that a subscription-based dark web site was publishing material depicting the abuse of boys under thirteen; the material was distributed to nearly *sixty-three thousand users worldwide.* Since then, said the article, offenders have been prosecuted "in Thailand, Australia and the United States…and police in nearly 60 countries are involved in the investigation."

Wikipedia cofounder Larry Sanger has been using Twitter and other resources to get the world to wake up to this "horrible reality." He warns that "many of the Beautiful People know about child sex trafficking by elites…some participate in it…the media and courts cover it up."

Hmm. A conspiracy theory?

Apparently not. In 2017, the Justice Department ended the two-decades-long crime spree of a group known as NXIVM, a sex slave cult that masqueraded as a self-help organization. The HBO documentary *The Vow* documents how NXIVM recruited more than sixteen thousand people into ESP courses that, in fact, were used to break those individuals down and turn them, and sometimes their children, into sex slaves. Actress Sarah Edmondson filed a complaint with the New York State Department of Health documenting how she was recruited, indoctrinated, and eventually branded near her pelvis by the group's founder, Keith Raniere. Allegedly, the daughter of a prominent newspaper owner in Mexico was persuaded to offer her own virgin daughter to Raniere. Even Mexican cartel murders of women and children have been linked to Raniere and his organization.

Thanks to the arrests of Jeffrey Epstein and, after his suspicious death, his confederate, Ghislaine Maxwell, pedophilia among the global elite is in the news. In July 2020, as reported by the BBC, the German state of North Rhine-Westphalia announced that it had uncovered a pedophile ring of at least thirty thousand members who share child pornography and advise each other on how to drug and rape children and even babies. And there is this, from a 2018 Snopes.com article:

> Operation Rescue, a joint effort involving the European Union Agency for Law Enforcement Cooperation (Europol) and law enforcement in thirteen different countries, was initiated in 2007, and in March 2011 Europol announced the success of the years-long investigation that had, at that time, resulted in the identification of over 200 victims of child abuse and the arrest of 184 suspected child sex offenders.

The pedophile ring in question is said to have had as many as seventy thousand elite members throughout the world. But the news is even worse than that.

In 2018, Natacha Jaitt, a model and socialite, tweeted this: "I am not going to commit suicide, I am not going to take too much cocaine and drown in a bath, or shoot myself. So if this happens, it wasn't me. Save this Tweet." Months earlier she had claimed to have evidence of a pedophile ring involving politicians, movie stars, and other celebrities. In a video available on the American Truth Today website, Jaitt names names and explains the pedophilia network, including incriminating the president of Argentina as the head of a sex trafficking network, and the pope as an enabler who hides pedophile priests in locations where they can continue their crimes. In August 2019 she was found dead in a nightclub with cocaine in her nostrils, LSD and alcohol in her system.

Nor is she the only individual to meet a similar fate after blowing that whistle:

- Actor Isaac Kappy spoke out frequently about "the culture of elite Hollywood ritual abuse and pedophilia," leveling accusations against such luminaries as Tom Hanks and Steven Spielberg. Kappy was killed when he allegedly stepped off a bridge and was struck by a car.
- Ex-cop Mark Minnie, who with his ex-cop friend Chris Steyn wrote the book *The Lost Boys of Bird Island* about children who were taken to the island and sexually abused, and possibly murdered, was found shot in the head nine days after his book was published.
- Soundgarden front man Chris Cornell and Linkin Park front man Chester Bennington, both of whom spoke publicly about either witnessing or experiencing child sexual abuse, were found dead by hanging.

Corey Haim, Corey Feldman, Elijah Wood, Todd Bridges, Brad Pitt, Angelina Jolie, and others have spoken of the same sickness that permeates their profession. Former *Little House on the Prairie* star Alison Arngrim claims that stage parents often facilitate the sexual abuse of their children: "In Hollywood, there are parents who will practically prostitute their kids in the hope they can make money and get ahead. It is a horrible trap that the kids are in… It's more common than you think."

And these are just the celebrity examples. Tens of thousands of others whose names will never be heard also suffer abuse. Not all child sexual abuse falls under the rubric of sex trafficking, but much of it does. As of mid-2019, the Department of Justice had arrested 12,470 people for the crime of human trafficking, and rescued 9,130 victims, but the plague continues like an out-of-control wildfire, slowed but never extinguished.

Still, I remain dubious about any connection between this information and the Gricar and Burchette cases. But whether it is or isn't connected, the epidemics of sex trafficking and child abuse remain a damning indictment against all humanity. That such rampant perfidy could ever be allowed to fester and grow casts our entire species in an odious light.

I do have to wonder, though, if this kind of information is precisely what Kennaday wanted me to find. Is this a game of connect-the-dots he has me playing? Whatever his motive, I am not enjoying his machinations. But I'm locked into this mystery now, and I have to see it through to the end, no matter how unpleasant the end might be.

15.

Secrets within secrets

By eleven that morning, I was exhausted from the research, but I still had some time to kill before showing up for my third interview with Phoebe. The day promised to be another anomaly: close to freezing at dawn but with a projected high in the low sixties by afternoon. My spirits were buoyed a little by the prospect of taking Candy out of the garage later in the day, so I resolved to keep my nose to the grindstone awhile longer. But where to look next in my quest—which had become nearly fanatical by now—to uncover Kennaday's true identity? There were two facts I hadn't yet checked out fully, the only *factual* clues in my possession: the address of Kennaday's rented house, and the license plate number on his rented Chevy Trailblazer.

I placed a call to one of my law enforcement contacts. The call went to voicemail, so I gave him the license plate number and asked if he would be so kind as to suss it out for me, with a bottle of Maker's Mark as his reward for success.

As I waited to hear back from him, there was little else for me to do. I could either nibble my fingers off, or I could turn my attention back to the house on East Wallace Avenue. I chose the latter. Apartments.com informed me that the single-family house currently had "no available units." Zillow and Trulia listed it as off-market, and Zillow added that "this property has missing facts, which can affect the accuracy of home value rates." Because it was off the market, no real estate agency was listed. And a property search turned up absolutely nothing. The house was not listed at all. As far as the county was concerned, the building did not exist.

But I had been *inside* the house, had walked through or looked into every room, and knew that it did exist. A call to the recorder of deeds at the county courthouse got me two minutes with a honey-voiced woman whose honey abruptly hardened when I asked, "How can that be?" in response to her assertion that there was no owner or owners of record for that building and lot. "It happens sometimes," she said flatly, then wished me a nice day and hung up.

My go-to contact in law enforcement proved as luckless as me in tracing the license plate number of Kennaday's SUV. "Unknown," he told me after his own search.

"So what does that mean?" I asked. "A guy rents an undocumented house with no owner and drives a vehicle with no registered owner. What does that tell you?"

"It tells me he doesn't want anybody to know who he is."

"And who would be capable of pulling that off?"

"You know that as well as I do."

"Are we talking an alphabet agency here?"

"You know the answer to that."

"Which one?"

"Ha, take your pick. Officially there are seventeen of them. Every branch of the military has their own secret agency, plus there are several more outside of the military, and each of them has its own affiliations with corporations and foreign companies. Unofficially? I doubt that any one person knows the real number."

"I can't believe it. A CIA or DIA or NSA or whatever safe house in little old New Castle, Pennsylvania?"

"What's that town called—the fireworks capital of the world? And once upon a time the murder capital of the country? Next door to Youngstown, Ohio, also once upon a time the murder capital of America. *Of course* the intelligence community has a presence there. I mean, c'mon, man, they have a presence everywhere."

That was when I remembered something. I tried to swallow but my throat was too dry. "Would you ascribe any significance to the fact that this so-called safe house is only a block or so away from a Scottish Rite cathedral?"

He laughed. "Sounds like an easy walk, I'll say that."

Once again, my head was spinning.

I spent the last hour before meeting Phoebe scribbling down every question in my head and every possible answer to those questions. Had Kennaday put me onto Ray Gricar because Gricar's death had something to do with the Burchette murders? Or was it because of Gricar's link to Sandusky, and Sandusky's link to pedophilia? Could Baby Doe be somehow linked to a pedophilia ring? Why had her disappearance and/or abduction never been reported, the identity of her parents never determined? Hadn't Kennaday told me that "it all starts with the baby in the woods"? But the baby was found *before* the murders. Had he been tipping me off to the fact that somebody from the Burchette house or in the Cirillo entourage had something to do with her disappearance? If so, why hadn't he come right out and said that? Why was he turning this into an Easter egg hunt? When *did* Baby Doe go missing? It seemed impossible that nobody, not even a neighbor, had reported a missing infant. And why in the world had Kennaday involved me in this nest of rattlesnakes in the first place, making me his what?

His puppet, that's what. But that still did not answer the *why* of it.

And what about the black SUV and its passenger who had, I felt certain, been trying to intimidate me outside of Kennaday's rented house? Was it simply because I had been witnessed sniffing around a safe house operated by a clandestine government agency? Or were the ties even tighter than that?

And now it occurred to me that Phoebe's spontaneous revelation of the rented house's address and the license plate number had not been spontaneous at all. *Of course* she had told me! She fed me that information because Kennaday had instructed her to do so. How could I have been so stupid? He was yanking at my strings through every word she uttered.

But did that mean I was going to forgo the third and fourth interviews? I wanted to. I wanted to turn my back on everything remotely associated with Thomas Kennaday. But I also knew myself well enough to know that if I did, if I cursed his name and turned away in anger and resentment, I would wake up in the middle of the night, if I slept at all, and resolve to follow up no matter what. I simply wasn't wired to let this sleeping dog lie. I was wired to keep going until I got my leg chewed off.

At least now I was armed with a little ammunition of my own. I would not be asking future questions of Phoebe from a position wholly in the dark. I was still half-blinded by what I did not know, but if I kept my one good eye and both ears open, maybe I could figure this thing out. Problem was, so far in this game, Kennaday had been three moves ahead of me since the very beginning.

Truth is, I was no longer expecting to win the game. What was there to win? A few shards of knowledge, that's all. But what was there to lose? Probably nothing that would come at the hands of Kennaday, but that guy yesterday from the SUV? Him, I wasn't so sure about.

16

The tenant, third interview

I was most definitely *not* in a calm state of mind when I took my usual seat in the Burchette living room for the third time. The house was quiet, as before. Phoebe stood behind the sofa.

———

P: Would you care for something to drink? I have bottled water, milk, and apple juice.

S: I'm not thirsty, thank you. Were you aware when you gave me the information that I wouldn't be able to trace the car or rented house to anybody?

P: I could make a pot of coffee if you'd like.

S: What the heck is going on here, Phoebe? What kind of game is he playing with me?

She comes around the end of the sofa and sits with hands folded in her lap.

P: All I know is that he told me that if you asked, I should give you the address and plate number.

S: There's no record of ownership for either one of them. How do you account for that?

P: [*shakes her head*] I can't.

S: Don't you ever wonder who he really is?

P: All the time. But he said there were things I couldn't know because it would put me in danger.

S: In danger from who?

P: He wouldn't say.

S: Well, not long after you tell me his story about Dan Aykroyd and the men in black, I have a similar encounter. Except that my man in black was dressed in dark blue.

P: [*eyes widen*] What happened?

S: He climbed out of an SUV and stared at me. An SUV with no license plate, by the way. You didn't know anything about that?

P: How could I?

The surprise on her face seems genuine, as does the glimmer of fear in her eyes. My tone softens a little.

S: The house where you said you met him? Empty. As if nobody had been there for a very long time.

P: Honest to God, that's where we met. Many times.

S: [*shrugs, then frowns, then shakes head*] Did he ever talk to you about a guy named Ray Gricar?

P: No.

S: Jerry Sandusky?

P: No.

S: How about a pedophilia ring?

She flinches. It isn't much, just a tiny, momentary flutter of her eyelids. Followed by silence.

S: He did, didn't he?

P: Maybe we'll talk about that next time.

S: I'd like to hear about it now.

P: I can't. Not today.

S: Then what am I doing here, Phoebe? In fact, why am I even involved in this? I'm beginning to suspect that he didn't run into me by accident at Joy Buffet, did he?

She lowers her gaze and says nothing.

S: I'll take that as a yes. Which means he had been following me or watching me or something. Right? And *that* is very, very creepy.

P: [*stares at the tips of her shoes*] He told me that a writer would come to ask me about what happened here, and I said how do you know that, did you already arrange it, or what? And he said... the truth has to come out. From somebody who won't hide it or cover it up. Somebody with an audience.

She smiles then as if remembering something more, then looks up at me again.

P: He said he'd go after the biggest fish he could but that the pickings were slim.

Ouch, that stings a little, but I must admit to the truth of it. Probably fewer than a dozen people in the entire county know I am a writer; far fewer would recognize me on sight. My books have a relatively small but (I like to think) discriminating audience.

S: In other words, I was the best he could find.

P: I think he made a good choice.

S: I bet you've never read a single book of mine, have you?

P: [*blushes*] I like to read romance novels.

It is impossible to not sympathize with her situation. If she is being honest with me, she is as much a pawn of Kennaday as I am.

S: So what can I ask you? What are you permitted to tell me today?

P: You can ask me more about Thomas if you want to.

S: How about if you just tell me everything you know about him.

P: He said you have to ask. Otherwise I should keep it to myself.

Even in his absence, Kennaday is an irritant.

S: Okay. Where did he come from? Where is his permanent home?

P: He doesn't have one. He goes wherever he is assigned.

S: Assigned by whom?

P: His employer.

S: And who would that be?

P: He said he works for a branch of the government that goes by several names.

S: Such as?

P: The Zed Division. The 13th Floor. The Nowhere Group.

If not for the fact that my law enforcement contact brought up our intelligence agencies and their myriad permutations, I would have laughed out loud at those cartoonish names. But cartoonish names shouldn't surprise me. Former officials such as Brennan and Clapper have already demonstrated how obtuse and chuckleheaded our so-called intelligence can be.

S: And what kind of work is this secret government agency involved in?

P: Stability and continuity, he said.

S: Of what?

P: The world, I guess. Everything.

S: Phoebe, please. What is that supposed to mean—the stability and continuity of everything?

P: He said that's as much as he was permitted to say.

The notion sends a shiver through me. I will admit to a healthy distrust of the whole Medusa-headed military/industrial/intelligence/congressional/corporate/media complex. Eisenhower warned about allowing that complex too much power. JFK and Reagan warned about it too. It's more than likely that JFK and his brother were assassinated because of their expressed intent to shut down or at least defang the CIA.

Unfortunately, the CIA's Operation Mockingbird, started in the fifties to wiretap journalists, has been successful in infiltrating and taking over the media and establishing a nearly permanent war economy. In a 1977 article in *Rolling Stone*, Pulitzer Prize–winning journalist Carl Bernstein reported that the CIA had placed over four hundred assets inside the country's most influential news outlets. How many are there now?

Trump claimed to want to dismantle the whole complex, which he called "the swamp" and "the deep state," but at the same time, in 2018, he pushed forward a deal with Boeing, a major war profiteer, on a $10 billion fighter jet. So it's difficult to be sure just which side the Donald was on. And Biden? Biden has been chest deep in the swamp from the very beginning of his political career, and lately has been buddying up to countries such as Iran and China, whose stated intentions are to destroy our country. And his hard swing to the left should be terrifying to every liberty-loving citizen. So yes, "the stability and continuity" of the whole world sounds, on its surface, like a good thing. The question is, how is that stability and continuity to be interpreted, and how is it being enforced? In 1951 the CIA allegedly doped an entire French village with LSD to test the mind control potential of that drug. Hundreds of innocent people were affected, dozens were sent to asylums, and seven died. All in the name of national security.

S: How do Kennaday and his employer go about keeping the world stable?

P: What do you mean?

S: What are their methods?

P: All I know is that he said they're involved in the possibilities of vertical time travel.

Vertical time travel?

S: [*groans*] Good lord.

As far as I was concerned, that assertion crosses the line into absurdity. And I grew up on a steady diet of Superman comic books. Not that I even understand the term *vertical time travel*. Thanks to Jules Verne and others, I have a good grip on time travel per se. But *vertical?* I draw a blank on that one.

I choose not to ask Phoebe about it; the way she enunciated the term suggests that she is in the dark with me on that one. I change the subject.

S: You told me in our first interview that Kennaday gave you a gun. It was the .38 Special you shot at Cirillo with, correct?

P: Yes.

S: And is that why Kennaday gave it to you?

P: Not exactly.

S: I'm all for exactness here, Phoebe.

P: What he told me was that I should shoot Justin with it.

S: Shoot as in *kill*?

P: Yes. I mean he didn't tell me exactly when I would need to do it or specifically who I should shoot. He just told me to keep the gun with me and be ready to shoot somebody, because I would know when the moment came. And the only moment that came was when Justin took a shot at me and Shonnie.

S: Hmm. According to the clippings I've read, you had to run back to your bedroom to get the gun after Cirillo shot at you and Shonnie.

P: [*nods*] I didn't like carrying it. Especially around the girls. That's why I screwed up.

S: You think you screwed up by not killing Cirillo?

Phoebe nods again, this time with tears in her eyes.

P: If I'd been downstairs when Justin and Eddie and Jo came that day, and I had the gun with me, maybe at least Diney and Shell would still be alive.

My heart goes out to her. I understand guilt. She will probably spend the rest of her life blaming herself for those deaths.

S: What will happen now that you didn't kill Justin?

P: I don't know.

S: Kennaday didn't tell you that?

P: He just said that I had to do it.

S: But not your brother or the Mrozek woman? You weren't supposed to kill them, right?

P: No, just Justin. I mean he said the time would come when I
would have to kill a man, because if I didn't, he would kill me and
Shonnie too. And she was the important one.

Did I hear that correctly?

S: What do you mean LaShonda was the important one? In what way?

P: She was the one I had to save. And I did. At least I did that by
shooting at him, even if I didn't hit him.

Something is missing here.

S: Can you explain that to me, Phoebe? What was it that made
LaShonda more important than everybody else?

P: I don't know for sure. Something she has to do when she's older.
He wouldn't say what exactly, except that things would be bad if
she wasn't around to do it.

S: Bad for who?

P: For everybody. Everywhere.

I don't want to hear this nonsense, I really don't. Kennaday knows
the future, or at least a possible future? This interview is giving me
a throbbing headache. If I put the pieces together in a certain order,
according to what I have heard from Phoebe so far, they line up like
this: Kennaday + secret agency + time travel + LaShonda Burchette
as an adult = future continuity and stability for the USA or the world.

It's ludicrous. Fantastical. Preposterous. Or so I keep telling myself.
And I'm the guy who spends most of every night treating insomnia
with the medicine of podcasts about near-death experiences and other

paranormal subjects. I am familiar with the territory. *Coast to Coast AM, Fade to Black, Dark Matter, Metaphysical Talk Radio, Supernatural, The Richard Dolan Show, Mysterious Universe*, and so forth.

There are those in the paranormal community who make their living by pushing outlandish ideas. One man claims that he has been time traveling for the government since a child, another that he is a time traveler from the future, another that he is a government-trained super soldier who battles monstrous aliens on the astral plane. But it is too easy to claim knowledge of the future when disproving such claims is impossible. How can you disprove what hasn't yet happened?

There are, among my late-night playlists, a few individuals who approach their subjects with a rational cynicism, but others of the hosts and guests so irritate me with their improbable speculations and anecdotes that I will switch to instrumental meditation music and, invariably, an easier sleep.

P: I'm sorry. That's all for today.

She stands and brushes the tears off her cheeks.

P: I can meet with you one more time. Come back on Wednesday, please. Not tomorrow but the Wednesday after that.

She turns abruptly, then heads for the stairs.

S: A full week? Why not some day *this* week?
P: [*walks briskly up the stairs*] You have things to do.

Seconds later, a door overhead closes with a muted thud. I remain seated, still stunned. Eventually I rise to my feet. My knees feel weak, my gait wobbly as I head for the door and outside.

17.

The buzzards gather

A part of me couldn't wait to get home and go to work researching the Zed Division, the 13th Floor, the Nowhere Group, and vertical time travel. I would also have to interview Cirillo and try my best to get a few rays of illumination from him, even though he was playing the role of a mute not only with the police but also with his public defender. For the moment, though, I needed to sit in a quiet, empty space for a while. It was the only way I could think of to keep my thoughts from careening around my skull like so many fuel-injected pinballs.

There were woods all around Bell's Grove, but I didn't know those woods, and I was in no mood to get as lost physically as I was cerebrally. Plus, I would have to leave Candy parked defenseless on the street, and that I wasn't willing to risk. Her body is made of fiberglass; the trunk and saddlebags could be smashed open by any cretin's hammer, screwdriver, or rock. Pearson Park, about three miles away, had a nice parking lot where she would be relatively safe while I ambled along the hiking trails in the woods, but those trails wound through a stand of trees trapped between the intersection of two busy roads, where the roar and rumble of traffic could never be avoided. It was a good place for burning calories but not for burning off one's confusion.

That was when I remembered the Scottish Rite Cathedral. Every time I traveled into downtown New Castle, whether alone or with Cara, whose favorite place for a chai latte is on Washington Avenue, we would both glance up toward the hill where the cathedral sits, a massive granite fort that tempted us with its secrets. I had parked across from the building just yesterday when I visited Kennaday's safe house, had felt the massive building's secrets tug even then, but had had other business to attend to. Not so today. Today I needed calmness, quiet, and solitude. The afternoon's events had shaken me.

In the past I have sought and found solace in other majestic cathedrals: the Salisbury Cathedral, not far from Stonehenge; St. George's Church in London's Hanover Square; the Cathedral of St. Michael and St. Gudula in Brussels. Closer to home I had spent revivifying hours in smaller but no less important churches. Cara and I spent part of our second date holding hands on a rear pew in the otherwise empty chapel on the campus of Westminster College in New Wilmington, maybe nine miles north of the Burchette house along winding country roads. I had also spent some time alone there after my son's graduation from that institution, and was able to exit the building afterward with more joy and pride and gratitude in my heart than the sense of loss that had driven me there.

But the Scottish Rite Cathedral was closer by half. Though not a church in the conventional sense, its size and majesty promised a greater opportunity for solitary contemplation than did a college campus. Plus, and this possibility intrigued me even more than the promise of solitude, the cathedral just might have a link to Kennaday's alleged employer.

I fired up Candy and aimed her south by southwest.

———

I parked Candy in the lot across the street. The sky, though still gray, was high and thin, and the day was warm enough that I peeled off my leather, packed it in the trunk, grabbed a note-book and pen, and crossed toward the Scottish Rite Cathedral. High above the building, three buzzards were cutting wide circles in the overcast sky. Jokingly, I thought, *I hope they aren't here for me.*

That thought barely had time to complete itself before one of the buzzards wheeled out of its circle and glided down to sit atop the building's cornice, high above and a few yards left of the entrance door. The slow flap of its long brown wings and then, as it perched, the bright red head and yellow beak, told me it was a turkey buzzard rather than the more aggressive black buzzard. Although ugly up close, the turkey buzzard is a graceful flyer, and in my youth I had spent many hours watching them soaring on thermals hundreds of feet over my head, zeroing in on roadkill or other carrion with their keen sense of smell.

And maybe it was my imagination, but as this bird stretched out its long, crooked wings, I could swear that it was peering down at me. I almost expected it to croak out a throaty "Nevermore."

I was so unnerved that I paused on the sidewalk before going up the steps, pulled my phone from my pocket, punched in my password, and asked, "Hey, Google. What is the symbolic meaning of seeing a vulture?"

Sometimes when I ask my phone a question, it gives me flap-doodle. This answer, however, seemed far too pertinent. "If a vulture appears in your life, it could mean many things. You are expending too much personal energy."

Oh yeah, I thought. *That fits.*

"You have numerous resources at your disposal, yet you still feel exhausted and ill-equipped."

On the nose with that one.

"The vulture spirit animal has no voice, which means that your actions speak louder than your words."

Well, yeah, but that's true for everybody, isn't it?

"Vulture symbolism also speaks of purification. It symbolizes that the time has come for you to right your wrongs and restore the harmony in your life."

Easier said than done.

"The vulture teaches you to embrace and truly understand the meaning of death, because for the vulture, the death of one means life for another."

Okay, enough of this nonsense. Who listens to their phone's advice anyway? Not me, that's who.

I shook off the shiver trickling up my spine and hurried onto the uncovered porch, then seized the thick door handle and gave it a yank, fully expecting it to yank back, locked. But it didn't. The door opened onto a high-ceilinged lobby with marble walls rimmed on three sides by eighteen Doric columns, massive arched windows along the front wall. Behind the pillars were, by my count, six dark doorways.

I stepped farther inside, allowed the heavy door to *shoosh* shut behind me, and immediately felt dwarfed—which is, I propose, the way a cathedral *should* make a person feel. But this was no traditional lobby and no traditional cathedral; this was where the most coveted secrets and rituals of an ancient organization had been shared and carried out. A traditional cathedral will make you feel dwarfed yet part of something infinite and good; this one just made me feel dwarfed.

Down at the far end of the lobby, not a short distance away, was a wine-colored settee pushed against the wall, the only place to sit in the cavernous lobby. I walked the necessary yardage, sat, fidgeted for a moment or two, then prepared to ease myself into the silence before putting my notebook and pen to use.

Within seconds, and with no visible, audible, or other discernible provocation, my heart kicked into warp drive and my lungs were sucked dry of all oxygen. It felt as if somebody had dropped a seventeen-gallon Shop-Vac atop my chest, plunged the hose into my lungs, and flipped the switch on. I tried gulping air but to no avail. Where had all the oxygen gone? As a dark dizziness took hold of me, I struggled to my feet and stumbled toward the door, which now looked a mile away. With my pulse thrumming in my ears like a tattoo artist's drill, I expected to topple unconscious to the floor at any moment.

Somehow I made it outside onto the concrete porch. But my breathing was still constricted, my chest in an ever-tightening vise, my heart hammering faster than I could count. I was gripped by an urgency to get away from the building, as far and fast as I could.

My legs gave out just as I reached Candy. Steadying myself against her front faring, I went down on one knee. Then turned and sat on the dirty pavement as I leaned against her wheel, hyperventilating. Darkness swirled around me.

Again and again I instructed my heart to slow down. I tried meditating, closed my eyes and counted each seemingly empty breath going in and out. I wanted to lie down but was afraid that the weight against my chest would crush me. For at least five minutes I tried without luck to fill my lungs and quiet my heart. Was I dying? The possibility seemed very real.

In his beautiful song "Radio City Serenade," Mark Knopfler sings, "every wounded soldier needs a lady with a light to help him through the night." He was singing about a city, but I have never been comforted by a city, I need a good woman for that. With excruciating effort, I worked my cell phone from a pocket and struggled through the tears in my eyes to send a text to Cara, my lady with a light who just happened to know a lot more about anatomy than I do: *What does heart attack feel like?*

18.

Brush with death #10

This seems like the appropriate place to tell you a bit more about Cara, who is, at this point, my girlfriend of a year or so. During her college years she worked with kids on the spectrum, kids with Asperger's syndrome, so she recognizes and accepts, and even shares, many of my "Aspie quirks," as she calls them. She finds them endearing. Sometimes. But her tolerance for my quirks has its limits too.

A veterinarian, Cara does business in a remodeled farmhouse in the township west of mine. The first floor is devoted to her practice, the second floor her living quarters. She spends her day tending to every kind of domestic animal you can name, most of them at her place but not rarely at a neighboring farm.

She is also a certified Reiki master, though not exclusively for humans; she is on retainer to a stable with a dozen show horses. Turns out they are very skittish animals by nature, though a regular energy massage will keep them mellow. I, too, can attest to the magic in her hands. (Fortunately she has not yet been forced to use any of her veterinary skills on me, though she did show me—"for future reference"—her collection of livestock castration tools.) In every other instance, however, she is a healer, a lover and protector of all life. She is, inside and out, a very beautiful woman, talented in a number of ways, kind and generous and more tolerant than any other woman I have known.

And now we return to the narrative: I, sitting on dirty concrete and being held semi-erect by my motorcycle as I pant for breath, have just now made a polite query of Cara by text, asking her to describe the sensation of having a heart attack.

I had barely tapped the Send icon before the phone started ringing. "Hey, babe," I groaned.

"What's going on with you? Where are you? What are your symptoms? What were you doing?"

"Doing nothing," I said between shallow gasps of air. "At Scottish Rite...Cathedral. Can't...get breath."

"What are you doing *there*? You didn't go inside, did you? I'm calling an ambulance for you."

"No amblance. I'll be o...kay."

"Where's the pain, baby? Tell me exactly what you are feeling right now!"

"No pain. Heaviness. In chest. Pressure. Heart too...fast."

"Oh my God, how fast? How fast is it beating?"

"Faster than on...treadmill."

"Oh my God oh my God, I'm calling an ambulance. Where are you exactly?"

"No amblance or...I won't tell."

"Baby please! Tell me exactly where you are!"

"No amblance."

"Damn you!" she said. "Then I'm coming. Where are you?"

"Parking lot. Me and Can...dy."

"Don't you dare get on the bike like that!"

"No worries."

"You're in the big parking lot across from the cathedral?"

"Yep."

"Doing what?"

"Trying to…breathe."

"How long have you been like that?"

"Minutes. Two…three."

"It happened when you were riding?"

"No. Went inside."

"*You went in the cathedral without me?*"

"Sorry."

"Did you protect yourself first?"

"Forgot," I said.

"Baby, do it now, you have to do it now! This could be a spirit attack. Do you remember what I taught you?"

"Yep."

"I'm going to call an ambulance—"

"No…amblance!"

"You can't even say the word right, you have no breath! Baby, please."

"No…thank you."

"You could be dead before I get there!"

"True dat," I said.

"Baby PLEASE!"

"No worries," I managed with the next exhalation. I sucked in another short breath and added, "All good."

She was silent for a few seconds, then told me, her words in a rush, "Don't hang up I have a ninety-pound Rottweiler on the table with his hip cut open so I need to put you on hold just ten seconds I promise. *Don't hang up!*"

I used those seconds to ask God, the Light, Jesus and the angels and all the saints and ascended masters and my dead relatives and my deceased dog Shadow to cleanse me of all harmful attachments, entities, and spirits, and to not let me die that afternoon in a dirty parking lot.

When Cara took me off hold, she said, "You have to start cleansing yourself right now, baby."

"Did it," I said.

"Okay, okay good. Can you do it again, out loud for me? I just want to listen, okay? Just do it out loud and stay on the line with me. I'm going to Reiki you from here, okay? But first I need to hear you cleansing yourself."

I felt a little silly mumbling my improvised chant loud enough for her to hear, but I also felt more than a little guilty for interrupting her day so abruptly. There was a significant difference in our ages, and ever since our first lovemaking session she had been expecting me to drop dead of a heart attack. For a while back then she would call a halt to the activity just as things were getting interesting, so that she could check my pulse or listen to my heart. When she first discovered a minor arrhythmia, a missed beat every six thumps or so, she had panicked, certain that I was wading into the River Styx. I assured her that a skip now and then just meant that my heart was taking a little hop of joy. She has never really accepted that explanation, but remains vigilant, every time we make love, for signs of my imminent demise. This time, it seemed that she might be right.

Soon a siren's wail cut through the distance. I stopped chanting long enough to tell her, with three pauses for breath, "I'm not... getting into...that thing."

She played dumb but I knew better, thanks to the increasing volume of the siren. And then the vehicle made the turn at the bottom of the hill, the whine reaching its earsplitting crescendo, then dying to a whimper as the ambulance slammed to a stop at the curb behind me.

Two EMTs came rushing toward me, the male carrying oxygen and a mask, the female with a bag of tools for probing my body. I laid the phone on the pavement and prepared to fight off the inevitable fondling of my less private parts. Unfortunately, releasing the phone took my last ounce of strength, so I sat there like a rag doll about to nod off.

The female, a small brown-haired woman in blue scrubs, knelt beside me and seized my wrist while the other one strapped a mask over my face and sent a blast of cool air into my nostrils. For a few moments, nobody talked. Then she spoke to the male. "One fifty-two," she said. She pulled a stethoscope from her pocket and listened to my heart.

To me, she asked, "Is that where it's been since it started?"

"Faster."

"How much faster?"

"A lot."

"What about the pain?"

"Just pressure. On chest."

"Is it still there?"

"Not as...bad."

"No pain in your arm?"

"Which one?"

"Either."

"No."

"Pain in the neck or back?"

"Every...morning."

"Do you have a history of heart problems?"

"No."

"Panic attacks?"

"No."

"Do you smoke?"

"Never."

"Drink?"

"Water. Coffee."

"How much coffee?"

"Two mugs. Morning."

She whipped a blood pressure sleeve out of her bag and slipped it over my arm and started pumping. "How's your cholesterol?"

The bottled oxygen was working its magic on me. "Don't know," I answered.

"You've never had it checked?"

"Not that I...recall."

"One thirty-six over eighty," she said, and let the air out of the blood pressure cuff. "I don't suppose you know what your blood pressure is normally?"

I offered a weak smile. "Just happy...to have one."

"When was your last checkup?"

"Years."

"How many years?"

"Fiftyish?"

"When you were fifty?"

"Years ago."

"You haven't seen a doctor in *fifty years*?"

"Doctor of...Literature."

She scowled and shook her head. Women are always scowling at me. "Have you ever had tachycardia before?"

I assumed she meant non-sex-related tachycardia, so I answered, "No."

"How long have you had this arrhythmia?"

I had first noticed it back in high school, during the second of one of our two-a-day football practices in suffocating August heat. I'd sat with a finger to my temple after running four laps in full uniform, gasping for breath, pretty sure I'd detected an irregularity underneath my fingertip. But I was seventeen then and invulnerable, so I'd chosen to regard it as just another of my endearing idiosyncrasies. To the EMT, I said, "Always."

I couldn't tell if she believed me or not. Her eyes were digging into mine. "What about your potassium and magnesium levels? Do you take supplements?"

"Had a banana this…morning."

She studied my face awhile longer. I was smiling stupidly now, happy to be alive, loving the oxygen pouring into me. She said, "You think you can walk to the ambulance?"

"Sure," I said. "But won't."

"And why not?"

"Not in my…playbook."

"What's not in your playbook?"

"Doctors and…probing and…tuff."

"Is dying in your playbook?"

"Last page."

She tried out a more severe scowl on me. "This isn't a game, you know."

But I'd seen worse scowls before. "Sure it is." I smiled under the mask. The oxygen was my friend.

"What do you have against the medical profession?" she asked. "The cost?"

I shook my head. "You guys do…good work. Nurses too. Orderlies too."

"You left out doctors," she said.

"Whoops."

"What do you have against doctors?"

"Quacks…killed my…parents."

She nodded. Kept trying to scare me with those steely-gray eyes. "And how did that happen?"

"Usual way. Incompe…tence."

Without going into the tiresome details, my mother had lived in pain since I was nineteen, having endured three botched spinal fusions after a fall, and died at seventy-nine of senile dementia because the pain had confined her to bed and curtailed circulation to a degree that she suffered a series of ministrokes. My father was still walking three or four miles a day at ninety-three, then slipped returning from breakfast at his assisted-living facility; the attendant helped him into his chair, where he remained, suffering in silence like the ex-Marine he was, his right leg numb and unresponsive, until I called him in the afternoon to say hello. He told me what had happened, and I immediately read the riot act to the woman at the front desk and demanded that my father be sent to the hospital for an X-ray. He had a broken hip. He remained in a coma for three days after the surgery, then was sent back to his tiny apartment for hospice care.

The EMT knew none of this, of course. Nor did she need to.

"Bad doctors are rare," she told me. "There are *some*, okay? But they are very, very rare."

"A million a year," I answered. My lungs were working much better now, breathing in, breathing out, only squeaking a little like a leaky accordion.

"A million what?"

"Patients who die of…complications in the…hospital. Look it up."

She shook her head and all but snarled at me. "Guys like you are a pain in the ass, you know that?"

"Copy that," I said.

She and the male, who had spoken nary a word since arriving, stayed with me until I was breathing normally again, heart rate beep-beeping at a leisurely gallop. I refused all suggestions of medication and/or institutionalization, thanked them, offered to buy them both dinner, was rebuffed and insulted a couple more times by the female, then thanked them again as I got to my feet and swung a quivering leg astride Candy.

"Where's your helmet?" the female asked.

I smiled weakly. "Messes up what's left of my hair."

"You know what else will mess up your hair?"

I held my smile and my reply. Turned the ignition key and pushed in the start button. The engine roared.

She took a long stride and closed the distance between us. Leaned toward me and said, "Do you *want* to die? Because if you keep riding that thing without a helmet, and you don't go see a doctor about that heart of yours, that's exactly what's going to happen."

She meant well, and I appreciated her concern, but the tone of her voice was one better suited to a dog that insists on pissing on a favorite rug. I answered, "I prefer to let my...body decide when it's time...for me to die. Not some quack doctor...getting rich on kickbacks...from big pharma."

She squinted. "Are you for real?"

"No," I said. "And neither are...you. We're all just cartoon characters...in a cartoon world."

She blinked. Shook her head. Took a step away from me, just in case I was contagious. "Don't blame me if you drop dead on your way home."

I nodded toward her partner. "I'll blame him. It's always the... man's fault."

"You need your head examined."

I had heard that diagnosis before, several times. So I allowed her the last word and answered only with a smile.

One more shake of her head. Then she strode away and climbed in behind the wheel and slammed the door shut.

Just as I was backing Candy up to make a turn toward the street, the male EMT came toward me. He fished into a pocket and pulled out a silver medallion about the size of a quarter. "Here," he said. "Take this and keep it with you."

I took my hand off the throttle and let him lay the silver disk in my palm. Unfortunately, my eyes were still slightly crossed, so I could not make out any of the tiny letters inscribed on the medallion.

He saw me squinting and bobbing my head like a pigeon, and said, "It has the names of the twelve archangels on it. For protection. You should wear it."

I tried to hand it back to him. "I don't want to take your—"

He pushed my hand away, moved a little closer, and said sotto voce, "If you're going to be messing around in places like that, you need protection. A lot of bad shit has gone down in that building."

"So I've been told. You mean like...rituals and stuff?"

"You name it, it's happened. And not just in there. This whole town is like..." He shook his head. Apparently EMTs do that a lot. "Just be smart, man. Protect yourself." He squeezed my fingers shut over the medallion, gave me a knowing nod, then walked away.

As the ambulance drove forward, I waved my hand in thanks, blinked the last of the tears from my eyes, and shoved the archangels into my pocket. Had I the breath and inclination to do so, I might have told the female EMT before she left that no, I did not have a death wish, I have a life wish. I want to experience life as fully and vividly as I can. But I am not afraid of the Angel of Death, no matter whether she appears as a radiant being of golden light or as a grumbling old drunk armed with a dirty shovel to scrape up my bloody, scattered parts. I don't mind a flirtation now and then but I certainly wasn't ready yet to do that final boogie into the tunnel of light.

I might have told the EMTs, whose lives are devoted to stealing people back from the edge of death, that the only experiences that give any true weight to life are love and death; the first experience suggests to us that we are a part of something more significant than our own egos, and the second experience provides the proof.

As a young man I was eager for that proof, for I had not yet come to a full appreciation of loving and being loved. I'm older now. A lot older. Now I want as much of the first experience as I can possibly get before the second experience wraps me in its embrace and carries me away. And of all the brushes with death I had had thus far, the one in the Scottish Rite Cathedral had brought me closest to the precipice, had me teetering on the very edge, and therefore engendered in me the greatest swelling of gratitude for the time and love I might have left.

Prior to setting off for home that day, I sent Cara a text that sounded a whole lot more coherent than I was: *Alive and kicking. Just needed a few slugs of the big O. Strong like bull. Me and sexy Red headed home. Thanks for caring, sweetness. See you tonight.*

Sometimes it helps to be a fiction writer.

19.

The sticky
gobbledygook of truth

Cara's hands-on Reiki session that evening helped a lot; they always do. I crawled off her table feeling like a new man. Or at least like an old man after a pleasant nap. We sat on her sofa then, holding hands, the trees outside her balcony mere shadows. She told Alexa to play my favorite song, Jackson Browne's "Sky Blue and Black."

"How do you feel?" she asked.

"Like Scarecrow after Dorothy stuffed his stuffing back in. Thank you, sweetheart."

"You slept through most of it again."

"I know, I'm sorry. I try to stay awake but…"

"It's okay. You were worn out."

"I was stupid. I shouldn't have gone in there without you."

"That too," she said, and laid her head on my shoulder.

I kissed her hair. "Any company tonight?"

"Six of them," she said. "In robes and hoods. I couldn't see their faces. But they put their hands on you too."

"I woke up once and felt your hands on my head. But when I opened my eyes, you were holding my feet."

She nodded. "I don't know who they were, but I'm awful glad they showed up. I was so afraid of losing you."

"Me too," I said.

It humbles a guy to think that higher beings actually care enough to attend to my health and welfare, just as it humbles me when Cara expresses her love. Truth is, I have always felt unworthy of anyone's love and attention, which is why I too frequently respond to it with sarcasm. I can't pinpoint anything in my past that might explain why I feel that way; it might be because of my father's emphasis on self-reliance, or because I grew up feeling dwarfed by my older brother, or because of past life or ancestral karma. But it is what it is, and despite my continuing efforts, it remains a tough tick to shake out of my fur.

But I try. I kissed her head again. "You're the best woman I know," I said. "And I'm lucky to have you."

She snuggled a little closer. "Best how?"

"Most honest. Most generous. Most caring. You're the only woman I've been with who never tried to exploit or take advantage of me. My mother would have adored you."

"Maybe she sent me to you."

I looked toward the ceiling. "Thanks, Mom," I said.

Cara let a few moments pass. Then, "She said to tell you, 'You're welcome.'"

"Did she really?"

"Somebody did."

"You actually heard a voice?"

"It's more like hearing a thought. So maybe it was her, or maybe it was just me."

"There's no such thing as 'just you,' sweetness."

We talked awhile longer that night. I was eager to hear a blow-by-blow recreation of the Reiki session, wanting, as usual, to learn as much about the process and its results as I could absorb. But Cara had an early morning coming up, and it was time for me to leave;

a man would be showing up at the clinic before seven a.m. to drop off a pair of iguanas on his way to work. She would use her healing gifts on them as well, running her hands over their bodies and feeling for any "hot spots," as she called them.

"And that always works?" I asked.

"It helps me to identify the problem. So that I know what to prescribe." I find it fascinating, but for her it is matter-of-fact. "Go to any doctor and they'll do basically the same thing. They poke and probe and ask you where it hurts and what it feels like. That's all I do, really."

But it isn't. There is mystery and magic to what she does.

For some, the mystery of space is the last frontier. For others, the mystery of what lies in the deepest parts of our seas. But those mysteries are out of reach for most of us. Those mysteries are the eggheads' and millionaires' domain. For the rest of us, there is but one last frontier we are capable of exploring. It doesn't require a lot of money or technology or even a single advanced degree. Its only requisites are desire and persistence. And that is the mystery I have been poking at since the age of seven or so, when I first saw, in my peripheral vision, my dead grandfather watching me from a few yards away. The mystery of the true nature of reality.

As I have often said to Cara, "Maybe spirits *aren't* real. Maybe you and I are a couple of wackos. But we manage to function fairly well despite it, don't we? Better, in fact, than a lot of people we know. So what's the harm in believing?"

20.

A real nowhere man

I should have slept like a stone that night, and I did…for maybe forty minutes. The rest of the night was a series of bad dreams and loud thumping noises that seemed to come from either my bathroom or just outside in the hallway. Each one woke me with a start, though I can't honestly say whether any one of them was real or each a part of a dream. After the first one, I grabbed a .357 revolver out of my sock drawer and went tiptoeing through the house room by room, switching on one light after another. Only after assuring myself that all was well, every entrance into the house secure, did I return to bed. After that I kept the revolver an arm's length away on the mattress. Every ninety minutes or, until I finally climbed out of bed at 4:05, another thump woke me, and my hand seized the revolver, ready to swing it toward the door at the first hint of a kicked-in lock.

After nuking what remained in the pot of yesterday's coffee, I went to work researching my meager list of clues from the day before, starting with the names of the alleged secret government agency that was the alleged Kennaday's alleged employer. Here is what I found in regard to the Zed Division: zed, the letter Z; a character in a popular video game; a division of Bloomsbury Publishing for "socially and politically meaningful books"; the zoning evaluation division of the Fairfax County Planning Commission; a digital services and data monetization provider; a chain of Brazilian-style steak houses.

The 13th Floor? A floor often omitted on multilevel buildings because of the association with thirteen as an unlucky number; a 1999 film featuring a computer-generated parallel world set in the 1930s; a Florida-based investment and real estate development company; a song, "Floor 13," by Machine Gun Kelly.

The Nowhere Group: a company, called simply "Nowhere," that designs corporate workspaces; a different company that provides sales data in the form of contacts, financials, and competitor information; a sixties and seventies cover band, the Nowhere Men, that now bills itself as the Washington, DC, area's premier band. And this, which led me to a tantalizing glimmer of illumination only to send me diving into a deeper layer of darkness:

In a 1997 movie titled *Nowhere*, an actor named T. L. Kennaday appears briefly in a nonspeaking role as one of the party dancers. The thumbnail plot of the movie, according to IMDb, is this: "A group of teenagers try to sort out their lives and emotions while bizarre experiences happen to each one of them, including alien abductions, bad acid trips, bisexual experiences, and a rape by a TV star." Kennaday is also listed as an associate producer. Had I uncovered any other bit of evidence that seemed the least bit relevant to my search, I would have ignored this listing altogether, seeing as how my Thomas Kennaday would have been born, by my estimation, no earlier than 1990. So how could he have played a teenage party dancer in a 1997 film?

But I hate coming away from any endeavor with more questions than answers, so I pulled up Amazon Prime on my BluRay and bought a viewing of the film for $4.99. The movie is only an hour and twenty-two minutes long, but it took me nearly double that time to spot T. L. Kennaday the party dancer's two seconds of fame. The kid, surrounded by dozens of others on a strobe-lit dance floor, has spiked hair the color of lime Jell-O and can be seen dancing alone wearing nothing but Elton John–style sequined sunglasses and a Mexican flag tied around his waist. He is a bit blurred in the freeze-frame, but could easily be mistaken for, or identified as, *my* Thomas Kennaday. But that, I told myself, isn't possible. Could it be his father, or maybe an uncle? An uncle possibly, though resemblances between relatives at that genealogical distance are seldom, if ever, so striking. And the kid in the film was way too young to have fathered a child in 1990 to 1995, the range I guessed for Thomas Kennaday's birth. So what the hell was going on here?

A call to Desperate Pictures, the production company of Greg Araki, writer/director/producer of the film, to inquire about associate producer T. L. Kennaday, brought yet another spoonful of what was becoming a very sloppy ten-layer parfait of confusion. After being switched to three different unnamed voices, each one answering with "DPC. How may I direct your call?" each one avowing no remembrance of Kennaday, a fourth, who might have been anyone from an intern to the janitor, gave me this: "I sorta remember him, yeah. Dude contributed a couple of ideas to the story line and a shitload of dinero. Started out with a nice secondary role but got demoted for trying to bang everybody on the set. Nada, no idea what happened to him afterward. No idea where he came from, man. Did his thing and vamoosed, from what I can recall."

I thanked him for his information, then asked for his name and position with the company. His answer, followed by a click that terminated the call, was "Hang loose, dude. Deuce out."

As to the nature of vertical time travel, my last topic for research, I did and did not find useful information—which is to say that I found information that seemed to make sense until I tried to deconstruct that sense. It was like peeling a tasty-looking orange and finding nothing but a ball of worms inside.

In an online *HuffPost* article, "Retreat and the Gifts of Vertical Time," by Bruce Davis, PhD, retreat leader at the Silent Stay Retreat Center, I read this:

> Most of us are busy trying to get from where we are to where we want to be... We live in horizontal time. There is another path. Instead of having to get someplace, there is the art of living in the present. This is vertical time... Vertical time is falling, falling into the arms of emptiness. We land in the great presence of the intimacy of life. The movement is inside as much as it is outside. Vertical time is tea time, a coffee break, a long walk... There is so much in vertical time... There are worlds and worlds, realms upon realms for us to know and enjoy as vertical time unfolds within each of us.

Is this the beginning of practical information or just new age gibberish?

A year ago I would have argued for the latter definition. But after meeting Cara, I am inclined to temper that judgment. She has more psychic gifts than she likes to admit. The first winter we were together, I was out running errands on a particularly icy day. While driving home, I received a call from her warning me of an accident at a certain small bridge a few miles from her place. "There are three or four vehicles blocking the bridge," she told me. "You might want to turn around and go home another way."

I have this character flaw that doesn't often allow me to retreat, especially when there is something as interesting as a multivehicle crash up ahead. So I kept going, and Cara kept asking my speed and urging me to slow down.

And soon I came to the bridge in question. It was empty. "All clear," I told her. "No wreckage or anything suggesting there has been one."

"That can't be! It just now happened! Not ten minutes ago. It can't be cleared already."

"Can't be but is," I said as I cruised over the bridge. "You must have the wrong place."

"The bridge across from that bar, Aces and Eights," she said.

"Yep. Just passed it. Apparently somebody got their facts—" And *bang, crash, bang, kaboom*! I looked in the rearview mirror. Less than fifty yards behind me, the accident was happening.

I started shaking. Pulled over onto the shoulder. And with a trembling finger put my four-way flashers on. "It just now happened," I told Cara.

"It *what*?"

"The accident. It just now happened. *Behind me*. A few seconds *after* I crossed the bridge."

How could that be? I can think of only two possibilities. Either Cara had entered a time slip when her patient's owner notified her of the accident, or I had entered one when I crossed the bridge *before* the accident happened. Either way, I had escaped possible injury, and it wasn't the first time. When I was nineteen and, as usual, driving too fast, a similar time slip spared me certain death. I and my vehicle miraculously jumped ahead in time and space by three or four seconds.

That was my first experience with the elasticity of time, and the accident at the bridge was my second. And lest you think that statement is yet another reason to label me a nutcase, here is what a writer had to say on the subject in the May 15, 2021, issue of London's *Daily Mail*: "Liverpool's Bold Street is so well known for time slips that there's a Reddit forum dedicated to discussing it, along with YouTube documentaries and Facebook pages."

Yes, they happen, and worldwide. Online you can find a myriad of other examples of time slips, along with numerous explanations of why they occur, many of them citing Einstein and Tesla and quantum physics. But the truth is that we all slip through time with every ticking second. We are all sliding forward. So for me the question isn't whether or not it is possible to hop forward in time by a few seconds, but why it seems to happen to some, including me, whenever their lives are in danger. And who is pulling those strings?

Maybe we are pulling our own strings, but we just don't realize it on the conscious level. For example, we know that photons do not move only as waves but can also move as particles. More recent experiments demonstrated that they can also exhibit both behaviors simultaneously, and even be in two places at once—as if the photon is making a conscious decision as to the best path to take! And since our bodies are essentially a bunch of photons held together within an energy field...

Okay, maybe it's best not to go down that particular rabbit hole right now. Let's get back to the subject of vertical time travel, which just might explain time slips: the second reference I found to that possibility—or, in this case, to vertical time—was in a *Mysterious Universe* podcast, in which the Aussie hosts talk about what they call "blank time." Blank time, they propose, is not horizontal time, i.e., the past, present, or future, but is vertical time. Vertical time is a kind of invisible tower of time in which every moment of time exists as the same moment in time. All time, in other words, is a single moment of time, and everything that has ever happened exists within that same moment. Only in vertical time travel can events be changed, altered, or revised without precipitating the butterfly effect or the grandfather paradox, both of which make horizontal time travel too dangerous and unpredictable.

In discussing the concept of vertical time, the hosts of *Mysterious*

Universe cited Wolfgang Smith, a philosopher and physicist who has devised a new interpretation of quantum mechanics. I won't go into his philosophy here, but if you enjoy complicated academic jargon, you can read more about his theory in the addendum on my website.

In any case, where did all this information leave me? It left me ready to slam my throbbin' noggin against the wall. Not only was I getting nowhere in my investigation into the true Thomas Kennaday, but I was also getting deeper into the multilayered nowhere surrounding the Burchette murders. I had started with an injured baby found in the woods, and with an obvious triggerman and his three victims, then somehow found myself also juggling a missing DA, a global pedophilia ring, a secretive organization that practices ancient Egyptian magic, plus an infuriatingly manipulative and enigmatic millennial smart-ass who appears to have been an extra in a 1997 movie about all manner of odd happenings. And oh yeah, the number four, the four Gospels and all of that business. What did the number four have to do with any of this?

The only person in the room who was smarter than me, yet just as capable of being as dumb as a cow flop, was the little lady inside my phone. So I posed my question to her, in frustration, with only a small modification to Tina Turner's famous musical query, *what's love got to do with it?* "Hey, Google. What does four have to do with it?"

Her answer was to toss up a screen titled "Set up Voice-Android-Google Voice Help-Google Support."

That's a cover-your-own-ass reply if ever I've heard one. But I empathize with her confusion. Throw in vertical time travel, Dan Aykroyd, men in black, and a probable spirit attack, and I was lost in a funhouse of broken mirrors, slanted floors, and hidden doorways from which a squealing lunatic with a rusty ax might spring out at any moment to lop off my throbbing head.

21.

Where did I put my tin foil hat?

My problem is not necessarily with believing in such things as time travel and mystical numbers, but in jibing it all with the Burchette house murders and the information I've received from Thomas Kennaday through Phoebe Hudack. I cannot verify either's honesty or even guess at their intentions. Past experience has taught me that I tend to trust people before they have proven themselves worthy of trust; in other words, I give them the benefit of the doubt. At the least, I often suspend judgment too long, a proclivity I have, on several occasions, regretted.

Try as I might, though, I cannot refute or deny any of the prognostications about my behavior and reactions that Kennaday allegedly made to Phoebe before he ever met me. How could he have known that I would act precisely as I did? He has either been extraordinarily well-trained in human behavior, or he possesses, as Phoebe claimed, knowledge of the future. Is he indeed a government-employed time traveler? Is that what the Zed Division/13th Floor/Nowhere Group is up to?

Evidence is concrete that the CIA, and probably other agencies too, has been conducting secret psi and paranormal testing for decades. Project Blue Book, MKUltra, and Majestic 12 are matters of fact. The navy has admitted to its ongoing investigations of UFO phenomena and has even released video and photos. Thousands of highly credible individuals—law enforcement personnel, pilots, astronauts, air traffic controllers, and even the former Canadian minister of defense, former Senate majority leader Harry Reid, and a former investigator of UFOs for the British Ministry of Defense have testified to the presence of extraterrestrials.

Most recently, Haim Eshed, who helmed Israel's space program and Defense Ministry, made the most startling claims yet. He told an Israeli newspaper, *Yediot Aharonot*, that there is "an agreement between the U.S. government and the aliens. They signed a contract with us to do experiments here." He also claimed that American astronauts and extraterrestrials meet in an underground base on Mars as part of a galactic federation. Furthermore, Eshed said, the galactic federation talked President Trump out of revealing all this to the public so as to "prevent mass hysteria."

Just to write those claims and present them to the public makes me feel like more than a fool. Surely only a fuzzy-brained fourteen-year-old would buy into such sophomoric cheese whiz. But to deny the truth of these and other claims is to label hundreds of senior government officials and other credible witnesses as liars or crazies. And to deny something out of hand only because we ourselves have not experienced that something is narrow-minded, to say the least. As a cynic in the original Greek sense, I am willing to credit the possibility of just about everything until even stronger evidence comes along to negate it.

Unfortunately for me, extraterrestrials is one of the few subject areas not specifically represented in my past week of activities. Unless the man in black I encountered was an extraterrestrial. And unless the global pedophilia ring has its roots in ancient rituals influenced by extraterrestrials. Neither of those assumptions would be without historical precedent.

Still, it seems a flimsy link in regard to *my* investigation. When I began this project, it was never my intention to investigate UFOs or anything else paranormal, only Justin Cirillo's motive for slaughtering three people, the identity of Baby Doe, and the true identity of Thomas Kennaday. But now I have to ask myself: Of those three individuals named above, attention to which one might have prompted my encounter with a man in black?

Kennaday, that's who. If he really is a member of a secret government agency, does his involvement with me mean that he has gone rogue, and that another member of his own organization doesn't want me learning too much? Has Kennaday been gingerly releasing information to me through Phoebe Hudack that some other organization, quite possibly an alien or alien-friendly one, is determined to keep secret? If so, are they capable of engineering a spirit attack on me? If they could pull that off in the Scottish Rite Cathedral, isn't it logical to assume that they can pull it off wherever and whenever they wish? Or had the attack been merely a warning or an attempt to frighten me, just as the man in black had been? Or am I starting to see connections where none exist?

This research carried me through an entire day and into the evening. Each new layer made my muscles tenser, neck stiffer, breaths heavier. I lay in bed that night examining every detail of my time since first meeting Kennaday, looking for greater significance and hidden meanings. The vulture that had perched on the Scottish Rite Cathedral's cornice, for example, its long wings held out and crooked as it looked down on me—was that bird signaling something with its peculiar posture? Was that carrion-gobbling bird more than a bird? Any organization, human or otherwise, that could control spirit activity could certainly control a vulture. Or project an individual *as* a vulture.

I was truly and deeply frightened. My legs ached, my neck ached, my stomach was boiling with sour bile. I tried meditation but it was of no avail, my mind would not stop chattering. I searched the medicine cabinet for a remedy, but, as an eschewer of nonhomeopathic remedies, all I had were a bag of cherry throat lozenges and a box of Band-Aids. The refrigerator was no help either, nor any of the cupboards. I crawled back upstairs and into bed.

There I started playing with various convoluted scenarios in hopes of tying my day's research together with the murders in the Burchette house and Kennaday's insistence that I explore the case. For hour after hour I moved the pieces around, hoping they would adhere to one another. In the end, only one scenario accomplished that, and it is such a Rube Goldberg construction, so far-fetched and rickety, that even I have to chuckle now as I write it out for the very first time:

Baby Doe was abducted as part of a pedophilia ring that somehow had ties with Cirillo and/or his primary target, Barry Faye, a ring that includes individuals of such prominence that a secret government agency involved in time travel—and therefore aware that LaShonda Burchette will be instrumental to the country and/or world's future well-being—sends one of its agents, Thomas Kennaday, to manipulate a malleable writer into exposing the whole conspiracy to conceal the true nature of reality from the masses, while a rival organization, possibly one in cahoots with malevolent djinn, works to undo Kennaday's work by scaring the daylights out of that hapless writer.

It is a laughable premise, I know. Utterly and completely unbelievable, harebrained, and absurd. But it is the only explanation that works.

I lay in bed for a long time that night, cursing the hour I spent with Thomas Kennaday. I wished I had never gotten involved in the investigation. Above all else, I wished for another premise to replace the only one that seemed to fit.

As on previous nights, I awoke several times with a sense of foreboding. Each time, rain was loud as it blew against the windows, the wind gusting, branches creaking. I remember that my last conscious thought before drifting into a final ninety minutes of sleep was that I hadn't had a full night's sleep since my early thirties, and in all likelihood would never enjoy that luxury again.

22.

Witchy woman, got any nines?

I spent the next morning on the laptop sifting through YouTube and other videos and reading articles professionally and/or abysmally written pertaining to every crackbrained conspiracy theory imaginable. Ninety minutes were used up by racing through an online course in the Kabbalah, which informed me—as if that morning's coffee hadn't made my stomach sour enough—that a cosmic evil force, called *sitra achra*, the Other Side, is not only real but is equally as divine as goodness. Both are elements of the energy we call God, and our job, to put it simply, is to balance out the evil with good. Evil exists, in fact, to provide us the opportunity to do good.

Yikes! In other words, evil can *never* be completely eradicated? We *need* it? That's a hard pill to swallow. Or, as the author of my online Kabbalah lesson states, "Letting go of the reality of separate evil, and really accepting that the sitra achra is a side of Divinity, is easy on paper and very difficult in reality."

Shortly after noon I returned to my bed to wallow in confusion, hoping that sleep would claim me. But instead, I started thinking about my aunt Sara. In the memory of her that first arose, I was nine years old and playing catch with the porch roof, tossing a softball up and letting it roll back down and plop into my hands, again and again and again as my grandmother lay dying on a roll-up bed in the dining room. I knew that she was going to die that day, knew it would happen any minute now, and the repetitious thump of the ball off the roof and then into my little hands felt good—felt like I was throwing the ball at God, bouncing it off his big implacable Old Testament face. I blamed every hurt and slight and fear on God back in those days. And would continue to do so well into my adulthood.

My mother's sister, Sara, lived next door to us when I was growing up, and was my babysitter until I turned twelve or so. She never owned a car, never married, and lived a very simple, even austere life in the tiny cottage on the other side of our driveway. She raised chickens for their eggs, tended a huge garden of vegetables every summer, plus a half-acre of strawberry plants and blackberry vines that I raided on firefly nights. When I or one of the other neighborhood kids, playing out in my yard, would smack a softball too far, or when I would lose control of my rubber band–powered balsa wood airplane, Sara would step outside suddenly and snatch the offending object up off her lawn and take it back inside the cottage before anyone else could get to it. She was so quick that she must have been watching from behind the curtains, though other theories, inspired by a steady diet of comic books, were floated too: She has super hearing! Her yard is bugged with some kind of secret alarm! She's part retriever! She's Superman's real mother! She's a witch!

A week later the snatched object would turn up on our porch. The other kids in the neighborhood, all of whom were three or four years younger than me and preferred the witch theory, were afraid of her; she was a tall, thin woman, like my mother, but where my mother preferred pedal pushers and sleeveless blouses, Sara outfitted herself almost exclusively in ankle-length dresses and wide-brimmed sunbonnets.

I loved Sara and she loved me. I was a lonely, overly sensitive boy, and her back door was always open to me. She and I must have played a thousand games of go fish together. On stormy nights when my parents were out, or on frigid winter nights when the wind blew like banshees and I was too frightened to sleep, it was Sara who would lay a Bible beside my pillow and say, "There you go, Chookie. Jesus will keep you safe now." It always did the trick.

Her nickname for me was Big-Eyed Chook, or usually just Chookie. Not until I was an adult did I think to ask her why she called me that. "Chookie?" she said. "Like chickie, a little chicken."

"And why big-eyed?"

"Because you were always watching, always wanting to be in on the action. I couldn't have a conversation with your mom or dad or even the meter reader without you standing around some corner wanting to hear every word of it. You had big ears too. I knew you'd grow up to be either a writer or a thief."

On the morning my grandmother died, Sara had come over to our house to be with her and my mother. Grandma was barely conscious the last time I saw her before running outside, moaning softly on her little bed, now and then arching her back a little. Since then I had been lobbing the softball at God's almighty nose, hoping to break something. After a few minutes of this, Sara came out of the house with a mug of tea in hand. She called me over to the porch steps and pressed the mug into my hand. "Drink this," she said.

The mug was very warm, the tea steaming. This was in July or August; I remember that my shirt was sticking to my skin. "It's hot," I told her.

"It's supposed to be."

"What is it?"

"Magic tea."

I looked into the mug. Lipton tea with condensed milk and a

bit of sugar, the tea bag's slender string and tag stuck to the side of the cup. "It doesn't look magic."

"Well, it is."

"Magic how?"

"It has your grandma's love in it, that's how."

That brought tears to my eyes. I loved my grandma every bit as much as I loved Sara. Sometimes when Sara was babysitting me, we would walk hand in hand the half mile to my grandmother's shack of a house, where all three of us would sit at her table with the red-and-white-checkered oilcloth over it and play go fish while we laughed and stuffed ourselves with jelly bread dipped in cups of tea sweetened with condensed milk.

My hands trembled and my voice quivered as I gripped the mug of tea. "Why does she have to die?"

"Because she's old, Chookie. And she's been sick a long time."

"Why can't we take her to the hospital?"

"A hospital won't help her."

"It's not fair."

"It's how things work. Sip your tea."

I shook my head. "I don't know why everybody has to die."

"It only looks like a bad thing," she told me. "But it's a good thing for your grandma. You want her to keep suffering?"

I shook my head.

"So this is how it works. Pretty soon she won't be in pain anymore. Won't that be a good thing?"

"I don't believe in Heaven," I said.

"Neither do I."

That surprised me, and my startled look told her so.

"It's just a word, Chookie. Heaven is just a word, and so is death, and so is God."

I had no idea what she meant by that. Was she saying that

her friend, Nora Ryder, another old maid and my Sunday school teacher, was a liar?

Again, she read my eyes. "What I'm saying is it's all about moving on."

"What is?"

"Life. You keep moving on to the next grade. Just like you're doing, right? Fourth grade in the fall?"

"Yeah."

"So that's what your grandma is doing. It's time for her to move on now."

"What grade?" I asked.

"I don't know, Chook. College, I guess."

"Grandma's going to college?"

"Something like that."

"She's old." My oldest cousin, Gary, eighteen, a loud, strong boy who could smash a softball into the deep weeds where nobody could find it, and who seemed to enjoy nothing better than punching me in the arm, had started college the previous fall.

"That's who this college is for," Sara said. "For people too old or sick or hurt to stay here any longer. It's a college where she'll get better, just like that." Her wrinkled fingers snapped.

"But I won't ever see her again."

"Of course you will. I'll see her first, then you'll come along later to join us."

"What about Mom and Dad?"

"Everybody," she said. "And sooner than you think."

"I want to go now."

"You have to pass high school first. Don't be in such a hurry. You have to get a girlfriend first and make babies and all of that nonsense."

"Yuk," I said.

She kept talking to me, kept me talking, and before I knew it, I had emptied the mug of tea. My belly was warm, my eyes wet. She said, "Let's go inside and tell her goodbye now, you want to?"

"No," I said.

"Okay, don't. She'll move on and tell everybody there what a little brat you are."

"No she won't."

"Well, I will if you don't tell *me* goodbye before I move on. You little brat." She pulled me close and held me, and a few minutes later we went inside together and whispered our goodbyes to my grandma.

My aunt Sara was ninety-one years old at the time I remembered all of this while gazing at my bedroom ceiling, yet she was still as sharp as a pin, and my last living connection to my parent's generation. For the previous eight years, ever since my mother's death, I had been visiting her once a month in her assisted-living apartment. It was a forty-mile drive each way, and I really didn't like the smell of the place, or the way most of the residents would stare at me and smirk as if to say, *Just you wait, kiddo. Your turn's a comin'.* But her tiny studio apartment was always meticulous and somehow managed to radiate the aroma of freshly baked bread and rolls, just as her little cottage had. That scent wafting across the driveway never failed to alert the younger and always hungry me that some treat was just a few steps away, and soon I would be at her back door with my mouth watering and one dirty little paw held out to accept another of her delicious handouts.

Remembering all this, my stomach still churning with acid, I felt an overwhelming urge to see Sara again, even though a visit would be fifteen days ahead of schedule. So I dragged myself off the bed, splashed some water on my face, and drove to the nearest state store, where I bought a bottle of Mogen David Concord wine, the closest match to the sickeningly sweet elderberry wine she used to make and sip when I was a boy. Then I drove forty minutes to a tidy redbrick building two blocks off Main Street in a town four miles from where I had grown up.

It was nearly two in the afternoon when I arrived. The day was warmer than the previous day had been, a temperate forty-eight degrees, but the sky was a marbled gray, like granite whipped into a froth. The air was still so humid that the wetness hadn't evaporated from the street or soaked into the saturated yard around the building. Everything was damp. The horizon in all directions lay hidden behind a misty veil.

I found Sara in what was optimistically called the solarium. It was, in fact, a small screened porch on the western side of the building. A dim floor lamp burned in the corner of the room, and that was where she sat in a white wooden rocker, facing the screen and the misty day beyond, a heavy, white knitted shawl wrapped around her thin shoulders. Sara, like me, was an introvert; I never once came upon her enjoying the company of another resident, but always either sitting alone in one of the public spaces or in her apartment. I approached her from behind and tapped her lightly on the shoulder, and when she looked up, her jaw dropping, I bent over to hug her and kiss her snowy head.

"Chookie!" she said as her arms went around my waist. "I was just thinking about you."

"Good or bad?" I asked, and pulled a chair away from a card table so that I could sit closer to her.

"Bad, of course. Why are you here now? What happened?"

"What makes you think something happened?"

"What did I just tell you? I've been thinking about you."

When my mother was in the early stages of senile dementia, the only observable symptoms a tendency to repeat herself and a desire to slip salt and pepper shakers and sugar packets off a restaurant table and into her purse, she told me that her sister had once made her living as a fortune-teller. We had been having a friendly conversation, my parents and I, remembering how Mom and Sara would stand shoulder to shoulder in our overheated kitchen every summer after the strawberry crop came in, one of them ladling boiling hot jam from the kettle into a Mason jar, the other pouring melted wax over top of the jam then quickly capping the jar.

"You know she was a fortune-teller," Mom said.

"She was what?" I asked.

My mother nodded. "Started out in a traveling carnival."

"She did not."

"She most certainly did. Then one of the fellas she was seeing in the carnival found out she was seeing another one at the same time. Second one went after the first one with a knife, so she run off from the carnival before he could do the same to her."

I looked to my dad, who was never a man to use too many words. He raised his eyebrows and gave me a little shrug, which either meant *Yeah, she did*, or else *It gets worse every day, son.*

"After that," my mother continued, "she took up with some fella owned a nightclub somewhere. It was in Chicago, I think. Or maybe Cleveland. Which one was it, hun?"

"Before my time," Dad said.

"It was Cleveland, I guess. One of them gangster types. He gave her a table in the corner of the room and she sat there every night telling fortunes to the rich men and their ladies."

"Seriously, Mom? Is this for real?"

"You're the storyteller, not me. But then that nightclub owner broke her heart, and she came back home to live. Told fortunes by telephone after that."

"Over those landlines we had?" I asked. "The ones where

you had to dial the operator first? Those were party lines, right? Everybody on the line could listen in."

My mother nodded. "Now and then a car would come by, but most of the time she did it by phone."

"I thought you said those were her nieces and nephews coming for a visit."

"Nieces and nephews would be your cousins, dummy. You never thought of that?"

"I guess I didn't," I said. Which caused Dad to chuckle. I said, "I always figured she was on welfare, like the rest of the neighbors."

"She'd rather have died of starvation first, same as your dad and me."

That part was true, I knew; my parents despised the welfare system, what they called "being on the dole." My mother blamed it for turning most of her brothers into useless alcoholics.

As for Sara's history as a fortune-teller, I have never known whether to believe my mother or not; her dementia would be a tiny bit worse every time I saw her. And Sara, after becoming my last living vestige of those days, had never insinuated that she was anything but an old woman patiently waiting to die.

Until now. Now she seemed to know that I was troubled about something. Was she, in fact, a fortune-teller, i.e., a psychic, or had she simply read the fatigue and worry on my face? Her eyes were warm but as gray as her hair. "Chookie," she said, "what kind of trouble are you making now?"

I had to smile. It was the same question she had asked nearly every time I'd showed up at her door for a slice of freshly baked bread smeared with homemade strawberry jelly. "I don't think I'm the one making the trouble this time."

"You need to tell me about it," she said. "But first"—and here she looked around the room, then lowered her voice—"did you happen to bring me anything?"

"Same as always," I said.

She grinned and, with my help, climbed out of her rocker. Her hand went immediately to the small of my back, where the bottle of wine, covered by my jacket, rested inside my waistband. I escorted her to her room, where I cracked open the wine, poured three inches into a juice glass, and handed it to her. Comfortable in her recliner, sipping and gently rocking, she was ready to listen.

I told her about the past few days, about the murders in Bell's Grove, about Phoebe Hudack, and about the man in black, whom I referred to simply as *some strange guy*. I spoke in broad strokes, adding none of the metaphysical elements, ending with the incident in the Freemasons' cathedral.

"Come stand over here close to me," she said.

I did.

"Now bend down a little."

I bent closer, and she laid her ear to my chest. After half a minute or so she pulled away and gave me a pat on the butt. "You're fine," she said. "But you need to mind your own business for a change."

I returned to my chair. "I'm trying."

"Try harder."

I smiled.

"I'm not joking, Chookie. You're messing with stuff you don't understand."

That one surprised me. "Are you talking about dark forces of some kind?"

She opened her mouth as if to answer, then closed it, pursed her lips, took a sip of wine, then stared out through the screen for a while. A few moments later, she looked at me again and said, "Go on over to that dresser and get something for me."

"Okay, sure." Again I stood.

"It's in the bottom drawer. A little purple bag with a drawstring."

I found the bag beneath what appeared to be white cotton pajamas decorated with periwinkles and primroses. When I attempted to hand the bag to her, she said, "Open it and take out what's in there."

It was a tiny golden medal, smaller and thinner than a dime, egg-shaped, and dangling from a thin chain. "You keep that," she told me. "And wear it. Don't you ever take it off."

A figure was engraved on the face of the medal, but it was too small for me to identify. "I didn't bring my reading glasses," I told her. "What is this?"

"It's called a miracle medal. That's Mary on it."

"The one with the lamb?" I joked.

"You could say so." That was another of the things I loved about Sara. She never talked down to me. She expected me to know things, and I usually did. The lamb was Jesus, of course. And the Mary was his mother.

"I really don't like wearing jewelry," I told.

"Then just keep it in your pocket. You need protection. At least until I die. You'll have me after that."

I certainly wasn't going to reject her gift, no matter what I thought about my need for protection, so I slipped the medal and chain into a pocket, then took a seat beside her again. I said, "You're the second person in twenty-four hours to give me a medal for protection." Then I told her the only detail I had left out of my spirit attack story, about the EMT giving me the archangel medal.

"Can't hurt," she said after I'd finished. "Keep them both with you. And next time you get in trouble again, which you will, you hold on to one of them and ask for help."

A chill went up my spine. "If those things really work," I said, "why aren't you wearing it?"

She gave me a sideways look.

"Okay," I said. "I know. People are supposed to die sometimes."

She nodded. "That little miracle medal saved me more times than you would know."

"Tell me about them."

"Better not," she said, and grinned a little. "Maybe when you're old enough to hear it."

I patted my pocket. "Where did you get it?"

"A man I knew gave it to me when I was in trouble once. I don't need it anymore, so I want you to have it."

"I'll treasure it," I told her. "But like I said, I don't wear any kind of jewelry."

"You'll wear it in your pocket then. Now quit being a baby about it."

It was true that I did feel safer sitting there in that little room with her. Despite her thinness there was always such a stolidity to her, a stubborn refusal to yield to adversity. My mother and father and grandmother had all been the same way. They never expected life to be anything more than it was, a hard, mystifying journey, and they never failed to meet it on its own terms.

"When you get into the kind of stuff you're into now," she told me, "you're opening doors that won't want to be shut again."

I leaned closer. "I would really like to hear more about that."

She patted my cheek. "You coming back next month like you usually do?"

"I will if you want me to."

"I'll see you then, Chookie. Unless I decide to die before that. Depends on how long the wine lasts." She took my hand and squeezed it. "You're going to be all right," she told me. "Just do as I say and you'll be all right."

She squeezed my hand a few moments longer, then let go abruptly, tossing it into my lap. "Drive safe," she said. "Watch out for the deer. You young people drive like maniacs these days."

At home, I took the miracle medal from my pocket and laid it on the coffee table beside the archangel medallion. Then, with my reading glasses on, I examined each of them more closely. In the center of the miracle medal was the figure of a woman with rays of light extending from her hands and around her head. Inscribed around her were the words *O Mary conceived without sin, pray for us who have recourse to thee.*

Around the edge of the medallion, eleven names were inscribed, with *Michael* inscribed inside that circle of names. Despite thirteen years of Sunday school, I recognized only Gabriel, Michael, and Raphael. It wasn't hard to find information about those three online. Michael is the warrior who fights Satan and his minions and who protects those who love God. Gabriel is the angel who stands at the left hand of God and serves as a messenger of God's will. Raphael's role is to heal the souls of humans and to bring them closer to God. The *el* at the end of each of the twelve names is Hebrew for *god*, or *the mighty*.

Apparently, there is no consensus as to the total number of archangels. The Roman Catholic tradition recognizes only Gabriel, Michael, and Raphael. Other sources recognize as many as twenty-two. Apparently, the EMT who gave me the medallion recognized only twelve, or else the person who inscribed it did.

In any case, I left both Mary and the archangels on my coffee table to keep each other company while I, still a cynic, neither a believer nor a disbeliever but hungry for any evidence that would turn me one way or the other, tended to other business. Even in the midst of turmoil—and mine was both spiritual and intellectual—there is laundry to wash and dry, floors to vacuum, emails to answer, food to purchase and prepare.

As for my aunt Sara, she passed quietly in her sleep, I was told, with no indications of illness or distress beforehand, three days prior to my next scheduled visit. After her funeral, when I returned to the nursing home to pack up her things, a member of the staff told me that they had found seventeen empty wine bottles lined up against the wall underneath her bed. She said, "I suppose it's too late now to ask if you have any idea where they all came from."

I smiled and said, "I suppose it is."

23.

Spinning my wheels

The day after receiving the miracle medal from Aunt Sara, I was still so unnerved by my memory of the spirit attack, or my near heart attack, panic attack, whatever kind of attack it was, that I began to grieve for the quiet life I used to have, and feared that I might never reclaim it. That kind of thinking can lead to despair and its downward spiral. For many years I had kept myself out of that black hole, safely just beyond the event horizon, by making certain that I always had a goal to work toward. What goal could I turn to now?

A vehicle inspection! Okay, sure, why not? My Jeep's inspection had expired the previous month, but I had been putting it off for weeks because it would require my sitting in an overheated waiting room for two or more hours while some mechanic got around to attending to my car. Try working on a laptop in such a place crowded with ill-mannered customers and their mannerless children complaining or chattering on cell phones or noisily masticating their Whoppers, incessantly going in and out of the door, all while clamorous mechanics shout to one another and bang their tools around in the echo chamber just a few feet away, and you will understand why I looked forward to the experience only slightly more than I looked forward to having my appendix removed with a rusty spoon.

But it was my only viable option, so off I went to my local garage, laptop in hand. Another damp, gray day, though no rain or mist was falling now. Fifteen minutes after assuming my position in the already crowded purgatory, and with two young mothers talking to one another across the width of the dirty floor while ignoring a total of five rug rats staring and/or standing in front of me and trying to put their sticky hands on my laptop, I called Cara and invited her to lunch at Mobogo's, a little Vietnamese restaurant a quarter mile from my place of torture. She said she could spend twenty minutes with me but no more because one of her two employees had not shown up for work that day. That was good enough for me, so I pushed my way through the moil of rug rats, laptop tucked under my arm, and gladly started the hike through the parking lot and traffic.

I should tell you a little something more about Cara, I suppose, just to better fill in the picture of her and of our relationship.

The first time we met, we both felt an unspoken kinship with the other. We then spent the next nine hours examining all the things we had in common: both of us grew up feeling like aliens stranded on a strange, hostile planet; both of us avoid noisy people and the venues where they gather; both of us love to travel and prefer to explore places off the beaten path; both of us have had numerous paranormal experiences over the course of our lives; both of us would be considered intuitives and empaths by the new age community, were we ever to fraternize with that community, which we would do only under penalty of a proctology exam.

Thanks to her innate talents and medical training, plus her training as a Reiki master, Cara's abilities are far more developed than mine. And my encounters with the nonordinary have all occurred spontaneously, out of the blue, whereas Cara is often able to induce them. All of her normal and paranormal gifts are more developed than mine, especially her compassion, her kindness, and her generally sweet disposition.

Not that she is a pushover. When we first started dating, we would often meet for lunch at a little diner separated by its small parking lot from an AAA office. Our kisses and embraces as we bid each other goodbye in the parking lot were apparently too lewd for the priggish AAA employees in the building next door, because one of them placed a call to the diner's owner to complain about our fully clothed displays of affection. The owner laughed it off as none of his business, but Cara, not wanting him to have to deal with further complaints, reluctantly allowed that I should keep my hands off her breasts except behind closed doors. However, the next time we met at the diner, she taped a sheet of printing paper to her Nissan's rear passenger window facing the AAA office. Here is what was printed on that paper:

Anal
Abiogenetic
Acetous

I had to look up the last two words, as Cara expected the AAA ladies to do too. *Abiogenetic*: sexless; asexual. *Acetous*: producing or smelling like vinegar.

That was almost a year ago. The sheet of paper mysteriously reappears on her window every time we visit the diner.

And the moral of that story? Don't piss off a woman in love.

That, my friends, is Cara. Over two orders of #11—large bowls filled with pickled shredded carrots, chopped cucumbers, bean sprouts, mint-infused lettuce, and charbroiled pork with sautéed scallions and onions, plus two crispy spring rolls each—I filled her in on my adventures since our last Reiki session, including the conclusions I had reached after hours of research on the 13th Floor, time travel, the djinn, et cetera, and my visit with Aunt Sara. She sat listening intently until I finished, then shook her chopsticks at me. "You better be wearing those medallions," she said.

"Yeah, you know me and jewelry. I just don't—"

"You put them on the moment you get home!"

"I don't like the feel of something around my neck."

She cocked her head for a moment, then said, "Maybe you were choked to death in a previous life."

I smiled. Just between you and me, sometimes I *do* humor her. "By whom?" I asked.

"I think you did it yourself."

"I can understand that."

"Or maybe it was me in a previous life. Sometimes I feel like doing it now."

"Sorry," I said. "Erotic asphyxiation has never appealed to me."

She released a heavy sigh, and it wasn't the first such sigh in my company. "Why do you always have to be so stubborn? It's not good for our relationship, you know."

"I think we have a very balanced relationship."

"You do?"

"I do. You complement my life, and I complicate yours."

She shook her head, rolled her eyes, all of the regular responses. "Seriously, though. Wear those medals. I can't be around you if you won't protect yourself. You're a danger to both of us."

"I'm just not sure I'm buying any of it."

She laid her chopsticks across the top of the bowl and leaned toward me. "A scary guy in a blue suit and sunglasses gave you a death stare," she started.

"I don't know that I would call it a death stare—"

"That's how you described it."

"Yeah, well, sometimes I exaggerate a little."

"You've spent a week talking to a girl about some mysterious guy who suckered you into a murder investigation—"

"I don't think I was suckered in, actually."

"You were suckered in. And then a man in black gives you a death stare."

"He was wearing blue."

"A man in black wearing blue, okay? Death stare. And then you go inside a Masonic cathedral with three vultures circling over it. *Three!* And one of them actually perches over the doorway like the raven in Poe's poem! But you go inside anyway, and you almost have a heart attack!"

"It wasn't a heart attack."

"Yes it almost was! You don't know what I cleaned out of you the other night."

"You mean when you Reikied me?"

"Yes."

"What did you clean out of me?"

"Something that shouldn't have been there."

"Shouldn't have been where?"

"On your heart! Where do you think?"

I sat up a little straighter. "Are you serious? You actually saw something on my heart?"

"It was ugly and sticky and black," she told me. "Like tar. And it stank like sulfur. It took everything I had to get it out of you. Somebody or something put it there to harm you."

"Okay. Well..." I have always allowed for the possibility that what Cara sees and experiences is real, at least on the spiritual level, but it has never been easy for me to credit unquestioningly that which I have not personally experienced. Even then I strive to find a logical, this-reality-based explanation. "You got rid of it, right?"

"*This* time!" she nearly screamed. "That doesn't make you immune!" There were tears in her eyes now, the tears of fear. She reached for my hand. "Please don't be stupid, baby. Please. Please stop what you're doing before it's too late."

I thought about it for a few seconds, then nodded. I pulled her hand to my mouth and kissed it. "Thank you for caring so much about me. I don't deserve you, and I know that."

"I'm the best thing that ever happened to you. Or ever will." She squeezed my hand again, then glanced at her Fitbit watch. "I have to go. You want my vermicelli and spring rolls?"

"Take them with you."

"I'm on keto again."

"Okay then, sure," I said. The garage hadn't yet texted that my car was ready, so I decided to linger in the restaurant despite Mama Phan's shrill castigations of her lazy good-for-nothing staff. As I enjoyed the extra spring rolls and rice and a cup of tepid green tea, it occurred to me that I could sort of keep my promise to Cara yet not give up my investigations entirely. Until I felt ready to write fiction again, I had to do *something*, and the project at hand was the best possibility.

Besides, something Phoebe had said kept playing over and over in my brain. *You have things to do*, she'd told me, her excuse for why we couldn't meet for a full week. I couldn't get the sentence out of my head. At the time she spoke it, I heard it as a throwaway response people sometimes use when they want to get away or don't have time to consider something, so they feign consideration for the other person. *You have things to do. You're a busy man.* But had it meant more than that? Did it mean, literally, that there were things I must accomplish before we could meet again? Was this another glimpse into the future from our farsighted Mr. Kennaday?

If so, what could it mean? What did I yet have to do? Only one answer presented itself: Justin Cirillo. That's what I had to do.

Thing was, a part of me knew that Cara was right. I had no footing in the spirit realm, no grounding in ETs that were djinn or in djinn that were shadow people and so forth. I was a lapsed Methodist with a contempt for organized religion but an enduring belief in an ultimately unfathomable creative power beyond this reality. Yes, I had had numerous unexplainable encounters with spirits ever since I was a child, but they had all been spontaneous, not one of them brought on deliberately by me. I could read ten thousand books and watch twenty years' worth of videos and still be a neophyte without more experiential knowledge. I didn't have enough otherworldly wisdom to be guru to my dog, if I had a dog, and at that moment I wished I did. Somebody who would look up at me with love and affection and loyalty and expect nothing more in return than a bowl of food, a bowl of water, a belly rub, and a place to curl up at my feet.

What if I forgot all about Kennaday and his implications about the metaphysical convolutions of the Burchette case, and got back to basics, what I knew how to do? What if I concentrated on the murderer and his motivations? Maybe I could write something along the lines of *In Cold Blood* or *The Executioner's Song*. A study of abnormal human behavior. I was good at that kind of thing. I understood people. Real, three-dimensional people, especially those broken and put together crookedly. Those with crossed wiring in their brains. Humpty-Dumptys and Frankensteins, that should be my subject, my métier, not hoodoo and devilry.

Yep, that's the kind of book I should be researching. A book like that would keep me off the event horizon of depression for quite a time to come. And should, if Cara was correct, keep the sticky black spirit tar from encasing my heart.

24.

Janky and jazzy perform

I like prisons only slightly more than I like funerals and hospitals. Hospitals kill nearly as many people as they save. As for funerals, well, let's just say that sometimes death is a cause for celebration rather than tears. Grief is a very selfish emotion, as is wanting to hold on to a suffering loved one as long as possible. Grief is little more than feeling sorry for yourself, and grief plays on a loop at funerals. I fully intend to stay away from all funerals forever, including my own.

Prisons and jails, on the other hand, serve a necessary purpose. I used to work in a county jail as a nightshift dispatcher and guard. This was back in the mid-1970s, long before cell phones and call tracing and 911. I was just a kid, really, both me and my colleague, whom I will call Jeff. We shared an office on the first floor of the jail, his desk and phone against the eastern wall, mine perpendicular to his. We took turns fielding the emergency calls and on strolls around the cells to make sure that the inmates were sleeping and not setting their mattresses on fire or tunneling through a concrete wall. Once I got used to walking past cells full of angry and often violent individuals who viewed me as an enemy, or worse yet, as prey, the guard aspect to the job was an easy one and even gave me opportunities throughout the night to stretch my legs. The dispatcher aspect was equally nondemanding: inquire as to the nature of the emergency, take down the caller's address, and send an ambulance, fire truck, and/or sheriff's deputy to the proper location.

Then there was the call that caused me to turn in my resignation. It still haunts me. A young woman, her voice shrill with panic, called in because her husband had collapsed in their yard, his face blue. I told her don't worry, I'll get an ambulance there immediately. And before I could ask for an address, she said "Okay!" and hung up. As I mentioned, we had no call tracing abilities back then. We did have ★69, which redialed the most recent number received on that phone. I tried it again and again. No answer. She was outside with her dying husband.

It wasn't until 1987 that 50 percent of the country had 911 service, and not until the end of the century that over 90 percent had access to enhanced 911 service, which automatically provides the caller's location to dispatchers. Those facts do nothing to keep the man's death from haunting me.

I hadn't been inside a lockup since taking that tragic call. But that's where Justin Cirillo was, in the Lawrence County Jail, so I had no choice in the matter. My hope was that Cirillo would give me some tiny bit of ammunition to hit Phoebe with so as to startle or frighten her sufficiently that she would drop the prescribed routine and tell me the whole truth as she knew it.

My job, as I saw it, was to forget about Kennaday and his motives for now. This left only two significant mysteries. Why had Cirillo done it, and what did Baby Doe have to do with it all?

I had no illusions that I possessed the skills to track down Baby Doe's mother or father before law enforcement could, but maybe, just maybe, I could coax Cirillo into coughing up a fur ball or two of intel. It wouldn't be the first time a scumbag had shut out the men and women in uniform only to bare his soul to a man with a pen—a man who, the scumbag often believed, could write the scumbag into the annals of history.

I thought it prudent to know as much as possible about Cirillo before contacting him. The newspapers were no help, seeing as how Cirillo refused to talk to them. But as luck would have it, he had posted a couple of amateur videos on YouTube. The first, two years old, showed him with a white hamster he introduced to viewers as Janky. He then put Janky through an obstacle course built out of corrugated cardboard, Pringles cans, bits of carpeting, and PVC pipe. As a reward for Janky at the end of the course was a sugar cube. The other video, filmed rather shakily eight months before the Burchette murders, showed Janky and a second hamster, Jazzy, running a more complex course built out of painted plywood, red bricks, PVC pipe, and other molded or manufactured materials. At the beginning and end of each video, Cirillo held the hamsters lovingly and called them his "babies." In both videos he was dressed in jeans and a T-shirt.

In light of the Burchette murders, they were strange videos to watch. Incongruous to my notion of what kind of person he was. His physical appearance, too, belied the gentleness evidenced in the videos.

Justin Cirillo stands about five eight, has a stocky but soft body, a moon face, and a head with thick black hair falling haphazardly over his ears and forehead. I found it difficult to keep a scowl off my face when watching him talk. He blinked frequently, his eyes squinting and brown and narrow set, cheeks scruffy with several days' beard. His mouth is too small for his face, his nose too broad. Whether because of his Mediterranean complexion or the scruffy beard, he presented an unwashed appearance. For a while it seemed that he was regarding the camera with one eyebrow permanently cocked, but then I noticed that his left eye is set slightly higher than his right, and this gives him the kind of asymmetrical face often seen in mug shots of the less successful criminals, those whose brains are not operating at maximum efficiency.

His voice was higher than I'd expected. Not Truman Capote high; more like the voice of actor Giovanni Ribisi when his character is being whiny. In real life Ribisi has a very distinctive but pleasant baritone voice, is a first-rate actor and one of my top three favorites in the profession. As an actor, no matter how dastardly his character, there is a likable, mischievous quality to Ribisi himself that always bleeds through. Not so with Justin Cirillo. The word *venomous* came to mind as I watched him. Churlish. Thuggish. Malign.

Yet he adored those hamsters. That too was obvious in the videos. I had to wonder what had become of the animals now that he was spending his time in jail. Maybe that topic would offer me an opening into a meeting with him.

According to the Lawrence County Jail web page, I could not visit Justin Cirillo until he added my name to his visitors list. Then I must call the jail the night *before* I wished to make a visit. My first job, then, was to get on Cirillo's visitors list. Could I call him directly and request an invitation? I couldn't find any information online to answer that question. *So call the jail*, I told myself. *Easy peasy*.

Except that no phone number was listed on the jail's website, only a comment box. And I didn't have three or four days to wait for somebody to respond to my written questions, if they ever did. The only number I could find was for the Lawrence County Government Center, which housed departments from the sheriff to the county commissioners to the register of wills and recorder of deeds. The business day was nearly over yet I hoped I could reach someone who might be of assistance. But of course I would have to get through a gatekeeper to reach any of them.

"How may I help you?" a honeyed voice asked.

"I have a few questions about visitation policy at the jail."

"The Corrections website should be able to answer your questions."

"Yeah, but it doesn't."

"The manual for inmates is also available on that website. You should find all the information you need in there."

"Yeah, I didn't. I read the manual and it doesn't tell me how a person can get his name on the inmate's visitation list."

"The inmate must first add your name to his or her list."

"I understand that. But how do I contact an inmate in order to make that request? Can I call him directly?"

"No. But he can make a collect call to you."

"And how do I make him aware of my request so that he will make that collect call?"

"What is your relationship to the inmate?"

"I have no relationship with him."

"Excuse me?"

"I've never met him."

"And so why would you want to visit him?"

"I'm a writer. I have a few questions for him."

She was silent for a moment, then asked, with a touch less honey in her voice, "In which unit is the inmate housed?"

"I don't know that. All I know is his name. Justin Cirillo."

Another pause. "Inmate Cirillo is awaiting trial."

"I know that too."

"Inmates awaiting trial are not permitted visitors."

"Are they permitted telephone calls?"

"An inmate is permitted to make collect calls."

"But I can't call him?"

"That is correct."

"Would you be able to relay my request to him?"

"I cannot."

"Does he have access to email?"

"No."

"Instant messenger?"

"No."

"How about carrier pigeon?"

She clicked her tongue. "Do you have any other questions?"

"Just the original one. How can I get in touch with Justin Cirillo?"

"You could try contacting his lawyer."

"And his or her name, please?"

"I'm sorry, but we are not permitted to release that information. Do you have any other questions I can help you with, sir?"

"I don't need help with the questions, I need help with the answers."

"Have a good day, sir," she said.

It took another forty minutes of watching video clips online to find out who was defending Cirillo. But, of course, he had a gatekeeper too.

Her voice was older and sounded as if she had been gargling bourbon. "I'm sorry but that is out of the question. We don't run a messenger service here."

"I just want to ask two or three questions is all."

"You can do that at the next press conference."

"And when will that be?"

"There is nothing on the schedule yet."

"Will I be able to talk to Cirillo at a press conference?"

"I'm fairly certain you will not."

"Then what good will a press conference do me?"

"I am sure I don't know. Is there anything else?"

"Yeah. Who's buried in Grant's tomb?"

My question was answered with a click.

Thinking isn't easy when you feel like punching holes in the wall. Not a single brilliant idea announced itself through the fog in my brain. So I didn't do any further thinking for the next thirty minutes or so. I opted for a lot of cursing instead, followed by some wet leaf kicking in the yard, then a short drive and a brisk, muttering walk around the local park. I hadn't even noticed while kicking leaves or driving that darkness was falling. That's how frustrated I was. But during my third lap around the park, my brain discharged a couple of crackling sparks, which I decided to call an idea. It too was not a brilliant one, but it was better than none.

25.

The father is brother
to the other

I remembered seeing once, but only once in all the clips I'd read, a comment from Cirillo's father about his son's crime. So out came the bulging accordion file again. By ten that night I was bleary-eyed and weary, but I'd found what I was looking for. It was a comment made by Cirillo's older brother, not his father. He looked old enough in the photo to be the younger man's father, and that was probably why I remembered him as a father. I had seen the photo and thought *father*, then had come across the phrase *the suspect's brother* but had read *the suspect's father* instead. That's how observation and memory work; neither is wholly reliable.

I had thought the man in the photo, Dennis Cirillo, was Justin Cirillo's father, but he was actually his brother. No big deal. Except that my error kept me feeling slightly off-balance as I reread the article, which had appeared not in a bona fide online newspaper but on the website of an individual who went by the pseudonym "Citizen Journalist."

Dennis Cirillo had said, when asked by the writer of that piece what his thoughts were upon hearing of the murders and his brother's arrest, "I knew when he was five years old he'd end up in prison someday."

The reporter asked, "And how did you know that?"

"He wouldn't listen to nothing or nobody. Had a stubbornness you couldn't beat out of him. And believe me, I tried. Everybody did."

"Everybody tried beating it out of him?"

"Again and again. Didn't do him a bit a good, though. He was what he was."

"And what was that?"

"Didn't I just tell you? There was something broken in him."

"Is there any chance that all of those beatings might have caused the breakage?"

"Ha. You got it ass backwards, bud, same as you people always do."

The article provided little in terms of encouragement in my quest to understand Justin Cirillo. But, as I mentioned earlier, I have always been a balls-to-the-wall type of person, even in those situations that promise another painful lesson. I looked up the brother's name in the telephone book. His address was well south of New Castle, a few miles beyond the old Cascade Park, an amusement and nature park that opened in 1897 and closed in the early 1980s only to reopen as a community park with walking and hiking trails. I had been there several times, so I knew the way at least that far. I would have to figure out the last few miles in the morning. It was time for bed, where another nightmare awaited.

26.

Another irrelevant allusion to Truman Capote

A t least once a week I dream that my boys are small and I
have lost one of them. In that night's dream I was driving up
an icy and very steep mountain road, both boys strapped into the
back seat, when the vehicle started sliding backward, sliding and
swerving until it crashed through a low stone wall, and we all went
diving down. Then suddenly the dream shifted, and I was climbing
the craggy mountainside, hands and feet scrabbling for purchase
but slipping because of the icy crust, one tiny movement at a time
as I screamed for my boys, trying to locate them. I knew they were
on the mountain somewhere but I could not see or hear them,
and I was desperate to rescue them, nearly hysterical with fear and
grief and the torment of imminent failure. My final scream, wild
and primal in my chest, stuck in my throat and came out as an
agonized groan that woke me. The rest of the night offered no
improvement.

After the nightmare, every time I fell asleep for a few minutes,
a loud thump would jerk me awake. This must have happened
four or five times before three a.m. I would lie awake, listening
for another sound from an intruder, my hand finding again the
.357 revolver that I had taken to leaving under the adjacent pillow except when Cara spent the night. The last sound to wake

me was a kind of low, prolonged scrape I instantly recognized as the *shooshing* sound of a window being forced up. Three seconds later I was fully awake and alert and moving quickly through the house, turning lights on in room after room, the revolver in my hand fully loaded and cocked.

But every door was locked, every window down. Where had that sound come from? Either my subconscious mind took great pleasure in tormenting me, or some outside force did. Because of recent experiences, the second option seemed more likely.

There was no use going back to bed. I filled a mug from the sludge in yesterday's pot, nuked it to within a degree of scalding, gulped half of it down and tried to meditate. But the mental vertigo I had experienced earlier continued, exacerbated by fatigue. I kept losing my place in my morning prayer of gratitude, kept repeating myself and half dozing, waking, and starting again. I spent the next four hours sweeping the floors, trying to read, staring at a laptop screen, and watching coffee drip into a glass pot. Finally a hazy daylight filled the house, and soon it would be a decent hour to go knocking on somebody's door. I took a long, hot shower, shaved and dressed and filled a thermos with fresh coffee, then stumbled to the garage gripping the slip of paper on which I had scrawled Dennis Cirillo's address.

An early morning ride on Candy would have blown the cobwebs out of my head, but unfortunately it was another damp morning, the air gray and chilly, heavy in my lungs. Cursing the weather as well as my insomnia, both of which I now viewed as lifelong antagonists, I climbed into my Jeep.

Prior to finding out that I would not be able to personally interview Justin Cirillo, I had composed a short list of questions I wanted to ask him. Only three questions really mattered: *Why did you kill those people? Do you know where Eddie Hudack and Jolene Mrozek are?*

What do you know about Baby Doe? I'd had no confidence as I first wrote those questions that Cirillo would answer any of them, given the rumor that he had clammed up tighter than a melted zipper, yet I felt compelled to try to get his brother to provide an answer or two.

Dennis Cirillo's battered brown-and-white mobile home, a single-wide with hardened streams of tar permanently dripping over the roof seams, was set inside a pocket of second or third growth hardwoods approximately two hundred yards off the twisty Route 18. From the looks of the algae growth on the trailer's exterior walls, sunlight seldom fell on the small clearing.

I checked the time: 9:13. The last fifteen minutes of my drive had met with wide shafts of welcome sunlight that sometimes broke through the cloud cover to warm the side of my face, but there was no sun in Dennis Cirillo's isolated enclave. I stood outside my vehicle, wondering whether to proceed the last twenty yards to the trailer or not. The humidity was high, the ground sodden. The air smelled of leaf mold. Tire tracks, seemingly fresh ones, ran across the yard, but the only vehicle visible was an old station wagon sitting tireless atop concrete blocks, its entire roof missing.

Yet a dim light was visible through the filmy window on the right end of the trailer. I pictured the brother sitting in there at the kitchen table, probably alone, smoking and sipping bitter black coffee, probably in his underwear. Or maybe he would be sipping from a bottle of beer he hadn't drained the previous night. How would he receive me?

You won't know until you know, I told myself. Not without trepidation, I walked forward, up the three metal steps to a tiny wooden platform, and knocked on the outer door's aluminum frame, rattling the torn screen. A significant part of me was hoping that Cirillo would ignore my knock.

But then the lock clicked open. I stiffened, and prepared to meet the surly individual from the online video. I couldn't have been more surprised had Heidi Klum greeted me when the interior door swung open. She wasn't Heidi, of course, but the woman looking out at me from the other side of the screen could have been Heidi's American cousin. Tall and thin and graceful, blond hair cut to her shoulders and neatly styled, she was dressed as if for a hike in the woods. Khaki slacks tucked into heavy cream-colored wool socks inside brown Ozark boots, a red wool V-neck sweater with a black crewneck T-shirt underneath. She wore no makeup and no jewelry, not even earrings. She didn't need any, thanks to those fern-green eyes and that soft, curious smile.

With a bit of surprise in my voice, I said, "Good morning, I, uh…I was hoping to speak with Dennis this morning."

"I'm sorry," she said. "He went to take Jake to the vet. He's likely to be gone awhile." Her voice hinted at a southern accent, Tennessee or Kentucky. She pronounced "awhile" as "awahl."

"Ah, well. At least I had a nice drive getting here."

"And you are who?" she asked.

"Oh, sorry." I told her my name, and that I was a writer, not a journalist but the other kind, whatever that means, and that I was, you know, just trying to piece things together in regard to what happened up in Bell's Grove, trying to figure things out—

Her smile widened a bit, and she saved me from swallowing my tongue. "You wanted to talk to him about Justin, I bet."

"Yes, I do. I, uh…I tried to arrange a visit with Justin in the jail but struck out."

"Only family and the lawyer," she said.

"So I was told."

"What was it you wanted to know about him?"

"About Justin? His side of things, I suppose. Though from what I hear, he hasn't been willing to say much to anybody."

She cocked her head a little. "What do you want to know for? You writin' a book about what he did?"

"Maybe," I said with a sheepish smile. "But it's going to be a very short book if I can't get anybody to talk to me."

She continued to smile. "Dennis don't trust people," she said, her first grammar faux pas other than the dropped g, but one that added weight to my impression of her as a backwoods beauty. How a man like Dennis Cirillo, given what little I knew of him, had won her favors was a mystery to me. But women and their choices in men have always mystified me.

"You can come on in if you want," she told me, and held the screen door open a little. "I just now made myself some tea."

"I wouldn't want to interrupt your morning."

"You're not interruptin' nothin'. I just got back from huntin' mushrooms."

"Any luck?"

"Come on in and see," she said, and pushed the door open wider. "I'm Holly, by the way."

"Golightly, by any chance?"

"I've heard that before," she said, laying a light, fragrant hand on my shoulder as I squeezed past her, "else I wouldn't know what you're talkin' about."

I stepped fully inside and was surprised again. The trailer was old but very neat and very clean. Her doing, no doubt. "The tea smells great," I told her as she closed the doors.

"That's my ashwagandha with lemon and ginger. I got all these other ones too. What kind can I get you?" She gestured toward a neat row of small boxes lined up on the kitchen counter.

I stepped into the kitchen to read the boxes: ashwagandha with lemon and ginger, ashwagandha with cherry, ashwagandha with ginger and peach, ashwagandha with mango.

"I guess I'll have an ashwagandha," I told her, "whatever that is."
She smiled. "Which one?"

"How's the one with lemon and ginger?"

"Strangely lemony," she said. "Not to mention gingery too."

Nice, I thought. *A sense of humor.* I hadn't been expecting that in Cirillo's home.

Holly smiled and took another mug from the cupboard, opened the box and pulled out a tea bag and set it in the mug. "Ashwagandha's good for the immune system. Some people think it's a aphrodisiac too. You take stevia?"

"Just a pinch, thank you."

"Gotcha." She moved to the stove, where a kettle was softly hissing. "The mushrooms is in the sink," she told me. "Have a look while I make your tea."

A red plastic sieve brimming with mushrooms of all shapes and sizes sat over the sink's drain, some of the fungi white, some light brown. "I don't know anything about mushrooms," I told her. "But it looks like a good harvest." I would have loved a tutorial on the identification and hunting of wild mushrooms. I make a mean mushroom French onion soup from store-bought baby bellas. I could only imagine how it would taste made with fungi fresh from their shady soil.

She nodded. "It's one of the reasons we live out here. I'm a mushroom fanatic, you might say."

She handed me a steaming mug of the fragrant brew and said, "Come on and set down and ask me your questions. I don't know if I can answer them or not, but I'll give it a try."

She settled in on one side of the blue vinyl banquette, and I slid into the other side. I used the excuse of a few careful sips to clear my head. Questions. What were my questions? "So…" I said. Another sip. "This is very good."

"And healthy," she said.

"So, my questions. Number one, I guess, is why did he do it? Why did he kill those people?"

"Okay," she said. "Now I'm just guessin', okay? Guessin' based on how well I know him, which is pretty well, and on what Dennis told me after talkin' to him."

"He talked to Dennis?"

"Dennis is the one that raised him, so yeah, he talks to Dennis some."

"I can't wait to hear what he's said."

"Well, it wasn't like a confession or anything. I mean he didn't need to confess, they already knew he did it. But as for the why of it…" She took a sip, swallowed, looked into the cup, raised it to her lips for another sip. Then looked at me sitting across from her. "What he said," she told me, "what he said to Dennis, I mean, is that Barry come at him first."

"Barry Faye?"

Another nod. "Barry come at him with a fork in his hand, he said. And what was he supposed to do, just stand there and wait to see if he got stuck in the throat with it? So he pulled the trigger and shot him. And after that he didn't know what happened, he said."

"Wow. Okay. I didn't know any of that." Sip of tea. "So what does that mean, he didn't know what happened next?"

"He don't remember any of it. Not a bit."

"He doesn't remember shooting Dianne or the little girl?"

"That's what he told Dennis. Said he never would've shot little Shelley for anything in the world. That he musta blacked out or something."

"Do you believe that?" I asked.

She shrugged. Waggled her head back and forth. "I know for a fact he don't care about shootin' the two grown-ups. They'd been on the outs for a while. What he told Dennis is that even though he don't remember most of it, he figures they got what they deserved. That he did the world a favor shootin' them. But he does feel bad about the little one. I know he does. So yeah. I believe him when he says he don't remember shootin' her at all. Though he knows he must've done it."

"Okay," I said. "But if he didn't mean to shoot Shelley, why did he take a shot at LaShonda and Phoebe?"

"He was surprised is all. The way I understand is, Eddie and Jolene went runnin' out of the house as soon as the shootin' started. So Justin didn't think anybody else was in the place. It wasn't until he went into the livin' room that he saw them comin' down the stairs there."

"You mean Phoebe and LaShonda?"

"Well," Holly said, "yes and no."

I cocked my head and waited.

"What he told Dennis is, he seen a tall black woman comin' down the steps ready to start shootin' at him. She was mostly shadow but…" She shrugged. "Like I said, he claims to have blacked out or somethin'. Said he wasn't seein' straight. Said he just took a shot in her direction then hit the street runnin'."

"Whew," I said. I was getting a lot more information than I had thought the morning would bring. But what did it mean?

I asked, "Did he say anything about why he even took a shotgun to the house that night if he didn't plan to use it?"

A quick nod. "It was to scare Barry into tellin' him somethin'."

I raised my eyebrows.

"He wouldn't say what that somethin' was, though."

"What do you and Dennis think it was?"

"We don't know."

"You must think something. Why was Justin on the outs with Dianne and Barry?"

"Well, they had a thing goin' on for a while."

"They being…?"

"Justin and Diney. They was fuck buddies until Barry come along."

"So it was jealousy?"

"I think it might've been, but Dennis don't."

"What does Dennis think?"

"He says it happened too long after Barry come into the picture for it to be jealousy. And Justin was already seein' somebody else by that time."

"When you say 'it happened'…?"

"Them being on the outs. For a while there after Barry come along, him and Eddie and Jolene was all still goin' over to the house now and then. Just like nothin' was wrong between them. Plus there was this bar over in Ohio they'd all sometimes meet at. Over in Lowellville. They knew the bartender there, and she'd sneak them free drinks now and then. But come last spring or so, he noticed somethin' in Justin's attitude toward him."

"Dennis noticed something in Justin's attitude toward Barry?"

"Right."

"So they were fine up until then? Barry and Justin?"

"Fine might be an exaggeration some. I don't think he kept goin' there to see Barry, to the Burchette house, I mean. But he tolerated him bein' there. He was more Diney's friend than anybody's, even if he might've resented her for takin' up with Barry. Plus I think he just liked the atmosphere of the place. The big happy family sort of thing."

"He didn't have that growing up," I ventured.

"Not hardly."

"What were his parents like?"

"Royal sons a bitches, to hear him and Dennis tell it."

"Neither parent is still alive?"

"They know for sure the mother's dead. That happened back in oh-three or four, I think. Overdose. The father disappeared the day after. Police were sort of suspicious he might've had somethin' to do with it, but there wasn't nothin' to prove it. He'd cleaned out the house of anything worth a dollar and just left. Dennis and Justin never heard a peep from him since."

I waited, but she seemed to be finished. Sipped her tea and smiled at me. I had only one more question. "Baby Doe," I said.

"Oh, that poor thing. My heart goes out to her."

"Is it possible that she has anything to do with this? With the murders?"

She shrugged. "I guess anything's possible."

"Is it possible that the mother of Baby Doe is the woman in Lowellville, the bartender? And that both Faye and Justin were having an affair with her?"

Holly's answer to this was another shrug and a crooked smile.

"You think she is, don't you?" I asked.

"Like I said, I wouldn't rule nothin' out."

"Does Dennis feel the same way?"

Another sly smile. "People have their theories, you know? They have to come up with somethin' to fill in the gaps. It's human nature."

"That it is."

"It makes things easier if they have an idea who the baby's mother and father is."

"It certainly would."

"'Cause the baby's biracial, you know. Or so everybody assumes."

"I did know that."

"I'm just sayin' that if they knew for sure who's white and who's Black between her parents, it might make things easier to figure out."

THE DEEPEST BLACK 183

"Things like who hurt her, and who abandoned her in the woods? And why?"

"Exactly."

"And what about the bartender? White or Black?"

"Oh, she's as white as snow after a soot storm."

"Interesting analogy. Are you and Dennis thinking that maybe Barry Faye *and* Diney Burchette were somehow a part of the baby's disappearance? Or only Justin and Barry? Or the whole bunch of them, including the mother herself?"

"Who can say?" she asked. "It's somethin' of a mess, isn't it?"

I remembered the newspaper left behind in Kennaday's rented house. Ray Gricar and Jerry Sandusky. The Penn State sex scandal. Pedophilia. A global cancer. Was there a link to that news clipping and Baby Faye? *I guess it all started with the baby in the woods*, Kennaday had told me. Why would he say that, then pique my curiosity about the Burchette murders, if the two subjects were *not* related?

Holly must have noticed my self-quizzing expression. "What are you thinkin' about so hard?" she asked.

I didn't answer for the moment. I was too comfortable sitting there with her, swapping ideas, answers and questions, thinking my thoughts. I set my half-empty cup on the table. "I'm thinking I've taken up too much of your morning already," I told her, and slid out to stand. "It's been a real pleasure meeting you."

She held out a hand. I took it. "You too," she said. "Good luck with the book you're writin'."

"The book I might or might not write," I told her.

"Either way, I bet it's nice havin' such an excitin' profession."

I have never thought of my career as exciting. Long stretches of sitting in front of a blank screen and trying to fill it. The necessary solitude. The few rewards that come along months and even years apart. The daily and very public criticisms by a world of nonwriters who think they can write better. "At the moment," I told her, and reclaimed my hand, "I'd rather be a professional mushroom hunter."

She chuckled. "Good luck anyway."

"And to you," I said, and made my way outside.

27.

Bee on your toes now

Had I made some progress finally?

The sky was clearer when I exited the trailer, the air warmer, the world brighter. The temperature had soared into the high fifties and the day was turning out to be a rare blessing. I intended to drive home without delay and trade the Jeep for my faithful Candy. I had a lot to think about, and I think more clearly on two wheels, with the sun and wind in my face, the white noise of the engine filling my ears. Unfortunately, more than a bike ride was waiting for me at home.

You know how you can come into your house sometimes, and everything is just as you left it, nothing out of place, yet you have a very uncomfortable feeling that somebody has been inside while you were gone? You can't identify any tangible way in which the rooms look different or smell different, but something definitely *feels* different about the place? And you just *know* that somebody has been there. You can feel it in your bones.

In most cases there will be a good reason for such a feeling. Maybe a family member has come and gone. Maybe your girlfriend accidentally left something behind on her last visit and came by to pick it up. But in my case, I live alone. My ex-wife has never been to my home. I keep my doors and windows locked. No one has a key to my house or knows the garage door code but for my sons, both of whom live hundreds of miles away, and Cara, who would never enter the house without my knowledge, though she has my permission to do so. Plus, I know her scent, and there's not a trace of it in the air. Yet I am absolutely certain that *someone* had been inside my house without my permission.

I spent a very tentative hour going from room to room, checking drawers and closets and under the beds, shining a flashlight into every dark corner, standing or sitting in the middle of the room trying to isolate the source of my suspicion. But not a scintilla of hard evidence revealed itself. Yet the longer I searched, the more certain I was that my privacy had been violated.

I checked my phone: no missed calls or texts from Cara, no reason she might have rushed here in a panic to see if I had died of a heart attack or tripped while hopping down the stairs. But just to be sure, I called her anyway.

"No, why?" she asked. "I'm at work."

"It just feels like somebody has been here. I've checked everywhere and nothing is different, but I still can't shake the feeling."

"Tell me what it feels like," she said in a half whisper, obviously not wanting any of her eavesdropping colleagues to hear.

"Heavy," I told her.

"Dark?"

"Yep."

"Like...evil?"

Before answering, I paused to take another measure of what I was feeling. "Like somebody walking over my grave," I told her.

"What does that mean?"

I could hear in her voice that I had frightened her. And I didn't want that. After what had happened at the Scottish Rite Cathedral, she was probably already drafting my eulogy. "Nothing really, I guess. It just feels like somebody was here, walking through the house."

"A spirit?"

"No. A real person. It's almost but not quite like I can smell him. He just walked around in here. That's all he did."

"That's awfully precise for a feeling. You said *he*."

"That's just how it feels. Masculine."

"Okay. I trust your feelings. What are you going to do, babe?"

"I don't know." But I did, because I'd just had another thought: my laptops! Both were there on my desk, both password protected, but maybe I could discern whether any of the files had been opened.

I told her, "Anyway, thanks. Just wanted to make sure you weren't worried about me for some reason."

"I'm always worried about you. And for good reason."

"Love you too, sweetie. Have a nice afternoon."

I ended the call and sat at my desk. Opened the first laptop, the one that held all the work I had completed over the past several years. The one containing my notes to date regarding the Burchette case.

I opened the My Documents folder, then spent a tense yet tedious ninety minutes checking the properties tab on well over two hundred files. None but the file labelled *Burchette case*, the first one I opened, had been accessed or modified since yesterday, and I had opened that file earlier in the day. That didn't mean that somebody else hadn't also accessed it while I was interviewing Holly. Other digital fingerprints *could* be there, but I was unable to see them.

I swiveled to my right to open the new laptop, but then felt a swell of defeat overcome me. That laptop was mainly used for doing my online searches and for listening to music while I worked on the other laptop. Somebody might have checked my browsing history, but how would I know? Besides, there was nothing significant they could learn from me in that history. Why waste another hour trying to track down invisible fingerprints and footprints? I leaned back in my chair, ready to cry uncle.

And that was when I saw it.

My new laptop is centered in the long part of the L-shaped table, surrounded on both sides by messy piles of notes and pens and reading glasses, books of stamps, bills needing paid, old birthday and Father's Day cards from my sons and Cara, plus the usual assemblage of office tools, such as a stapler, rolls of tape, a small wire bowl full of paper clips, various mementoes, and any other detritus I hadn't yet trashed. By comparison, the only objects on the short extension of the desk, my workspace, are my old laptop, the thick, black-covered *Beatles Complete*, and the most recent *Yellowbook*. *Beatles Complete* is a hefty book of sheet music I leaf through on occasion while trying to build a linear structure from twenty or so songs for a novel I want to write; I keep the *Yellowbook* handy as a source of names for my characters.

And just to the right of the *Yellowbook*, sharing the very corner of the desk where the short end and long end come together, is a table lamp and, beneath it, the Blue Yeti microphone I use when I'm being interviewed by radio podcasters. And there, perched atop the microphone's volume button, lying belly and legs up, was the only item that had not been there when I left my desk a few hours earlier. A small dead bee.

I put on my reading glasses and leaned closer. Gave the bee a little jab with the tip of a pencil. Yep, it definitely was a bee, and definitely dead. It resembled a yellow jacket but smaller.

The volume button has a diameter of approximately three-eighths of an inch. The bee, with its yellow-striped thorax curled up, measured about five-eighths. Was it possible for a bee to land on that tiny perch, die, and roll onto its back without falling off the button? Could it possibly have died in flight and landed securely in that position atop the miniscule pedestal, as perfectly placed as a—as a what? I couldn't think of an appropriate analogy.

While examining the bee, I also noticed that the volume setting on my microphone had been changed from just shy of halfway— which I knew from experience was the best setting for me—to all the way off. *That* I could have convinced myself was an oversight on my part, even though I had been careful not to touch the setting through any of the last several interviews. What I could *not* rationalize was the bee's condition. Very delicately I picked it up between finger and thumb to move it to the waste basket. It crumbled to my touch. Newly dead bees do not crumble. Only a long dead, dried-out, brittle, desiccated bee will crumble. And dead bees do not climb or fly onto a microphone button, nor do they fall out of the ceiling, or spontaneously materialize out of thin air.

Yes, somebody had been in my house while I was out that morning. And they wanted me to know it. And it hadn't been a Merry Maid.

Fiction writers tend to think in metaphors. At least this fiction writer does. So I had to ask myself: Were the condition and staging of the dead bee supposed to suggest something to me? That I was being listened to as I sat at my desk? That I was going to get stung if I wasn't careful? Or that I, like the unfortunate bee, was destined to end belly-up if I didn't turn off the volume and shut up?

28.

Bang buzz ow!

N ot only did I not take Candy out of the garage that day, but I hid out in my media room for several hours, only half watching a marathon of *Breaking Bad* episodes in lieu of succumbing to the nervous breakdown that wanted so badly to erupt. With every little creak of the house I reached for the .357 on the adjacent chair, my finger resting a millimeter from the trigger.

There was little sleep that night, but a lot of tossing and turning. Eventually I wore myself out with one overblown fear after another, and, around 3:30 a.m., fell into a restless sleep. Less than an hour later I woke with a start from a loud clap inside my head. I knew immediately that it had happened inside and not outside of my head, a sound like a door being slammed shut, accompanied by a whoosh of pressure in my eardrums. It wasn't the first time. It had happened to me maybe twenty times in the past, beginning when I was in my early thirties. I had even given the affliction to my fictional detective, Ryan DeMarco. The phenomenon is called "exploding head syndrome" and it is much worse in name than in actual effect.

Presumably much worse, I should add. Wikipedia describes it as "an abnormal sensory perception during sleep in which a person experiences unreal noises that are loud and of short duration…

People may also experience a flash of light. Pain is typically absent."
Various other sources have proposed causes ranging from tempo-
ral lobe seizures to spirit attacks to a blast from an energy weapon
to a noisy goodbye from alien abductors. WebMD recommends
clomipramine, an antidepressant, as a possible treatment. Or yoga,
relaxing music, or a warm bath before bed. I don't take prescription medicines, especially not those of the synthetic kind with their
litanies of side effects more dangerous than the actual condition,
so that was out. And who wants to do yoga or any other exercise
four hours before dawn? That would only make me more awake.
I sometimes listen to music before bed, but it has to be the spacy,
repetitive, nonlyric type or else I might start singing along.

In any case, my head exploded that morning, but the walls of
my house remained intact, the ceiling still in place. I climbed out
of bed in the dark, found my robe at the foot of the bed, and pulled
it on. I disconnected my cell phone from the charger and slipped
it into a side pocket and made my way downstairs, wobbling like a
stiff-legged drunk. There wasn't enough coffee left from yesterday
to fill a mug, so I made a new pot and waited there listening to the
gurgle long enough for twelve or so ounces to drip through the
filter and into the carafe. The first cup of a new pot, if I am quick
enough to grab it out of the pot before it gets watered down, is
wickedly strong, and just what I needed that morning. The first sip
threw my eyes wide-open like a whiff of ammonia from a capsule
of smelling salts. Good stuff.

Still, I skipped meditation that morning; no way was I in the
right frame of mind for it. In my office I stood looking down at
my laptop as if it were booby-trapped. Maybe it was. Maybe every
keystroke was being registered on somebody else's screen miles away.
Years ago I had taped a couple of Post-it notes over my laptops'
cameras, but now I had to wonder if that was enough protection

from prying eyes. Was the television watching me from behind? Were there fly-sized cameras in my lampshades?

When my cell phone vibrated inside my robe's pocket, I almost leapt whole body away from it, but it kept rattling like a viper until I recovered enough to pull it out. A phone call so early could only mean trouble. *Please not my boys, please not my boys*, I prayed as I fumbled with the phone.

The time was 4:27 a.m. The caller: *Unknown*. "Hello?" I said, my voice hoarse and tight.

No voice returned my greeting. Nothing but a weird noise, loud and grating and oscillating. The nearest equivalency I can come up with is the sound of a sink disposal grinding up something hard, such as a seed, a wooden spoon, or a bone. This continued for half a minute. Then, in the silence, the headache erupted.

I had never in my life felt such a fierce, shrill, sharp, jagged, incessant, unrelenting screaming son of a bitch of a headache. I tossed the cell phone onto the carpet. Leaning against my office chair for support, I went down on my knees, fell forward, and drove my forehead into the carpet. With both hands I pushed against my skull, but the blindingly painful shriek continued unabated. And with it came the nausea. The rigidity of every muscle in my body. I felt certain that an aneurysm had burst inside my brain and that my skull must surely split wide-open to vent the tremendous pressure. I felt certain that I was about to projectile vomit across the room. I felt certain that I was about to die.

And then it stopped. Gone in an instant. My skull was suddenly empty. I could feel it deflating.

I toppled onto my back, knees still tucked to my chest, and blinked at the ceiling.

Jesus fecking Christ, I thought. Then I apologized to Jesus, and added, *but I'm sure you understand*.

I straightened out my legs eventually and lay there quivering with both anger and fear. It was a while before a coherent thought formed: *The call log!* I grabbed for the phone. Unfortunately, all evidence that a call had actually happened was gone too.

Obviously, the call had been intended as another threatening message. Which meant that my actions *were* being monitored—maybe not there inside the house, but at least earlier, yesterday. Had I been observed entering Dennis Cirillo's trailer to talk with his girlfriend, Holly? Had our conversation *inside* the trailer been monitored? Had my visit put her in danger too?

The wisest course of action was for me to drop the whole thing, even though I had only a vague idea of what constituted *the whole thing*. I was holding a jumbled bag of pieces and nothing more. Could I drop the bag now, after all the work and energy I had invested?

But really, what was any of it to me? A story, nothing more. Always looking for another story. But I had dropped story projects before, many times. Ideas that blazed brilliantly in the beginning only to sputter out, void of dramatic potential. Could I do it this time? Could I leave the truth alone? I resolved to try.

Alas, I'm just not wired that way. I don't like being pushed around and told what to do. Long ago I wrote an essay about the necessity for a writer to follow no trends, accept no censorship. One of the first rules I drew up for myself as a writer and a human being had been to allow no saddle on my soul.

How could I live with myself if, after all these years, I surrendered to a few threats? Especially when I had no idea from whom those threats were emanating.

29.

No dog, no Jake,
no cha cha cha

For an hour or more I lay there on the floor, eyes staring at nothing, seething. Usually I enjoy being alone, solitude my preferred state of being, but that morning I longed for company. But who could I go to? My sons would think their old man had finally gone off the deep end and they would start reading brochures for assisted-living facilities. Cara had her animals to palpate and stitch and inject, and if I mentioned my woes to her, her loving concern would drive me the rest of the way to insane. Who was left?

My only living male friends are both FBI agents, one of them in Michigan, the other in Hawaii, both of them very practical, logical guys. "There is no X Files unit," they had assured me time after time, usually with a bit of a sigh and a roll of the eyes. They know my "out there" interests and are willing to tolerate them, but they certainly weren't going to waste taxpayers' money on investigating dead bees and vaguely threatening phone calls and exploding heads.

I couldn't think of a single person I could turn to for a bit of friendly advice. And several days remained before I could visit Phoebe for our final interview. I considered driving there and demanding that she talk to me but feared that she would clam up entirely and never speak to me again.

In the end, I had to admit that my lifetime of cultivated solitude had left me with exactly what I deserved: me, myself, and I. The three amigos. Friends to the end. Although sometimes even they can't stand each other.

Fortunately, the day was warming quickly, just as yesterday had. The sky seen through my front window looked relatively clear, no threat of rain. I pulled up the day's weather outlook on my cell phone. Around noon the clouds were predicted to take a PennDOT worker's cigarette break and go MIA for a few hours, which would allow the sun to heat the air to an amazing seventy-three degrees. The kind of miraculous day when one might give in to the urge to strip off jackets and caps and to roll around in the grass like an itchy puppy. But, said the weather forecast, the sun and warmth would be just a tease, a cruel trick, because soon the clouds would return to fill the sky with their crematorium smoke. With darkness in the early evening, the temperature was predicted to plummet along with a bone-chilling rain.

But, I told myself, then was then and now is now. *Seventy-three degrees?* And in the last week of October!

And with that thought I realized that I *did* have a confidante. At least for one more day. My sexy, top-heavy, four-cylinder beauty. I would spend the day with her, and maybe together we could come up with a way out of this mess that me, myself, and I had gotten us into.

Waiting until the temperature reached the probably-no-frostbite-from-windchill mark was a chore. Had my yard not been buried in dead leaves, I might have set off earlier and risked hypothermia. Instead, I bundled up and rode my lawn tractor back and forth over the leaves for a while, slicing and dicing them into a sodden mulch. Then I rushed through a quick shower and shave, dressed, and headed to the garage.

While packing Candy's trunk, I thought of Holly and the possibility that my visit might have put her in danger too. I had no real destination in mind for the day, so I decided to drive first to Dennis Cirillo's trailer south of New Castle so as to warn her, and maybe Cirillo too, about the forces attempting to silence me.

Being on the bike again was like getting a lung transplant, sucking in the fresh, unstifling air, cruising beneath a dome of blue. For a while, all was right with the world. Optimism returned. I imagined that Holly would maybe convince Dennis Cirillo to speak with me. He would tell me all about his brother's past, his fears and desires. He would open up the family scrapbook, show me photos, and while sipping another cup of aphrodisiacal tea I would learn everything there was to know about the unfortunate, misunderstood murderer.

Unfortunately, nobody responded to my knocks on the door of Dennis Cirillo's trailer. From Candy's trunk I took a pen and tablet and scribbled a note. *Holly*, I wrote, *thanks for the visit yesterday. There are a couple of things I forgot to mention. Give me a call when you can.* I left my cell phone number and signed the note *Randall S.* Then I folded it twice and jammed it between the screen door's aluminum frame and the doorjamb, then set off on what I believed would be a healing, revivifying ride.

From Dennis Cirillo's trailer I headed southeast toward the Laurel Highlands, where for four delicious hours I cruised up and down through three counties, taking one sun-shot, leaf-strewn blue highway after another, into and out the other side of a dozen or more sleepy hamlets and villages, following no map or GPS but only whim and fancy and curiosity. A couple of times I parked and dismounted: once to buy a pumpkin gob and coffee at a farmers' market, and then, thirty minutes later, to hotfoot it into the woods to answer the call of nature.

Upon returning to my bike from the last stop, I noticed two

things: I was running very low on gas, and there were four missed calls and one voice message on my phone, all from the same unfamiliar number. I assumed it was Holly's.

I opened the voice message. It was short, to the point, and loud with testosterone: "Hey, Silvis, whoever the fuck you are. What's with this note you left on my door? Next time write down the right fuckin' address, why don't you? I don't need any more assholes bothering me than I already get."

Apparently, Holly had failed to inform Cirillo of my visit. I would have to make amends. I dialed the number. And instead of a friendly hello, I received an angry salutation of, "Is this Silvis?"

"It is," I said. "Is this Dennis Cirillo?"

"You know damn well who it is. What I want to know is who are you and what's with this note you stuck on my screen door."

"I'm sorry, Mr. Cirillo. It's probably nothing but I just thought it prudent—"

"And who the hell is Holly? I don't know nobody by that name around here."

My stunned pause gave him just enough time to add, "I don't appreciate people comin' up to my place without me givin' them the okay to do so. You understand? I don't care if it's by accident or not."

"I'm sorry but…I talked to a woman named Holly at your place just yesterday."

"Not at my place you didn't."

"Green-and-brown trailer surrounded by woods? A couple of hundred yards off Ellwood Road, maybe three miles south of Cascade Park?" I recited his address.

"That's where I live," he said, "but that ain't where you stopped if you was talkin' to a woman named Holly or anything else."

"She said you had taken your dog, Jake, to the vet."

"Jake?"

"That's what she told me."

"Buddy, I don't know what kinda junk you been sniffing, but I don't have no dog named Jake. I don't even own a dog. And if I did I sure as hell wouldn't of named him Jake."

I shook my head. Something rattled inside. "Holly is very pretty, maybe five eight or so, blond hair?"

"You ain't listenin', bud. Now pay attention. I don't have no dog and I sure as hell don't have no girlfriend. I like guys, if you have to know the truth of it. Tall, skinny, nineteen to thirty or so. You one of those?"

"I was about forty years ago."

"Then this conversation's over and done. Don't call me again."

"But, sir," I started.

"I mean it, bubba. You call this number again, you're gonna be eating your next meal through a straw."

And just like that the call ended. I sat astride Candy for a long time afterward. Then I fired up the engine and rode off, but with a new fog of confusion filling the space between my ears.

With every mile north, the sky thickened more and more with a ponderous parade of heavy clouds, their bottoms flat and dark, their tops like whipped mounds of filthy spindrift. Not until a dusk nearly as dark as night did I pull into my driveway, my face wet from the first chilly drops of rain. And now I had to enter a house that no longer afforded any semblance of sanctuary, any hint of personal safety. I crept inside as if entering enemy territory.

30.

Does a moth even have lips?

A night of drumming rain brought a Sunday morning as cold and miserable as the previous afternoon had been wondrous. In the glow from my deck light at five a.m., a new blanket of sodden leaves dark yellow and brown over my deck and yard made me want to drop to my knees and scream.

But I had a better idea. I would run away.

Every year, beginning usually in September, my wanderlust begins to build, that old familiar ache for a two- or three-month-long road trip. Each year I tell myself to just go, you might never have another chance. Then winter comes and socks me in with nothing but mutters and curses for company.

I am already older than Steinbeck was when he, at fifty-eight, and his poodle, Charley, age unknown, took their memorable road trip through the America of 1960. They made the trip in an ugly green pickup truck sporting even uglier green rims, with a propane-equipped camper atop the bed of the truck. Steinbeck's health when he climbed behind the wheel was shaky at best; a lifelong smoker and drinker, he'd already had one or two minor strokes, not to mention three rocky marriages. I am older, in fact, than he was when he died eight years after the trip. Not that I am comparing myself to Steinbeck in any way other than age and health, though I have long admired his versatility as a writer, his curiosity and analysis of human nature and the natural world. Plus, we share a proclivity for short novels. He could write opuses like *The Grapes of Wrath* and *East of Eden*, but many of his books were slender volumes that could be read in a day: *The Pearl, Of Mice and Men, Cannery Row, The Red Pony, The Moon Is Down, Tortilla Flat, To a God Unknown*…

When I make road trips—none of them since 1981 covering as much distance as Steinbeck and Charley did—I travel as I live, avoiding people and the places where they congregate. Road trips are supposed to be energizing, and nothing energizes me like nature in its natural state. Nothing enervates me like the dirt and stink and noise of our "civilized" places. One day in the Badlands is worth a hundred trips to a museum or Broadway play or overpriced restaurant.

Steinbeck embarked upon his last road trip in hopes of taking the pulse of a changing America, but found that pulse weak and feathery. According to one of Steinbeck's biographers, Bill Barich, the author had reported to his editor that America was in the midst of "a kind of wasting disease." This was in the election year of 1960, Nixon vs. Kennedy, me in fourth grade, the year I got glasses and was first shipped out of a friendly one-room schoolhouse and into a multi-floored, multigrade, monolithic alien landscape. In 1960 I first began to see my school, and therefore my country, as a dangerous, chaotic, and wholly unpleasant place. In 1960, Steinbeck saw Americans as "overly invested in material toys and saddled with debt…bored, anguished, discontented, and no longer capable of the heroism that had rescued them from the terrifying poverty of the Depression."

I wonder what he and Charley would think about *this* America's heroism with its "safe places" for individuals who are so easily offended by everybody and everything, its tilt toward a totalitarianism that aims to censor individual thought and speech and actions. He would probably turn to Charley sitting in the passenger seat and ask, "What the hell, Charley? Did we cross a border somewhere? What kind of upside-down democracy is this?" And Charley would answer primly, as only a poodle can, "Pull over, if you please, my good man. I need to take a piss."

These thoughts of Steinbeck, coupled with a new distrust for even my own home, made me hungry to hit the road again, if only for a couple of days. If nothing else, a road trip would make me a moving target and keep my tormenters guessing about what I was up to.

Normally I wouldn't disturb Cara's slumber on her day off. But I was hungry for movement, the morning was wasting, so at 7:01 I woke her with a telephonic kiss.

She picked up after the third ring. "What's wrong? Are you okay? Where are you?"

"Simmer down, sugar pea. All is well. How would you feel about a road trip to Point Pleasant today?"

In 1967 the Silver Bridge leading into Point Pleasant, West Virginia, collapsed during rush-hour traffic, killing forty-six people. Ever since that tragedy, the little town has been linked to the red-eyed winged creature known as Moth Man, who was spotted nearby several times before and after the collapse.

Cara's office manager, Sheila, who listens daily to a tarot reader online, had informed Cara a week or so earlier that she and her romantic partner, yours truly, were, according to the tarot reader, about to be "kissed by a moth." When Cara told me this, my first question was, "You let her listen to tarot at work?"

"She says she does it only during her lunch break, which I doubt. But she gets her work done. She's actually a very reliable employee."

"Why does she listen to *your* reading?"

"She listens to mine, hers, and Hannah's too." Hannah is her vet tech. "They're not long, ten minutes or so each. And they're fun to hear."

"Kissed by a moth?" I asked. "What's that supposed to mean?"

"Who knows?"

"Maybe it means you're about to get a big sloppy one from Moth Man."

"Or maybe you are," she said. "Could be either one of us. Just be ready to pucker up."

We had joked about trying to track Moth Man down in his old stomping grounds, so, when I proposed that morning that we make the joke a reality, she was game for an adventure. "I love road trips!" she said, though a bit sleepily. "But how long will it take? I work tomorrow."

"Can't you call in sick or something?"

She thought about it for a few seconds. "Hannah does owe me a day of work," she said. "Gimme a sec while I pull up my schedule."

A few moments later she said, "It's all worming and shots. Plus a couple of vaccinations."

"She can handle that."

"What about an emergency, though? I've never left her alone with one of those."

"She can send them to New Castle, right? What's another eight miles?"

"I don't know," she said. "I might lose a patient because of it."

"You need a break, babe. I need a break. We, you and me, we need a break together."

Again she pondered it for a few moments. "Can we go to Hocking Hills too?"

And so it was decided. We hung up and stuffed a few pieces of clothing and other essentials into our bags. Twenty minutes later I pulled up in front of her place in my Jeep. From there we set off for Point Pleasant, arguing pleasantly about which of us was Steinbeck and which was the poodle.

The drive was long but relaxing. In southwestern West Virginia the landscape began to look good again, the colors brighter than back home, most of the trees still fully leafed, the hills and valleys still decked out in autumn's finery. And the temperature was doing its best to reach fifty degrees. The sky remained overcast yet seemed brighter despite the cloud cover. As the temperature rose and the miles disappeared behind us, the side of my face soaked up the gentle seepage of vitamin D through the window, and my mood swung toward the positive pole. It put both of us in a sanguine mood.

Just a few miles from our destination, however, the landscape changed abruptly from the pleasing hues of fall in full leaf to a chaotic, disorderly panorama of what appeared to be blighted foliage and hills that had been overturned and scattered and grown high with tangled weeds. The trees still held their leaves but the leaves were limp and dull and, like the grasses in private yards, edged in brown. In an instant I felt the change in the heaviness of my breath and a sense of foreboding. I kept muttering, "There's something wrong with this place, this is wrong, this is bad."

It wasn't long before Cara felt the same tightness in her chest. "We'll drive through it," I told her, and sped up. "This can't last forever."

When we finally arrived in the narrow little town of Point Pleasant, some of the oppressive feeling lifted, but not all of it. Even there the air seemed permeated with depression, and the few faces we saw on the streets had a sorrowful look of resignation to the town's economic despair. Many of the businesses had closed their doors, while most of the others were desperate to capitalize on the celebrity of its red-eyed harbinger of doom. Cara and I remained only long enough for her to take a few photos of the metal Moth Man sculpture in one of the otherwise empty streets.

Finding no eatery appealing enough to draw us in for lunch, we headed west across the Ohio River. Not far from Point Pleasant, on Ohio 7 north now, we spotted one of those huge, upside-down concrete funnels often associated with nuclear plants. This one was part of the Gavin Power Station, the largest coal-fired facility in Ohio. It was belching out massive clouds of what is probably purported to be only steam hundreds of feet into the air, but it was easy to see a toxic glint of yellow limning the clouds. Whether this output had anything to do with the blighted landscape on the other side of the river, I have no idea. I only know that as I drove toward and then past the Gavin Power Station, my throat got scratchy and my eyes burned. Again my foot went down harder on the accelerator. It was a shame to leave Point Pleasant so soon after a four-hour drive, but neither Cara nor I wished to linger.

Around dusk we pulled into a Holiday Inn parking lot in Logan, Ohio. Still shaken from the overwhelming negativity we had sensed before leaving West Virginia, we ate some heavy Mexican food and finally bedded down with the intention of visiting Hocking Hills State Park next morning.

Neither of us was quick to close our eyes that night. It was clear that the blighted landscape preceding and immediately following Point Pleasant had left its mark on us. Cara suggested that maybe I *had* been "kissed by the moth" when I so quickly experienced, physically and emotionally, the dark foreboding of the countryside. Usually she is much more sensitive than I am, but this time I had sounded the alarm a good three or four minutes before she felt or noticed anything amiss. Unfortunately, since neither of us was able to explain what is meant by "kissed by a moth," or what had caused the visual and perceived *wrongness* of the landscape we had encountered, her suspicion will never be verified.

31.

All talk and no satisfaction

Morning brought a magical change. The sky was cloudy and the streets damp as we pulled away from the Holiday Inn, but the forecast called for a temperate sixty-two degrees. Cara and I arrived at the state park a little after eight a.m., my Jeep one of only six other vehicles in the parking lot. We then spent two full hours climbing and descending all along the Gorge Trail, snapping photos of the rock outcroppings and caves and other geologic features. The hike, which we made twice to be sure we had explored all of the available trails, did a good job of washing out the dark stain of the previous day's activities. I love rocks and I love the trees that grow out of and around them. Rocks have the oldest memories, but trees have the kindest hearts. Both rocks and trees are connected to Mother Earth in ways we humans no longer are.

As much as I enjoyed Hocking Hills, a restlessness was building inside me again. I couldn't stop thinking about Holly and Kennaday and Phoebe, enigmas yet to be cracked. Cara wanted to explore other trails and local sites, but I demurred. We had a long drive home, I told her. I don't like driving in the dark, I said. We'll come back again, I promised.

The last three hours of the drive home were subdued, especially after a brief conversation initiated when Cara asked, "So where do things stand with your investigation?"

Not wishing to worry her further, I had said little of my activities since the incident in the Scottish Rite Cathedral, so she knew nothing of the dead bee placed atop my microphone by an unknown intruder, or of the late-night phone call and the excruciating headache it induced, or of Dennis Cirillo's renunciation of Holly as his girlfriend. I had to be careful in response to her question.

"Progressing," I said.

"When do you talk to Phoebe again?"

"This Wednesday."

"And that's the last one?"

"So she says."

"What are you hoping to hear from her?"

"Something about who Thomas Kennaday is, I guess. And whatever she knows about why Cirillo committed the murders."

"And what Baby Doe has to do with it."

"Correct," I said, and hoped the conversation would end there.

"You know what I think?" she asked after staring out the side window for a few seconds.

"What's that?"

"I think you're being punked."

"By Phoebe?"

"Her and Kennaday."

"It's a possibility."

"Remember you telling me about those kids who kept calling you a few years back? All those late-night calls?"

"I do." For most of a week I had received at least two calls a night, always after midnight, by a young man who refused to identify himself. He would ask a silly question, such as "When you write with a pencil, is your wood soft or hard?" Then I would hear other youthful voices laughing in the background. I repeatedly warned him to knock it off or there would be consequences, but my words fell on deaf ears. After several nights of interrupted sleep, I spent a groggy hour tracing the number to a residential landline in a town some thirty miles away. I then phoned that town's police department and reported the harassment. Someone from the department checked it out, then called me back midmorning to let me know that he had pulled a fourteen-year-old out of school and had "a serious sit-down with him and his mom." He asked if I wanted to press charges, and I said that I would if it ever happened again. It didn't.

"The thing is," I told Cara as we made our way north, "Kennaday and Phoebe are both in their twenties at least. They should know better. And don't you think it's pretty sick to use three cold-blooded murders to punk somebody?"

She shrugged. "There's no age limit on stupid," she answered. "Or on sick behavior."

"True dat," I said.

She seemed satisfied, and said nothing more on the subject. For me, knowing the whole truth of what I had endured thus far, there was no satisfaction at all.

32.

A foul weather friend

Dusk fell softly, but night came with a thud. With the evening's soft light fully extinguished, I dropped Cara off at her place. I walked her to her door, where we lingered over a few slow, soft kisses. Then, alone in my idling Jeep, I sat in her parking lot for a few minutes, not wanting to go home to its threatening darkness. That was when I noticed that the indicator on my gas gauge had snuggled up against the E. Lucky for me a gas station was a mere mile and a half away.

Minutes later, pump in hand as I watched my money pouring into the tank, a blue pickup truck came roaring into the lot, its horn blasting out a long shriek. The vehicle made a fast, wide loop around the pumps, and just before it went roaring out onto the highway again, the truck's passenger stuck his head and shoulders out of the window and called to me, "Randooooooooo!"

I couldn't believe my eyes. The man, in my brief glimpse of him, had looked identical to an old friend, Louis Burbage. The same tinted sunglasses, the same bad toupee of brown, curly hair. Lou had been the only person in the world to call me Randoo.

The last I'd heard of Lou, he'd been arrested in Tucumcari for drunken driving—in his battered blue pickup truck!—and had then been found to be suffering from dementia and was taken to an Alzheimer's ward somewhere in the city. We had talked only once since then, and it was clear to me that he barely remembered me, if he did at all. That was back in 2012.

The former founder and director emeritus of a large Midwestern university's creative writing program, and a transplanted New Mexican, Lou had been, for most of twenty years, my best friend. He was a brother to me, an older brother by ten or so years, and a man whose writing accomplishments I admired. He was a talented, intelligent, witty writer then and an excellent teacher and editor and a generous reader and critic and champion of my work. Thanks to him, I spent four wonderful summers teaching advanced fiction and creative nonfiction to eager students, adults, and Kiplinger fellows.

During those gigs, I stayed in Lou's spare bedroom in his house thirty minutes from the university. Those were warm, fecund, enriching summers for me. Hoping to return some of Lou's generosity, I later convinced my editor at *Destination Discovery*, the magazine of the Discovery Channel, to offer Lou a writing assignment about the weird flora and fauna of Australia, an assignment I had declined after my own assignment to the Arctic Circle had worn me out and made me miss my sons so badly that I couldn't bear the thought of being away from them again so soon. Lou, unmarried and childless, eagerly accepted the assignment and never stopped thanking me for it.

We had been close, Lou and I, as close as I had ever been to another man. But around 2010 or so, the last time I visited him in New Mexico, I'd noticed signs of deterioration. During our walks, he kept listing to the left and bumping into me. And sometimes he seemed confused when we talked, as if he didn't remember certain colleagues or had forgotten parts of earlier conversations. He attributed those lapses to getting old: he was in his early seventies then. In truth, his life of alcoholism and antidepressant medication was catching up with him.

A year later his emails and calls became even less coherent. Then he stopped returning my communications altogether. It took me another fourteen months to track down an individual who knew what had happened to him, and where he was. I called him at the Alzheimer's ward, but, as I said, he had little idea who I was. A second call a month or so later brought only confusion on my part—a series of brief conversations with individuals who spoke no English and could reply only "No aquí! No aquí!" when I inquired of Lou's condition. In the years since then, I have missed his friendship terribly.

So how could that individual I'd seen hanging out of a blue pickup truck in Hermitage, Pennsylvania, have been my friend Lou? And if it were, why would he let the truck speed away from me? It was impossible. And yet…his familiar "Randooooo!" gave me hope.

I banged the pump handle back into place, jumped into my Jeep and sped off in pursuit of the pickup truck. After weaving in and out of traffic for a few miles, I finally spotted the truck two vehicles ahead of me on South Keel Ridge Road. It zoomed straight through a yellow light at the intersection with Route 62, and I, blocked by the vehicle ahead of me, was stopped at the red light.

"Come on, come on, come on," I muttered to the light as I choked the steering wheel. And finally the light changed. The vehicle ahead of me turned left and I floored the accelerator, straight through the intersection, the blacktop two-laner empty ahead of me.

Fifteen seconds later I came abreast of the Serbian Orthodox church just in time to see red taillights disappearing around the rear corner of the building. I almost took out the *Apple Strudel $10 drive-thru only* sign when I sent the Jeep squealing down the drive to the big parking lot behind the church.

The lot was empty but for the blue pickup truck parked at the back end of the lot, not far from the giant spit where an unlucky lamb was roasted every August for the Chetnik picnic. Other than the open-walled building that housed the spit, the sparsely wooded area was furnished with only a half dozen picnic tables, which my headlights showed to be empty.

I climbed out, left the motor running and the headlights on. A murmur of low voices seemed to be coming from near the spit building. "Lou?" I called. "Louie, is that you?"

I was answered by a deep baritone chuckle.

I started toward it, straining to see inside the building. "Louis Burbage, is that you?"

I stopped ten feet short of the building. Squinted. Blinked. Peered left and right. Told myself, *You should have put the headlights on the building, dumbass.*

Did I see movement in the back of the building?

I was just beginning to realize the staggering odds against my friend recovering from his condition, traveling more than two thousand miles from New Mexico, recognizing me at a gas station in western Pennsylvania, calling out and waving but not stopping to say hello, and then hiding from me behind a lamb spit at a Serbian Orthodox church, when a soft male voice whispered in my right ear. "Hey."

I spun around, directly in the path of a flying fist; it caught me just above the left eye. Suddenly the sky was filled with stars, the woods alive with a thousand buzzing cicadas. Then another fist slammed into my rib cage from the left. I went down on my knees, then onto my side, and then…I remember the kick in my stomach, but nothing else.

33.

Too many cops for comfort

I don't know what time it was when I was shaken awake to find myself in a hospital bed. It took half a minute to recognize the hand shaking me as belonging to a police officer. He was leaning over me, his face so close to mine that I could smell his aftershave; it reminded me of my father's Old Spice but with a sour, limey edge to it. He was grinning, which I thought odd. My eyes seemed to have become slightly crossed, my tongue thick and stuck to the inside of a cheek, but my mind was well aware of the pain scorching through my ribs and how it had come to be there.

"How you doin', pardner?" the officer said.

"I'm not sure. Who are you?"

"Deputy Smith, Hermitage Police Department. Do you remember what happened to you?"

I tried to focus my eyes on the upper sleeve of his gray shirt. A round insignia with white lettering. I blinked, squinted, tried to remember, and then it came to me. Hermitage had switched to black shirts a few years earlier. And their insignia was not round but eight-sided. "You're wearing the wrong shirt," I told him.

"Ha," he said. "You musta took a hard one. Did you see who did it?"

I tried to sit up but he pushed me down again. I said, "I need to see your badge."

And now he put his face very close to mine. His breath smelled like Black Jack gum, a scent I hadn't smelled in decades. "It's probably a good thing you don't remember nothin'," he hissed. "You'll live a lot longer that way. Capisce?"

I couldn't help it, I laughed out loud, and it hurt to laugh. A lot. But he had gone from a redneck cop to a Mafia thug in two sentences. I figured that I must dreaming. I said, "Go away and let me sleep."

He drew back a few inches, then headbutted me. It wasn't hard enough to put me all the way out again, but hard enough to make me wish it had.

When my head cleared sufficiently to allow a bit of common sense to return, I pushed myself up on my elbows and looked around. The bed parallel to mine and a yard and a half away was occupied. The side of the guy's face suggested he was maybe in his midthirties. His eyes were wide-open as he stared at the ceiling.

"Did you see that guy?" I asked.

He blinked but otherwise remained still.

"He headbutted me. Did you see that?"

No movement, no response whatsoever.

I buzzed for a nurse. "That man," I told her.

She turned to glance at the guy in the other bed.

"Not him. The phony deputy."

"Did you just now wake up?" she asked.

"I wasn't dreaming. Ask him."

She looked at my roommate again. Then turned back to me. "He doesn't like to be disturbed."

"You didn't see him come in here? A guy pretending to be with the police?"

No, she hadn't seen anyone enter my room. Of course she hadn't.

I asked, "What hospital is this?"

"Sharon Regional."

"How did I get here?"

"Father Jaksic called the police about somebody squealing tires in the parking lot. Do you remember what happened to you?"

"Enough of it, yeah. Anything broken?"

"Bruised ribs," she said. "And a nasty bump on the side of your head. And this other one right in the middle of your forehead. Where did it come from?"

If she didn't believe that I'd had a visitor, she wouldn't believe that he had headbutted me. "I must have rolled over and hit the rail. Have the police been called?"

"They're going to send somebody to talk to you when you're awake. Are you awake?"

"The jury's still out on that. Can you call them, please, so that I can get out of here? I need a ride back to my vehicle."

"You're staying the night," she told me, and gave the red knob on my forehead a closer look. "Does that hurt?" she asked, and pushed it with a fingertip. I yelped. "I'll take that as a yes," she said. She pulled a little flashlight from her tunic's pocket, turned it on and blinded me with it, first one eye and then the other.

"Do you feel dizzy?" she asked.

"No more than usual."

"Nauseous?"

"No."

"Any double vision or blurriness?"

"No."

"Are you telling me the truth?"

"Nothing but," I lied.

She nodded. "What's your level of pain right now? Between one and ten."

"Three," I answered, but only because I didn't want any mind-numbing painkillers shot into me. "A couple of ibuprofens will do me."

"And how are we supposed to make any money off you from that?" she joked, but I wasn't in the mood to laugh.

"You'll charge me fifty dollars for each of them. And a thousand dollars to use the bathroom."

She smiled, but she didn't mean it. "Is there anybody you need to call? Let them know you're here?"

"Just the police."

"Nobody who's going to miss you tonight?"

"Nope."

She stood there looking down at me, probably trying to work up a bit of sympathy, but then decided it wasn't worth the effort. It was anybody's guess what she was thinking of me. A man drives into a church parking lot, leaves his vehicle running and door hanging open, obviously doesn't plan to stay very long, then dashes into the darkness behind the church only to get pummeled. No wedding ring, still has money in his pocket—or at least did until the hospital staff stripped him to his Fruit of the Looms and ransacked his pockets. The man appears clean, had been casually but neatly dressed, well groomed, apparently doesn't have a girlfriend or wife at home. Only a couple of situations would explain something like that.

"Ibuprofen?" I asked.

She blinked. Turned and walked away.

Twenty minutes later, just as the ibuprofen was kicking in, a real deputy showed up. He introduced himself as Deputy Bracken. I had met enough small-town deputies, police chiefs, and sheriffs in my life to recognize a real one. In general, they come in two varieties, either smug, suspicious, and looking for a chance to throw their weight around, or, more often, humble and wanting to help.

Deputy Bracken was of the latter variety, about five ten and slender limbed, his brown eyes looking tired.

"Man," he said, and leaned a bit closer to peer at my face, "you took a couple good ones, didn't you?"

"I'd like to say 'you should see the other guy,' but I can't."

He pulled a small notebook and pen from his shirt pocket. "Start at the beginning," he said.

"You'd be better off recording this with your phone," I told him.

"Long story?"

"Long enough."

He nodded, put the notebook and pen away, pulled out his cell phone, fumbled for a few moments finding the voice recording app, then tapped it on. "Shoot," he said.

I told the story in broad strokes. I was a writer and had been researching the triple murder in New Castle. Apparently, I was making some enemies. The attempted intimidation by a man in a dark-blue suit. The certainty that an intruder had been in my house. The late-night phone call and ensuing lightning crease through my brain. The man who looked like my friend suckering me into an ambush behind the church. And then the headbutting phony deputy just thirty minutes earlier.

Bracken's eyes kept getting wider the longer I talked. "That's how you got that?" he asked with a nod to my forehead.

"Yep."

"Can you describe him for me?"

I did so.

"Anything else?"

"That's about it," I said.

He nodded and shut off the recording. "So what we can do is to try to locate the guy who headbutted you."

"You won't," I said.

He shrugged. "Probably not. But because of all the other stuff, I'll need to let New Castle know about this too."

"I understand," I said.

"You haven't talked to them yet?"

"It's on my to-do list."

"All right, then. I'll take care of it. Anything else I can do for you?"

"Find out where my car keys are and if the vehicle is in a safe place?"

"No problem." He took out a card and laid it on the tray table beside the bed. "What kind of books do you write?"

"These days mostly mysteries."

"My wife loves mysteries," he said.

"I thank God every night for wives who love mysteries."

He chuckled. "I hope you feel better soon."

I thanked him; he left. A while later Nurse Ratched came in to tell me that the Hermitage police had brought my Jeep back and that it was parked safely outside. She laid the keyless remote on the tray table and looked down on me with what appeared to be real sympathy this time. "Are you sure you don't want to let anybody know you're here?"

"It would only upset her. I'll tell her tomorrow."

"So there is a she, huh? You know she'll be ticked off that you didn't call her right away."

"I know. But I can't stand being fussed over."

She shook her head. "Men," she said, but not without a half wink before she turned and left me alone for the night.

Unfortunately, I'm a light sleeper. Even in my own bed in a pitch-dark bedroom I rely on repetitive meditation music from my Fire tablet to bore me to sleep. In the hospital I couldn't even use my phone because the battery was already low and I had no earbuds with me. Light poured in through my open doorway. And the guy in the other bed, who hadn't looked at me or uttered a word since I'd been brought in, was now lying facing me, mouth open, horrendous snores issuing like walrus farts from deep in his throat.

I took it till midnight. Then I climbed out of bed and sneaked out the door in my bare feet and headed away from the front desk. Not until I passed into the next wing did I find an empty room. I settled into the vinyl chair and tried to relax, but with little success. Then I told myself, *Screw this. You're paying to stay here and it won't be cheap. You deserve a couple hours of sleep.* I got out of the chair, pulled the privacy curtain around one of the beds, curled up and tried to find dreamland.

The slap of footsteps in the hallway was nonstop. Bells dinged and doors banged shut. Voices echoed like shrieking Valkyries. And it seemed that every time I dozed off, my bladder would wake me and send me to the bathroom. A little before five I waved the flag of surrender—the rear slit in my hospital gown—and crept back unnoticed to my own bed so as not to be charged for the use of two.

34.

A tired story told again

I had been sitting beside the window in one of those orange vinyl hospital chairs for most of three hours, fully dressed in my blood-spotted long-sleeved T-shirt and dirt-splotched jeans, waiting for the alleged doctor to show up and sign my release, when the phone rang on the little table beside my bed. *Uh-oh*, I thought. *Some snitch told Cara where I am.* With an apology already forming on my lips, I picked up the phone and said hello.

"This Silvis?" a man's voice asked.

I swallowed the apology. "Who's calling?"

"Detective Smathers. New Castle PD. You getting released this morning?"

"That's supposed to be the plan."

"You wanna swing down this way before you head home? Have a couple of questions I need to ask."

"No problem," I said. "Though I'm kind of at the mercy of—"

He cut me off with "303 East North Street. See you then," and hung up.

It was 9:03 a.m. The world outside the window was gray and wet. I waited another fifteen minutes for the invisible doc to materialize, but he didn't, so I shuffled out to the front desk and told the pretty blond nurse sitting there, "I'm cutting out. I can't wait for

Dr. Who to finish his five-course breakfast. You have something for me to sign?"

There was a bit of complaining from her but when I turned and started listing toward the exit she whipped out the proper form and collected my signature. "That and four dollars will buy you a cup of bad coffee," I told her with a smile.

It took me too long in the low greasy fog to find my Jeep in the lot. Every movement hurt, and every black SUV I tried to unlock wasn't mine. I hit the panic button on the remote and made my way toward the shrill beeping. It sounded like a dying goose calling its mate, and I felt like a dying goose as I shuffled toward it. I climbed in shivering, damp from head to toe with the morning's spit, and cranked the engine. First stop: hot coffee. In the biggest cup I could find.

Caffeinating on the fly, I followed my phone's directions to 303 East North Street. It was a twenty-minute drive, which allowed me to swallow most of the coffee before pulling up at my destination. The police department's building was less intimidating than I expected, a long two-story redbrick facility that took up most of the block. It looked more like the bank in whose parking lot I was parked than like a building filled with stern men and women in dark uniforms. And now I was supposed to go inside that stolid, practical building and tell my story to an equally stolid and practical detective. I would consider myself fortunate if he didn't order up a battery of Rorschach tests for me. I was sane enough to know that I might not pass.

I drained the rest of my coffee, then headed across the street and inside, where I inquired at the information desk for Detective

Smathers. I found him at his desk in a metal stall with three walls. I would have appreciated a window of some kind, but as it was, I had the choice of looking at him or the inside of his gray box.

"You Silvis?" he said when I stepped into his doorway.

"Unfortunately."

"You look like roadkill."

"Roadkill can't walk. I still can."

He jerked his head at the chair positioned in front of his desk. It was one of those hard, molded fiberglass chairs we used to sit in at school. I came into the cubicle and gingerly lowered myself onto the seat. I'm pretty sure I winced.

"You hurtin'?" he asked.

"Pain is life's way of letting us know we're still alive."

"Huh," he said. I couldn't tell if the sound was his laugh or a refutation.

At first glance he reminded me of a black Philip Seymour Hoffman. He was wearing a pair of half-frame glasses, his face broad and fleshy, hair thinning on top but needing a trim around the ears. At nine thirty in the a.m. he was already in shirtsleeves rolled to the elbow, the knot of his blue tie pulled loose, top button on his yellow Oxford open. Truth is, he looked as wrinkled and weary as me.

He leaned back in his chair and laid a hand against a jowly cheek. "So how'd you get into this mess?"

"Which mess are you referring to?"

"You got the crap beat out of you last night."

"That I did."

"You know who did it?"

"No, sir, I do not."

"You know why they did it?"

Now I leaned back, or at least tried to; the seat held me fairly straight. I blew out a long breath.

"I'm here all day," he said.

"Didn't Deputy Bracken fill you in already?"

"I like to hear things from the horse's mouth."

"The chance of us having a second date is slim if you keep calling me names."

He scowled and flipped a hand through the air. *Shut up and start talking*, his hand said.

So I began, again in broad strokes, giving Smathers only a little more than I had given the deputy. I was aware that Smathers would have been briefed by Bracken and was therefore comparing those two stories as I spoke. Six minutes later, I finished. And for the next two minutes, Smathers did not move, did not speak. He breathed. Breathed like a leaky accordion and kept staring at me.

Fortunately, as a writer of crime fiction, I know some of the tricks. I know that silence will often make the guilty and even the innocent give up more information than they mean to. The more awkward the silence, the more a person will chatter away. Me, I smiled pleasantly. And to keep my mouth shut, I sang inside my head. Paul Simon's "Still Crazy After All These Years." I know every word of it.

Smathers puffed out a breath, leaned forward, and clasped his pudgy hands atop the desk. "So this friend of yours," he said. "The one from Texas."

"New Mexico."

"Same difference. You're fairly sure he's deceased?"

"Deceased or at least incapacitated. He was put into a dementia ward about nine years ago. As far as I know, there's no cure for that."

"Then why would you follow him behind a church?"

"Because it really did look like him. And because he called me by a name that only he ever used."

"So maybe it *was* him."

I shook my head. "Lou was a very gentle guy. Skinny as a rail and not in the least athletic. He couldn't have beaten up a kitten."

"Then why, I ask again, would you follow some guy behind a church?"

Good question, and the same one I'd been asking myself for the past twelve hours. "I *wanted* him to be Lou. He was my best friend. I thought if there was any chance at all...I don't know. I needed to find out."

Smathers said nothing for a few beats. "So why would somebody pretend to be a friend who's probably dead just so he could get you somewhere private and beat the crap out of you?"

Another damn fine question. "It does sound a little far-fetched, doesn't it? And yet, here I sit."

"How many guys were there?"

"Two for sure. Anyway there were two I could see in the truck when it first went past me. Lou and the driver. But behind the church it felt like at least three guys. Let's round it off at three."

"What'd the driver look like?"

"I have no idea. The Lou guy was the one nearest me. Honestly, I didn't see the driver at all. But I have to assume that there was one."

"Then how do you know it was a guy?"

"I don't. But he punched like a guy."

"You been punched a lot?"

"I grew up with an older brother. And my dad was an ex-Marine and amateur boxer. He taught me how to box."

"You still box?"

"I never did officially. But I held my own as a kid. I could make a speed bag sing."

He pursed his lips, nodded. I wondered if he knew how to smile.

He said, "You find anything missing afterward? Wallet? Money? Any personal belongings?"

"Just my pride."

"How about in your car? Anything missing there?"

Only then did I realize that I had never thought to check the Jeep. It had smelled of another person when I climbed into it that morning, but I chalked that up to the fact that either Deputy Bracken or one of his colleagues had driven it to the hospital. To Smathers, I said, "I didn't think to check. But I don't keep much in it. Nothing that would be of use to anybody else."

"Registration card? Insurance? Everybody keeps those in their car."

"Yeah, I, uh…I guess I need to check."

"As soon as we're done here. Call me from the lot if you find anything missing."

"Will do."

Another few beats of silence. I was just about ready to start head-singing again when he said, "So tell me about the fake deputy."

"Well," I began, "the first thing that threw me was that his uniform was off. He was wearing the old gray one. I asked to see his badge and he ignored me."

"And he wanted what from you?"

"Ah…fear, I guess. I mean, he asked me a couple of times if I had seen whoever attacked me. But I didn't answer. That's when he said it's a good thing if I don't remember. And then he headbutted me. Or maybe he headbutted me first and then said that. I'm still a little fuzzy on the chronology of things."

"You remember what he looked like?"

"Yeah…not very well. He seemed big, but he was leaning over me on the bed. And I'd been shot up with something, some kind of painkiller probably."

"Caucasian?"

"Ahhh…I'm going to say *yes probably* to that."

"That's it? That's all you can remember?"

"He smelled like Old Spice."

"The aftershave?"

"My dad used it, so I know the smell. But this guy's was slightly different. Sour, kind of."

"Sour how?"

"I don't know. Like there was lime juice in it."

"Why would somebody put lime juice in Old Spice? Is that a thing people do?"

"No, this was in addition to the Old Spice. Like an undertone of sour lime."

"An undertone, huh?"

"Sorry. That's the best I can do."

He sat motionless and silent for several seconds.

I said, "And Black Jack gum. I just now remember that too."

"Say again?"

"His breath smelled like Black Jack gum."

He almost rolled his eyes at that, but brought them back down again. "You take drugs, Silvis?"

"Not voluntarily."

"You sure?"

"I take an ibuprofen now and then, but that's it. I have faith in the body's ability to heal itself."

He grunted. "How long you been a writer?"

He must have googled me. I said, "I started wanting to be a writer when I was twenty-one. My first book was published when I was thirty-three."

"That's twelve years. Took you a while to get there, didn't it?"

He was starting to irritate me. I smiled. "It's the journey, not the destination."

"Yeah," he said, "that never made any sense to me. Why go somewhere if you're not really going somewhere?"

"You don't ride a motorcycle, do you?"

"Death traps," he said.

So okay, end of *that* conversation.

"Is this all part of your next book?" he asked.

"What do you mean?"

"This whole crazy story you're telling. The fake deputy, the old friend smacking you around? Did you get somebody to hit you a couple of times so you could make all this up and have something to write about?"

Yeah, he irritated me. "Is that something you would do, Detective?"

"Or maybe you went behind that church looking for a little hanky-panky."

"I have a girlfriend for that. We don't need a church."

"You wouldn't be the first guy goes out at night looking for a little fun on the side."

I stood. "Have a good day, Detective." I turned to exit the cubicle.

He said, "Check your vehicle, Silvis. Call if you notice anything."

"Ten-four," I said over my shoulder, and made my way to the exit. I needed another mega cup of coffee to quiet my withdrawal shakes. I also needed to get rid of the previous cup, which was already putting the squeeze on my bladder, so I figured I could do both at the Speedway on Jefferson a few blocks away.

But first I threw open the front doors of my Jeep and searched every crevice and compartment and cranny. Only one thing struck me as unusual. Anomalous. Possibly terrifying.

I didn't notice it until I climbed in behind the wheel after checking under all of the seats and satisfying myself that nothing was amiss. A dead bee. Belly-up, perched on the top of my steering wheel.

Yep, another dead bee, just as desiccated as the previous one.

Either these bees had a facility for flying through sealed windows and dying in flight and then drying out as they dropped supine atop precarious perches, or this one had been placed in my locked Jeep while I was speaking with Detective Smathers. I plucked it off the wheel, dropped it outside onto the pavement, and crushed it beneath the toe of my shoe, grinding it while I looked all around, hoping to spot a grinning face at a window.

But I saw no faces. I saw nobody. Still, I could feel eyes on me. Who the hell was watching me?

Then I looked down at the bee again. Powder with wings. *That was stupid*, I told myself. *You should have saved it, preserved the evidence.* But evidence of what? Maybe the bee had crawled in through a vent. Maybe it came in while I was checking under the seats. Maybe there was some kind of dehydrating-bee epidemic going around.

I left without calling Smathers. What was I going to say—I found a dead bee belly-up on my steering wheel? But I smushed it? Yeah, that would have done me a whole lot of good.

35.

Shut up and start typing

After an uneventful afternoon and night, quiet but for the rampaging paranoia jarring me alert every time the house creaked, I spent Wednesday morning writing up all of my notes, trying to build a cohesive narrative out of fragments of craziness. I wasn't doing it for publication but only so that I might be better able to discern a pattern of some kind. My sanity, at this point, depended on it.

I would eventually have to tell the police more than I had told Bracken and Smathers. What I'd given them so far was just a small pile of bricks dumped at their feet. If I wanted any of it to make sense, I had to line those bricks up in a few orderly courses, with plenty of details—the mortar to hold them all together. Left-brain people like Smathers would no doubt still think I was on the loony side of credible, but at least I would have done my civic duty. And maybe then I could return to a quiet, solitary life at my desk.

I didn't want to walk into Detective Smathers's office again just to be peppered with more questions. He had gone easy on me the first time. It's usually the follow-up conversation that goes from interview to interrogation. All cops have tricks for squeezing information out of people. A good friend who is also an FBI agent once showed me some of the technique by interviewing me as I played the role of a suspected murderer. It didn't take long for my friend—a guy I really like and admire and trust—to rattle me so much that my blood pressure spiked as I involuntarily fell into a confrontational attitude. Body language, intonation, word choice, they all go under the microscope when a cop interrogates. A gesture as subtle as an eyebrow twitch can give a cop a frisson of illumination. I hadn't done anything illegal—with the exception of letting myself into Kennaday's rented house—and I didn't want Smathers or anybody else treating me as if I had. A fully detailed written account of my activities and observances seemed my best protection from the good detective's stink eye.

It was an appropriate morning for staying hunched over my laptop. The house was chilly after the cold night, the sky dingy white from horizon to horizon, and everything I could see through the back door's glass—the deck and rails, the trees and some of the yard—was wet and determined to remain wet. In other words, nature did not call to me that morning. I had no desire to go shuffling and shivering through a deep bed of sodden leaves. I typed and revised, thought and remembered and typed and revised until my cell phone's alarm dinged. Time to get washed, brushed, dressed for my last interview with Phoebe Hudack. Time to switch gears and start thinking like an interrogator myself. This time, damn it, I wasn't going to leave the Burchette house and the little village of Bell's Grove without a few answers.

36.

The tenant, fourth and final interview

The first thing I noticed when I stepped inside the house was its absolute stillness. It had been fairly quiet during the previous three interviews, but this was a different kind of quiet. A stillness more felt than heard. More sixth sense than sensory.

Walking into the house was like walking into a depressurized building. I felt it immediately, then felt it coming from Phoebe too, nothing but nothing. No tension, no lingering residue of violence, no nervousness, no sorrow, no bitterness. No nada y nada. It was eerie, and it deflated the confidence I had earlier psyched myself into feeling.

"Something's different," I said in lieu of hello.

Phoebe smiled and gently closed the door behind me. "Our last goodbye," she said.

"Yeah. Something like that."

I had never seen her prettier. She was not, as I mentioned earlier, a strikingly beautiful young woman, but that afternoon she seemed an inch or so taller, more poised, and wholly in control of herself and the surroundings. She wore a dark, wine-colored skirt, black flats, and an untucked white blouse. There was something familiar to that look that I couldn't put my finger on at first, but as I assumed my seat in the usual chair, it struck me: my mother dressed for church. Church had been the extent of my mother's social life; the rest of her time was work. But for Sunday morning church she commandeered the single bathroom in my boyhood home for most of ninety minutes, and always emerged with her hair perfectly coiffed, fingernails self-manicured and painted a shiny red, her nylons straight and makeup deftly applied. And there would be a soft, indefinable calm to her as we walked the half mile to our little country church at the bottom of the hollow, as if, for this morning at least, all of the toil and tragedy and loss and grief of her life were taking a few hours off.

And that was Phoebe that afternoon, except for the nylons. Her legs were smooth and shiny and bare. She arranged herself in her usual seat, knees and feet pressed together.

———

S: I have three areas of information I want to explore today. The first is Justin Cirillo and his—

P: [*interrupts*] I'm sorry, but today it's important for you to sit and listen. Would you care for something to drink? I can offer bottled spring water or tea. I have a new tea that you might like—ashwagandha with ginger and lemon.

She might as well have slapped my face with a wet towel, that's how startled I am by her words. The woman who had called herself Holly, in Dennis Cirillo's trailer, had served me a cup of ashwagandha with ginger and lemon tea.

S: Where did you get—

P: [*interrupts, holds up a palm*] Please.

S: Do you know a woman named Holly?

She inhales deeply, closes her eyes for a second, then opens her eyes and smiles at me.

P: It's important that you just listen. All right? Otherwise, we can't meet today.

S: I can't ask any questions?

P: If you do, or interrupt me, then we're done. No exceptions. I'm sorry but those are my instructions.

S: From who? Thomas?

P: [*smiles*] Will you agree or not?

I am quiet long enough to hear my pulse throbbing in my right ear.

S: I guess I have no choice.

P: [*holds her smile*] So nothing to drink?

S: I'm good.

P: The water for tea is already hot. Ashwagandha is good for stress, and it strengthens the immune system.

S: Some people claim it's also an aphrodisiac.

P: That too. May I get some for you?

S: Not right now, thank you. But you go right ahead if you want some.

P: I'm good too.

She pulls herself very straight then and lays one hand atop the other in her lap.

P: I will now tell you everything I am permitted to tell you. I don't know anything more than this, so please don't bother asking. If you do, we're done, and you will have to leave immediately. Okay?

I nod, but with eyes squinting in suspicion. Where has the real Phoebe gone?

What happens next is just as odd as what has already happened. Phoebe closes her eyes, inhales deeply again, exhales through a thin slit between her lips, then opens her eyes and starts talking. Her eyes remain clear, not glazed over as if she is channeling or in a trance, but her gaze seldom meets mine. Instead she looks past me to some indistinct spot on the wall. I have to bite my tongue to keep from speaking. I want badly to write down or record her words, but of course that is taboo, a rule she established at our very first meeting. So I sit as motionless as possible so as not to allow my attention to veer away from the sound of her voice. I want to hear every word and can only hope that I will remember them all.

P: [*voice calm, steady, confident*] The first question is this: Why did Justin kill Diney, Barry, and Shelley? And the answer to that question is that it all starts with Baby Doe.

The very same words Thomas Kennaday first spoke to me! I twitch with the need to speak. But I hold my tongue.

P: What the police don't know is that a week prior to the murders, Barry Faye and Justin got into a fight. Barry's a lot bigger and stronger, and he hurt Justin pretty bad. My brother, Eddie, tried to intervene, but he isn't worth much in a fight and he got knocked out of it right at the start. What did Barry and Justin fight about it? Both of them believed that they were Baby Doe's father, because her complexion is dark. Not Black, not white, but somewhere in between. The mother is Caucasian. She lives about twelve miles from New Castle in Lowellville, Ohio, just across the border. She was fooling around with both Barry and Justin.

This immediately brings to mind what the woman who called herself Holly hinted at in Dennis Cirillo's trailer. That it would be a lot easier to figure out what had happened to Baby Doe if her parents were known, specifically which of them was Black and which white. And then Holly had told me, just as Phoebe now confirmed, that Baby Doe's mother is Caucasian. Both Barry Faye and Justin Cirillo were "fooling around with her." Has Phoebe just now insinuated that the father of the biracial Baby Doe is Barry Faye?

P: The problem is, people only *think* Baby Doe is biracial because she's darker complected.

Did she read my mind just now? Or did Kennaday accurately predict my thoughts? Or did he somehow eavesdrop on them from the future?

P: [*continues*] But so is Justin. He's full-blooded Greek. Maybe the hospital has tested her and they know whether she's definitely biracial or not, but none of us out in the public knows for sure.

Okay, so maybe Faye is not the father. But has Phoebe now revealed that either he or Cirillo definitely *is* Baby Doe's father? It certainly seems that she has. If only I could ask a question!

P: So they were fighting over that. Both of them thought he was the father. I don't know if Diney knew any of this or not. The fight happened in Creekside, not at Diney's house. I heard about it from Eddie. So if Diney *did* know, she never mentioned it to me. The thing is, she must've known the woman too, the baby's mother, because the whole gang of them would meet sometimes at the bar where that woman bartended. I never went 'cause I'd stay here and babysit. Plus I don't drink anymore and never wanted to go.

My head is spinning. If Faye and Cirillo were both having an affair with the bartender, and Cirillo had an affair with Burchette before Faye came along, and if Diney Burchette, along with Eddie Hudack and Jolene Mrozek, all partied together at the Lowellville woman's place of employment, is it too much of a stretch to suggest a kind of sex-swapping association among all six of them? But even if it does suggest that, is that point of any consequence? Can it explain how Baby Doe ended up injured and abandoned in the pine woods? And why she had been left so conveniently in the exact place, and on the same day and time, where two Amish teenagers regularly had sex?

Just as I am about to pull my hair out in frustration, Phoebe hits me with another bag of rocks.

P: Another thing nobody knows yet is that Barry Faye isn't his real name. He's not from around here originally. He's from out around Flint, Michigan. A good while back, the police there were looking at him pretty hard in regards to a couple of Amber Alerts. He was seen in the vicinity where two little children had disappeared, on two different occasions maybe six months apart. Neither one of them has ever turned up. Thomas says he knows they never will.

Thomas says *who* knows they never will? Thomas himself? Or Barry Faye? Or both? Damn, I hate ambiguous pronouns!

And how did Thomas Kennaday come by this information in the first place? What *is* Barry Faye's real name?

P: Thomas said it wouldn't take the police long to find out Faye's real name if they knew to look for it. They took everybody's word around here that Barry Faye was Barry Faye. Nobody knew otherwise. I doubt that Diney did or she never would've let him around her girls.

Is Faye the connection to pedophilia I've been looking for? To a pedophilia ring suggested by the planted newspaper in Kennaday's rented house?

Then something else Holly said occurs to me. She'd said that Justin liked to visit the Burchette house because it gave him a sense of family. If this is true, would a young man who longed for a family do harm to a baby he thought of as his own? No, but he might snatch that baby from somebody who *would* harm it.

Had Justin Cirillo somehow learned of Barry Faye's past, or of his sick intentions toward Baby Faye, and snatched her from the yet-nameless mother? Had that mother been aware of, and possibly in collusion with, Faye's plan? And what exactly was that plan? To sell Baby Faye to a pedophilia ring?

It shouldn't be difficult to identify Baby Doe's mother. A pregnant bartender in a small town would be easy to remember. I resolve to race to Smathers's office with this information straight from the visit with Phoebe.

P: The baby's mother took maternity leave from her job before and after the baby was born. Then a month or so after the birth, she told her neighbors that she was having a hard time going it alone, so she was taking the baby and moving in with her sister in Columbus. What nobody knows is that she doesn't have a sister.

If nobody knows that, how does Phoebe know it? From Kennaday, of course. So now the mother is missing too?

I sit there wondering, mind reeling, until I realize that Phoebe has not interrupted my thoughts for several minutes. She is done talking. Her head is lowered, eyes on her hands, completely motionless. She reminds me of a wind-up toy that has wound down.

S: [*softly*] May I speak?
P: [*blinks, then lifts her head*] I'm going to get some tea now. Would you care for a cup?
S: Yes, please.

37.

The convo convolutes

While I waited for Phoebe to return with the tea, I took a quick look at the time on my cell phone, and sorely wished I had secretly reneged on my agreement not to record our interviews. I probably could have gotten away with it. Now everything depended on my memory. But a promise is a promise. I shoved the phone back into my pocket.

It was past time for LaShonda to have returned from school. Yet the house remained eerily silent but for the *ssshh ssshh* of Phoebe's soles over the low carpet as she came back into the room, a steaming mug of tea in each hand.

I accepted mine, watched her sit and take a sip of hers. In a low whisper, I asked, "Is it okay if I talk now?"

She nodded. "But not about anything I've already said. We're finished with that."

I tried to smile in agreement, but even I could feel my smile's crookedness. "Shouldn't LaShonda be home from school by now?"

She took another sip, then held the mug just below her chin and looked at it instead of at me. "She's upstairs in bed. She has a sore throat and a little fever, so I kept her home today."

So, Phoebe had fallen into the role of mother quite easily. I had no doubts that she would make a fine one. But wasn't LaShonda supposed to leave for Hawaii soon to live with her biological father? Where was he in all this mess, anyway? "I hope it's nothing serious," I said.

"It isn't."

Hmm. Not *I hope so too?* Or *I don't think it is?* I found the adamancy of *it isn't* very interesting. Phoebe worked on a checkout line, not as a nurse. Where had she come by such medical confidence?

I said, "I want to thank you for all of the time you've given me over the past couple of weeks. I know how difficult things are for you and LaShonda now."

She nodded. "It helps to know that everything is going to work out all right."

Another odd statement. Doesn't one *hope* that things will work out all right? Only someone who knows the future can *know* what the future holds. Now that she had no script to follow, her words had become incautious. Could I get more information from her before the tea ran out?

I said, "I wish I could sit down with Thomas again and discuss all of this with him. I feel like I don't know him at all. I mean, I don't even know if he's a good guy or a bad guy."

"He's good!" she said. And then her eyes filled with tears. "He's *so* good. And I miss him so much."

"Did he say if he'd be back sometime?"

"No questions about him," she said, but it was a weak protestation.

"I'm sorry; you're right. It's just so hard not to ask. We both want to see him again, don't we?"

She nodded, and for a few moments I thought she might burst into sobs. But then her eyes brightened and she said, "I have a piece of paper he wrote on."

"Really? Is there any chance I could have a look at it?"

She shot me a conspiratorial smile, set her mug on the coffee table, stood and went into the kitchen. A drawer scraped open and closed again. She returned holding a sheet of white paper torn from a medium-size writing tablet and laid it in front of me on the coffee table.

"You're letting me read it?" I asked in surprise.

She gave me a little shrug. "It might help you, I don't know."

A little voice in my head told me not to touch the paper. I set my mug of tea aside and leaned forward to read. The handwriting was in blue ink, in a strong and steady hand but also seemingly rushed, as if he hadn't had time to write complete sentences. It was dated the morning of the last time she saw him. I read it through once, then looked up at her and asked, "How did you get hold of this?"

She blushed a little, smiled shyly, and said, "I went through his jacket when he was in the shower. I was hoping to find an address or phone number or something. He'd already told me that he was leaving forever after we had sex one more time. And I just, I don't know. I wanted something of his to keep. Something to remember him by."

I wasn't sure if I believed her or not. But it seemed typical of a young woman's behavior, a young woman in love, or otherwise under his spell. I read the note a second time. Here is what Kennaday wrote:

Woke 03:12. Masturbated. Back to sleep.

Woke 05:27. Went downstairs and worked for couple of hours on laptop. Slept on sofa till 11:30.

Showered, dressed, went out to meet the man. What a goober! Sick fuck is def out of picture soon. Tired of his bullshit. Left him and went for light

lunch but double zero prospects there for afternoon delight. Needed release bad, so asked chubby Asian server girl to trade a bj for whatever she'd make that day slinging stir-fry. She threatened to tell her old man, who's the cook and looks like Sumo wrestler, so I whispered a sweet nothing in her ear and that ended that.

Got home 14:30, worked out on weights for an hour then to bed to refresh T levels for PA219 later.

18:48. PA219 arriving in a couple of minnies. Will button things up and do her one or two last times. Need to vamoose by midnight, will be tied up next 48 running mouth for the team. Then back to Btown for debriefs. I better get a gold star for this gig or things be getting ugly.

I read it a second time, then asked Phoebe if any of it meant anything to her. She shrugged and answered, "Only what it says."

Unlike her, I couldn't take Kennaday's words at face value. The syntax was uneven and not at all similar to the way he had spoken to me at Joy Buffet. And why had he employed military time? "Are you PA219?" I asked Phoebe. "You arrived at his place a little before seven that night?"

She nodded.

"Do you know why he referred to you that way?"

"I assume the PA might stand for Pennsylvania. But I really don't know. He always called me by my name, or Pheebes. Like on *Friends* on TV. Phoebe or Pheebes or babe. I liked when he called me that."

"You liked when he called you babe?"

She nodded again. "I had a boyfriend in high school who called me that. It was nice."

And now I felt a heavy air of loss emanating from her. She had changed right before my eyes, going from a superefficient business-woman to a lonely, heartbroken young woman, but one working hard to hold herself together.

She sniffed a little, then nodded toward the paper. "You're permitted to take a photo of it, if you wish. But only one."

What? I was *permitted* to take a photo?

Her word choice clearly signaled that she was still following Kennaday's directions, maybe improvising verbally but still sticking to his script. It would mean that Phoebe really *hadn't* lifted the note from his pocket while he was in the shower, that the note was a plant, like the newspaper in his rented house.

In any case, I was not going to decline the offer. I took my time with the photo; my hands were shaking and I didn't want to blur the shot. In the end, it turned out clear enough.

At that moment I had no idea what to make of the note, other than that Mr. Kennaday was either a very libidinous young man or a very insecure one. All of those references to sexual acts—code of some kind? Or just a young man hoping to impress a much older man with his sexual prowess?

I recalled that in an earlier conversation with Phoebe, she had corroborated that they often had sex three or four times on an evening. "I really don't know why he liked me," she had said then. "He's such a special person, and I'm just a plain old nobody."

The answer to her question was now clear to me, though I would not have articulated it to her. She was his stooge, his puppet, his punch, just as I was. He was using both of us. But why? For what ultimate purpose?

Other questions arose as I continued to stare at the note on the coffee table. Does his use of military time signal a past, or current, history with the military? Who is "the man" referenced in the letter as a goober? And why is he destined to be *out of the picture* soon? What exactly did Kennaday mean by that phrase? Who are *the rest of the team* to whom Kennaday will be running his mouth? About what? What does he mean by *a gold star*? Is that shorthand for a promotion or raise? And where is Btown? Boston? Baltimore? Belgrade?

The word *debriefs* was also worthy of attention. It suggested that he had been on assignment in Bell's Grove, and now, at the time of the note, that assignment was reaching completion. At this point I was convinced that Kennaday had deliberately composed the note and instructed Phoebe to feed it to me with the fiction that she had come upon it surreptitiously. The problem was, I couldn't make much sense out of it.

As for Phoebe, an even deeper calm seemed to have descended over her. Maybe it was the tea. I hadn't yet touched mine except for an initial sip, and decided that I shouldn't have any more, just to be safe. She sat there with a soft smile on her mouth, her eyes looking sleepy and satisfied as she gazed at a spot on the floor a couple of yards from where she sat. Without looking up at me, she said, "I should go check on Shonnie now."

"Okay," I said. But neither of us moved.

Then her eyes opened wider and she lifted her gaze to me. "I almost forgot!" she said. "Thomas left a gift for you." She stood and went quickly into the kitchen.

Again a drawer slid open, then closed. She came back into the living room carrying a plastic sandwich bag, crossed to the front door, opened it, then turned and held the bag out to me. I stood and crossed to her. Inside the bag was what looked like thin brown strips of dried leather.

I took the bag gingerly, finger and thumb, and held it up to the light. "Is this what I think it is?"

Another soft, sleepy smile. "Thomas said it can help you. To understand. If you really want to."

Just holding the bag made me feel a little dizzy. For a long while now Cara and I had been talking about trying magic mushrooms. Unfortunately we had no connections, no way of knowing whom to approach. I had read extensively on psilocybin's ability to lift the veil, as we called it. To take the user to a level of higher conscious- ness, and possibly into communion with higher levels of being. As a young man, the only drugs I had experimented with were weed and a single sniff of cocaine. I didn't like the time dilation effect of weed, or the paranoia it engendered in me, and the cocaine had produced no effect at all. I soon stopped using any substance to get my highs, including alcohol, preferring a good cup of coffee for a temporary lift, and a long, solitary walk in the woods for taking me to a higher plane of consciousness.

I had had two spontaneous and very brief out-of-body experi- ences back in my twenties, but nothing I had tried since then could duplicate those experiences, though I had read several books on the practice of astral projection and followed all of the instructions.

It was Cara's belief, echoed by other psychics who knew me well or not at all, that I was "trying too hard." That has been my modus operandi throughout life. Not much has come to me easily; I have to keep pounding away at it. So it is a difficult habit for me to let go of. I needed help, and the literature I'd read on methods of expanding one's consciousness suggested that magic mushrooms might be the safest and surest path to just letting go and allowing the magic to happen.

Phoebe must have seen me staring at the bag of mushrooms, fro- zen in thought, because she laid a hand on my arm and said, startling me, "God be with you, Randall." Her touch and her words sent a shiver into me, and a chilly tingle raced up and down my spine.

Then she laid a hand against my back, and with a gentle pressure nudged me out the door. I stepped out onto the porch feeling woozy and unable to say even a few words of goodbye.

The door closed softy behind me. Beyond the porch the afternoon light was soft, the sky just as clouded as when I had entered the house, a fine mist of rain now falling. Yet, at that moment, everything felt changed. I can't say *how* it was changed, or what exactly had caused that change, or even if the change was real or merely the result of the previous hour. But I drove home with that little bag of mushroom strips on the seat beside me. How to explain their sudden and unexpected appearance in my life? How to explain Thomas Kennaday? How to explain life and consciousness and desire and the whole convoluted riddle of existence?

I felt as if I knew Kennaday even less at that moment than when he'd sat down across from me at the Joy Chinese Buffet. I also knew the world less than I had then. As for reality itself, well, let's just say that I walked out of the Burchette murder house that afternoon and down into the misty rain, walked under the leafless trees in a dead woman's yard and through the scraggly wet grass, walked down the sidewalk where its cracked, heaving chunks of concrete made the path to my Jeep a kind of obstacle course, and it all looked and felt so very strange to me, everything familiar and common but questionable now, everything suspicious, everything a tawdry mask for something indecipherable and probably dangerous underneath.

I no longer felt an urgency or obligation to visit Smathers again. Not immediately, anyway. He wasn't signing my checks. Nor, sadly, was anybody else. I owed no man my fealty. What I owed was a debt to myself—an obligation to allay the confusion, to plow ahead, to keep on keeping on. In short, to survive. As a man and as a father and as a writer. Thanks to my own father's example, that had been my itinerary throughout my entire adult life. He'd never expected or asked for quarter, nor could I.

38.

The Kennaday narrative et alia

The next morning, I was at my desk early, and remained there throughout the afternoon and evening. Cara texted from work a couple of times to ask how my day was going, and I must have texted back, because the words are right there on my phone, three responses, all of them lies, the first at about 11:00 (*Tickety-boo, babe. How you?*), the next around 4:30 (*Finished a nice walk. Cool and damp but refreshing. How's the animalian state of affairs today?*), and the final one at 9:02 that night (*Sweet dreams, sweetness. Love you madly.*). I don't remember writing any of them.

By midmorning the next day, the Kennaday Narrative, as I now thought of it, was coming together. A comprehensive delineation of the past weeks was essential were I to find some understanding of those events. And a degree of understanding was essential were I to leave those weeks behind and return to a state of near normalcy. I needed to get another novel under contract and soon, or else my meager savings account would bleed out. But until I emptied my head of this chaotic congestion à la Thomas Kennaday, my imagination would remain AWOL.

My plan was simple: complete the Kennaday Narrative to my own satisfaction, toss a copy of it onto Smathers's desk, and, in so doing, wash my hands of him and all things Kennaday.

Yet even as I typed and revised and told myself how much more revision the narrative needed and how much information was missing and all of that, a little voice in my head kept whispering that it would never be possible again, my former life, my sense of achievement with each new novel, my stupid belief that I was the captain of my own ship, the master of my soul.

My life would never again have an air of normalcy to it. The shallow pleasure I had taken in crafting pretty sentences, and all the fictions I'd written and wanted to write before I die, now seemed a frivolous ambition in light of what had happened over the past three weeks. I now understood what Graham Greene meant when he wrote that human nature is black and gray rather than black and white. Humanity is indeed steeped in evil. Egotism, arrogance, greed, avarice, deceit, betrayal—our evil reveals itself in sundry ways. As a species we possess more vices than virtues. Most of us try to be good as long as things are going well for us, but in the clinches we too are more than capable of doing evil, though we are likely to justify it as necessary. For example, I would not hesitate to kill anyone who threatens my children's lives, and I would feel no remorse for doing so. Is that evil? To the family of the person I murdered, it is. Which means that there is no such thing as absolute good among our species. The best in us and the beast in us share domain.

And then there was that noisy little bag of mushrooms on my desk too; it lay there staring at me, calling, admonishing, beckoning, taunting: *Silvis, hey! Over here! Yeah, remember us? What are you waiting for, man? When are you going to take the ride? It's what you want, right? Through the veil? Red rover, red rover, send Randall over...*

39.

It's your problem now, Gumshoe

I t was close to four on Friday afternoon when I deemed the narrative done. *Fini!* Like it or not, it was the best I could do. In the bathroom I splashed some water in my face, scrubbed the souring coffee out of my mouth with a quick brush and gargle, and, as the printer churned out the report, threw on some clothes suitable for public inspection. Then into my car and back to 303 North East Street I went.

I wasn't surprised to notice that the day was nasty cold and windy, gray and wet and unremitting in its bitterness. I tried not to take it personally. Unfortunately, my stomach was churning and bubbling from a diet of little other than coffee.

I found Smathers in an even more sour mood than my stomach's. He had his chair turned to the wall when I stepped into his cubicle, was staring at the blank gray metal while either massaging his cheek or picking his nose. I slapped my packet of pages atop his desk and said, "I put this together for you. You can believe it or not, I really don't care."

He lowered his hand from his face, turned, and regarded me with a look just shy of contempt. Then pushed up his glasses and peered down at the papers. "The Kennaday Narrative?" he read. "Did you write me a little story or something?"

"If you have any questions, call me. Otherwise, have a nice day, Detective."

I turned to leave, but he said, "Whoa. Hold on a minute."

I looked back and saw him paging through the papers.

"Have a sit," he said without looking up at me. "This won't take long. I'm a fast reader."

I sat and watched him read. There wasn't anything else in the cubicle to look at, just the gray walls, my shoes, and Smathers hunched over the papers, his stubby finger sliding across the lines as he read. I gave each of those vistas equal time.

Early in the narrative he looked up at me and asked, "This RS in here. That's you?"

Duh, I thought. "It is."

"Why not just say *me* or *I* instead?"

"It gave me some emotional distance from it. I felt that was necessary."

"Uh-huh," he said, then returned to his reading.

What Smathers read was a full fifteen single-spaced pages, yet still a much-truncated version, a mere summary, of the events I have detailed in this book. The introduction to the narrative opens this book. I would have preferred to leave out any references to Thomas Kennaday in the shorter narrative, but since he was the source for much of what Phoebe told me, it was necessary to include him, though I attempted to minimize the more incredible aspects of Kennaday's profile by relying on bullet points and an objective, voiceless style. The inclusion of a copy of Kennaday's note, the one Phoebe allegedly pickpocketed, plus the address of Kennaday's alleged safe house and the license plate number on his vehicle, were all intended to augment a profile that Smathers could otherwise have viewed as pure fiction. A double chronology of events, followed by a hypothetical conclusion, were added in an attempt to direct

Smathers's thinking toward the conflicting motives behind not only the murders but also my own personal experiences relevant to, if not a consequence of, the investigation.

I provide here the conclusion to the narrative, though I do so with no expectations that you, reader, will accord it any more credibility than Smathers did.

Conclusion

The murders in the Burchette house, when viewed through a lens capturing only the cold, hard facts, can be seen as just another example of the many ways we humans damage and destroy each other. When the mysterious Thomas Kennaday is factored into this puzzle, however, along with the clues he appears to have planted for RS to find, along with the information he seems to have stipulated that Phoebe Hudack should feed to RS, coupled with the harassment and injury visited upon RS as an investigator of the above, the mess of unverifiable information in the previous pages becomes wholly indecipherable. But what if this information is reduced even further? What if it is distilled, as it were, to its seminal elements, and these elements are rearranged? It is conceivable then that these parts do cohere, if yet only loosely:

Barry Faye and the bartender in Lowellville conspired to sell Baby Doe to one or more pedophiles who might or might not have connections with a larger ring. Justin Cirillo discovered this plan, or merely desired to raise Baby Doe as his own daughter, and consequently abducted Baby Doe from the unidentified mother's residence, probably with the assistance of Eddie Hudack and Jolene Mrozek. It is quite possible that Baby Doe was injured in this abduction; the stress fracture could have been caused by one party holding on to the baby's leg while another party attempted to yank her free; if the baby had been dropped or accidentally banged against a hard surface during the struggle, a concussion could have been sustained.

Justin Cirillo, given his proclivity for aggressive retaliation, would have blamed Barry Faye for this outcome, and sought revenge by shooting Faye.

If you prefer a simpler explanation: Baby Doe was injured by mishandling by Faye or the mother, and was then abandoned in the woods to die.

The viability of that explanation, however, is diminished by the fact that the baby was abandoned within yards of where two teenagers regularly conducted their trysts. So perhaps those who abandoned the injured Baby Doe did not wish for her to die, but to be adopted by an Amish family; the Amish are notoriously secretive and would be unlikely to inform anyone outside of their own community of the circumstances surrounding Baby Doe's discovery.

Who is most likely to have abandoned Baby Doe intending her to be found and saved? Cirillo, I believe, would not have done so to a child he considered his own daughter. He would have, at the least, left her at a hospital. Then who? My money is on Eddie Hudack and/or Jolene Mrozek. Or the mysterious Mr. Kennaday himself.

The question then arises: Why implicate RS in any of this? Kennaday must, of course, have had a reason to do so. I suggest that this agenda was spelled out in his following statement when I first questioned his motives for alerting me to the case: "The truth. I feel like it needs to come out. The whole truth and nothing but."

And what is the whole truth that he wished to reveal through me? I can only make an assumption based upon the clues he led me to discover. The truth Kennaday suggested by his actions, and which is affirmed by a multitude of sources available online, is that a global pedophilia proclivity, if not an actual unified ring, does indeed exist that includes Hollywood elite as well as known politicians and other one-percenters, many of whom are affiliated with the Freemasons and, as the theory goes, a military/industrial/intelligence community/congressional/media complex whose ultimate goal, control of the world's population and resources through surveillance, mind control, fear, and other manipulative tactics, is enforced by men and women in black, and is perpetuated through the practice of ancient Egyptian rituals, including pedophilia and cannibalism. Conspiracy theories abound that also link this confederacy to extraterrestrials. Incredible? Of course. Difficult to believe? Certainly. *Impossible* to believe? If you choose to ignore the tonnages of anecdotal and circumstantial evidence, yes.

When I break down my own personal experiences during the weeks previous to the writing of this narrative, including the information derived from those experiences, they appear to fall into two categories: those that were aimed at increasing not only my knowledge of Baby Doe's identity, but also, and perhaps most importantly, my knowledge of the larger forces at work behind the scenes of Baby Doe's abandonment and rediscovery; and those aimed at restricting or curtailing such knowledge through intimidation, threat, and physical injury.

Participants in the first category would include Thomas Kennaday, Phoebe Hudack, and a woman I know only as Holly. Although Kennaday's methods seem unnecessarily cryptic to me, I don't feel as if they were ever meant to harm me. As much as I resent the subterfuge in both him and his second, Phoebe Hudack, I have to appreciate the information I derived from those methods. Holly, the woman who claimed to be Dennis Cirillo's girlfriend, also provided useful information. Therefore, she too must be added to the first category.

The second category includes, in chronological order: the so-called man in black; the unknown intruder in my home; the late-night caller; the individual who posed as my friend Lou Burbage and then, with a confederate or two I am unable to describe, attacked me behind the Serbian Orthodox church; the bogus deputy who headbutted me in the hospital; and the unknown individual or individuals who left a dead bee on my steering wheel while I had my first meeting with you.

The spirit attack I experienced in the Scottish Rite Cathedral adds an otherworldly dimension to this second category, as does the information regarding Dan Aykroyd's UFO experiences, but since I cannot say with any certainty that the spirit attack actually was a spirit attack and not simply an alarming physical anomaly, and because I have experienced no verifiable UFO or extraterrestrial encounters myself, I will offer no opinions as to whether or not any of the forces at play in this drama are of an otherworldly origin. It is worth noting, however, that much of the literature on the subject proposes that men in black are, in fact, the otherworldly enforcers of a combined alien-human conspiracy to control Earth's population and resources. Pedophilia is often included as one of the tactics used in this conspiracy; this provides a possible link to Barry Faye. If you check into Faye's history, you will discover, according to Phoebe, that Faye, under another name, was once a suspect in the disappearance of two children.

But again, I can offer no hard evidence on this matter. The relevancy of this and the alien connection theory remains too nebulous at this point to factor in the case in question.

But let's say that one chooses to include these theories in his considerations. What, then, does it all mean? As I see it, it can mean only one thing:

a war is being fought on this planet for the minds and souls of all of us.

And now, Detective, you are free to laugh out loud. But perhaps your laughing will subside, as mine did, after a few hours of open-minded evaluation of the wealth of evidence available online. If you would care for a list of sources for further research, I will be happy to provide one.

I will not venture an opinion as to whether Kennaday's alleged employer is an organization attempting to counter the nefarious agenda of the others, or if it is a part of the perfidy. If the latter is true, it suggests that Kennaday has gone rogue and is working on his own or from within a small maverick group, working through me and no doubt other civilians to make the truth known. Either that, or I have been duped by a master of duplicity. I see the odds as fifty-fifty. Both options are terrifying.

I would welcome further discussion of these possibilities with you and your colleagues, but only if that discussion includes open-minded individuals whose agenda is an unveiling of the truth. Otherwise, I would rather proceed alone—not with a continuing investigation into the Burchette case, which, I concede, requires no further investigation, but into the matter that has concerned me for most of my life: the mystery of the true nature of reality. You are free to call such an investigation a fool's journey. You won't be the first or the last to do so. Frequently, I do so myself.

Good luck to you in your continuing efforts to preserve peace, justice, and the American way—or what used to be the American way.

It has been said, Detective, that the truth is out there. I concur, in spades. It's everywhere. All you need to do is to open your eyes and ears to it.

———

All through Smathers's reading of the report, I sat motionless, steeling myself for that moment when he would burst into laughter and toss me out of the office. Five minutes I waited, ten minutes, and another twenty minutes. I watched as his forehead beaded with sweat and his frown deepened. I watched his hand twitch now and then, his moving fingertip seeming to hit an invisible protuberance or pothole on the page.

When he finished reading, he looked into my eyes only briefly. Then his gaze lifted an inch or so, and I got the feeling, as a small smile graced his mouth, that he was staring at my forehead. "You write fiction, yeah?" he asked.

"Mostly fiction. Though I've done a lot of nonfiction too."

He inhaled through his nose, then exhaled through a slit between his lips. "So this guy you're supposed to have met. This Kennaday guy. Give me that description again."

I did so. Smathers then proceeded to ask a few other questions, mostly innocuous ones whose answers seemed to me irrelevant or repetitive. You met Ms. Hudack how many times? And where did that happen? Anybody else in the room with you at the time? And you're sure you didn't record any of it? And so forth. All of that information had been spelled out in my report, but I answered with as much equanimity as I could muster. And finally he dismissed me with a monotonic, "Okay. We'll toss this into the mix and see what bubbles up. Thanks for coming in."

And that was it. No laughter. No accusations. No challenges to my veracity or sanity or intentions. I stood and walked outside, but not without feeling off-kilter somehow, as if the other shoe I had been expecting to drop, a size fifteen at least, was still dangling in the air.

40.

Looking a gift horse
in the kisser

S ome long-ago philosopher said that the path to happiness is not
to know too much. Well, I had already lost that opportunity.
And I can never get it back. You can't return to ignorance once
you lose it, nor to the relative bliss that accompanies ignorance.
Once you learn with a degree of certainty that the universe is a
complex, convoluted, multidimensional puzzle impossible to piece
together, and that it is peopled by legions of self-serving individuals
with no regard for anyone but themselves, you're pretty much
fucked for life when it comes to a happy ignorance.

So what was I to do? Keep the truth to myself? Swallow the blue
pill? It was already way too late for that. But you can't live with
knowledge such as I had acquired in the previous weeks without
having it eating away at you all the time, you just can't. Not unless
you want to end up like one of those bastiches yourself, the kind
whose ambition becomes a sickness, a rampaging cancer. All I can
do until the Grim Reaper sweeps me up into his wagon is to concentrate on what I love—my sons, my future grandchildren, the
sweetly forgiving and revivifying embrace of nature. The healing
love of a good woman. Good food, good music, good work, good
books and movies. I can still have all that, yes? The products of my
own and other good citizens' labors.

A good night's sleep, alas, will probably always remain out of the question for me.

For several days after my meeting with Detective Smathers, I sat at my desk each morning, trying to finish the half-done novel or start another one. My hard drive holds at least a hundred ideas for new books, and I read them all, even started to write out a few of them. But they went nowhere. And the more often they went nowhere, the deeper I sank into a recognition that I was washed up as a writer of fictions. I was empty. Within a few months I would have to sell my house at a loss and move on. But to what? And to where? I wasn't cut out to live in an apartment or to take in a couple of roommates. My idiosyncrasies would eventually drive everybody to murderous thoughts. And I would never allow myself to become a burden to my sons or anybody else.

The truth, as I came to see it, was that without writing, I didn't fit in anywhere. Without writing, I couldn't survive, nor, honestly, did I want to.

But then, out of the blue, a peculiar occurrence interrupted my misery. The UPS truck pulled into my driveway. But instead of bringing me books from my publisher or a new tire for one of the motorcycles, the driver handed me a bulky cardboard box maybe five feet long, less than two feet wide, and about eight inches thick.

I carried it inside and examined the labels. They told me nothing of the box's origin. That in itself made the delivery even more suspect.

For the next hour, as I sat at my desk, trying again to concentrate on my notes, the box lay unopened atop my coffee table. Every time I leaned back in my chair and glanced at the box—just to make sure, I suppose, that it wasn't oozing a deadly gas, or that the tarry black form of a djinn wasn't leaking through the taped-over seams—I told myself, *Don't open it.* There is not a lot of educational value in the second kick of the mule. If you don't learn anything from the first kick, you won't learn much from the second. And I had already suffered a half-dozen kicks. I told myself that I should do with that box what I should have done when Thomas Kennaday slid into my booth at Joy Buffet: get as far away from it as possible. Yet I didn't.

Yeah, I decided to open it. At my age, why not? I have never been able to resist a mystery, especially one staring me in the face. So, with one hand clamped over my nose and mouth, and my body poised to make a twenty-foot leap if a spitting cobra or diminutive man in black leapt out at me, the other hand, quivering and uncertain, slipped the point of a steak knife down the center of the box and unzipped the shipping tape.

Unfortunately, the blade also cut a two-inch scar into the black guitar case just under the cardboard. And inside that guitar case was a beautiful black dobro, what some people call a resonator guitar. The dobro is a type of acoustic guitar that uses aluminum cones instead of a sounding board to amplify the sound, which, on a dobro, is a bit warmer and richer than the sound from a standard acoustic guitar.

And the dobro I received that day was not just any dobro, but the very one that had popped up a couple of weeks earlier on Facebook Marketplace. Oh, I had lingered over the photo of that dobro for quite some time, and even came back to it several mornings in a row. I had wanted that dobro with all of my heart, just as I have long wanted a violin and cello and a saxophone, even though I don't know how to play any of those instruments either. Then one day the word SOLD appeared on the dobro's listing. Ever since, I had done my best not to kick myself too frequently for failing to act when I had a chance.

And now here it was in my living room, that same beautiful dobro, the face black and the metal registers gleaming. It had come to me all shiny and strung and even in tune, with a fancy leather strap and marble slide bar included. And a handwritten note: *Nice work. Enjoy.*

Only one word took form inside my head: *Huh?*

Have you ever stood looking at something that seems so out of place that you go woozy with disorientation? That's what happened to me. I had never mentioned lusting after that dobro to *anybody*, not even to Cara. She already thought I was too profligate with my money. So how could anybody know that I had pulled up that Facebook Marketplace page a dozen times? Well, anybody from Czar Zuckerberg on down in his organization could have tracked my drooling desire, but why would one of them gift me with the object of that desire? No, it had to have been Kennaday, or one of his sneaky spying colleagues.

For a couple of days I didn't touch the instrument except to examine it for a bug, using a powerful little flashlight and dental mirror. Was it some kind of Trojan horse? Was it so tuned that my first chord would release a swarm of deadly bees?

Then I decided, what the hell, why not enjoy it? I didn't intend to play it naked, didn't plan to send coded musical messages to anyone, had no intention of using the instrument for anything more nefarious than learning to play "Runaway Train." My seething distrust of the government and its clandestine tentacles would never enter into my use of the dobro.

So why even pretend to hide from spying eyes and ears? There were already satellites high above that could peer into my bedroom, servers that record every email sent and received, cell phone towers that grab every text and voice call out of the air; so why not enjoy my beautiful dobro no matter the sender? The dead bees had already established that I was being surveilled and monitored by somebody. Though I have always kept every one of my shades closed, and long ago taped Post-it Notes over my laptops' cameras, and have avoided downloading any apps into my phone, there was no escaping the invasion of privacy. Edward Snowden told the truth, and now he is paying the price for it.

And maybe someday I would too. But in the meantime, why not play the dobro? As long as it doesn't blow up in my hands, I might as well take some pleasure from it.

So far, no boom. So far, the dobro makes only beautiful sounds, even in my clumsy hands.

I haven't yet touched the mushrooms, however. They remain in the sandwich bag, half-buried under miscellaneous papers on my desk. I sometimes lift the papers away just to look at them. They intrigue and frighten me. Yeah, they make me woozy too. But sooner or later, one of those emotions is going to win out. At this point, though, I still don't know which.

41.

Detective Smathers redux

My body has a habit of getting sick after the conclusion of anything that has caused me stress. During a book tour, for example, I'm just fine, and will usually present myself and my work well, but at the end of the tour, after the first night home in my own bed, I will wake up feeling like three-day-old roadkill. It's a nameless malaise that manifests itself in fatigue, sore joints, an upset stomach, head and chest congestion. Very flu-like but without the vomiting. The longer the event lasts, the more severe my symptoms. A two-hour book signing or reading might have me waking up with a mild hangover, even though I don't drink. A five-city book tour, with a total of six flights over four or five days, will render me useless for most of a week. My time in the company of Kennaday, Phoebe, a man in black, the Scottish Rite Cathedral, Smathers, and my several unknown assailants, coupled with my nightmares and confusion before and after, left me feeling and looking as if I'd gone ten rounds with Mike Tyson and his pet gorilla and never got in a punch. There were purplish bruises on my chest and stomach and under my right eye. I hadn't been able to swivel my neck more than thirty degrees since the beating behind the church. My cracked ribs made me wince with every deep breath. I had puffy, bloodshot eyes, a head full of mucus, a stiff gait, and labored breathing. Even my hair hurt. But not as much as my teeth.

That was my condition for a full six days. It was no better on the morning I received a call from some female-voiced individual at the New Castle Police Department. Detective Smathers requested my appearance in his office. Four p.m. would be good.

I agreed, though another visit with Smathers was the last thing I wanted to do. But I believe in facing what is unavoidable. As a timid young man I had walked away from so many situations, had literally *sneaked* away, disappearing like a ghost from job offers, parties, romantic entanglements, and anything else that demanded abilities I knew I did not possess. But the self-loathing that overtook me every time I avoided something uncomfortable eventually prompted me to change my ways and face the things I feared. Over the years I learned to do all of the things normal people do on a daily basis, but I still can't pull it off without an overbearing critic ceaselessly chattering in my head.

So, at 3:59 that afternoon, my sorry self filled the open doorway of Detective Smathers's cubicle. My head was congested, nose running, bloodshot eyes squinting, lungs wheezing like a broken baby doll. The good detective looked up at me and asked, "What's the matter with you? You been crying about something?"

"Sinus infection," I said.

"You on antibiotics?"

"The body will heal itself if you let it."

"What are you, some kind of religious nut?"

"Sort of. A nut without a religion."

"Whatever," he said. "Just don't breathe on me."

I dragged the plastic chair toward the back corner and sat. "How's this?"

"I suppose it will have to do."

In comparison to me, the messy and slightly overweight detective looked the picture of health. There was even something different about his eyes this time; they seemed almost merry, but in a sad kind of way, like those of a father who has given away his beloved daughter in marriage to a man he believes to be a lout—glad to see his daughter looking so happy, but with an ominous hunch of trouble ahead. He tapped the small stack of papers lying atop his desk blotter. My report. "Interesting reading," he said.

So he had read it again, probably more than once. "A positive review on Amazon would be much appreciated."

"Huh," he said, his version of a laugh. "I suppose you plan on publishing this in some form or another."

"I am a writer, after all."

He leaned back in his chair. "I hope you realize there's stuff in here certain people out there won't appreciate seeing in print."

"People you know?"

He shook his head. "Everybody I know is a sweetheart. I'm just saying. You might be rocking some boats with this."

"Isn't that what writers are supposed to do? Rock the boats that deserve to be sunk?"

"And maybe sink yourself with it."

"Are you saying you believe what I wrote?"

"Did you hear me say that?"

"I heard you imply it."

"No you didn't," he said.

"Then what did you think of it?"

He sat mulling it over for twenty seconds or so before speaking. "That girl you talked to in here," he said, and tapped the papers again. "You have any idea where she might be?"

"Excuse me?"

"We went to see her the day after you gave me this. The house is empty. Furniture's still there but not much else."

"Are you talking about Phoebe Hudack?"

"That's what you called her anyway."

"Are you telling me that Phoebe and LaShonda are both gone?"

"Would you please stop asking me what I'm saying when you know very well what I'm saying?"

"I had no idea. She gave absolutely no indication that she was planning to go anywhere. LaShonda was supposed to go live with her father when the holiday break started."

"What father?"

I cocked my head.

He said, "We pulled her birth certificate. You want to know what her father's name is?"

"I was told it's Christy."

"Blank."

"His name is somebody Blank? As in Mel Blanc, the animation guy? Bugs Bunny and Elmer Fudd?"

"As in the space on her birth certificate where the father's name is supposed to go was left blank."

"Is that legal?"

"It can be left blank, marked Unknown, even filled in with a made-up name. The girl's was blank."

"I was told that he lives in Hawaii. Has a new family out there but wanted LaShonda to come live with them."

"You believe everything that girl told you?"

"I guess I believed that she believed it."

"Yeah, guessing can get you into a lot of trouble sometimes."

My head, as dense as it was with mucus, swirled with confusion. "Why wasn't any of this reported? I mean, don't reporters look into this kind of information?"

The detective shrugged. "Sloppy journalism. Gets worse every day. They report what they hear, same as you did."

Guilty as charged. My already feverish face flushed a few degrees hotter.

Smathers said, "You were right about the baby, though."

"Yeah? In what way?"

"She's Cirillo's. Not that it will do her any good."

"What about the mother?"

"Another ghost."

"*She's gone?*"

"If by gone you mean dead, yeah, she's gone."

"Baby Doe's mother is *dead*? When? How?"

"Dead by the absence of life. That's how death usually happens."

That was probably his idea of a joke, but I was too dumbstruck to laugh.

"The fire department in Coraopolis pulled a floater out of the river a while back. Down by the Dashields Dam. She'd been in the water for several days. One of our guys saw it on the blotter, name, address, place of employment in Lowellville. He had a hunch and ran with it. DNA a dead-on match with the baby."

I still couldn't find any words. Nothing existed inside my skull at that moment but for mucus and one big fat swirling question mark.

"The cause of death was strangulation. By whose hands is anybody's guess."

"And Cirillo?" I managed.

"What about him?"

"He has nothing to say about it?"

"According to his lawyer, he doesn't plan to say anything about anything now or ever. He admits his guilt. Said he always knew it was his baby. Other than that… The lawyer insinuates he's afraid of somebody."

"The lawyer is afraid?"

"Cirillo is, dumb shit."

Okay, I could buy that. Cirillo knows things he is afraid to talk about. But what things? What things might get him killed in prison? Things like Barry Faye's history? Faye's connections? His association with larger forces of some kind?

Maybe that was going too far. Though maybe it wasn't. I doubted I would ever know the truth of it. Like Baby Doe, for instance; did she play *any* role in the larger metaphysical mystery? Or was she simply a catalyst that allowed Kennaday to point me in the direction of the global pedophilia outrage? Other than Barry Faye's rather nebulous connection with pedophilia, there was no concrete proof whatsoever that Baby Doe had been tagged to be a victim of that conspiracy.

When it came to Baby Doe, there was only one fact that I knew—strike that; *felt*—with any degree of certainty. "You know," I told Smathers, "I really don't think it was Cirillo who hurt the baby."

"And why would you think that?"

"From what I heard, he wanted a family. That's why he liked going to the Burchette house. Because it made him feel like he was part of a family."

Smathers studied a fingernail. "And who told you that?"

He already knew who. Holly. The woman who wasn't who she claimed to be. It was in the narrative I had given him.

And then I got his point. I nodded. Nobody was to be trusted. Nor was my sloppy investigation.

"So," I asked, "where does that leave you?"

"In pretty good shape, actually. Cirillo and Faye both claimed to be the baby's father, they argued about it, got physical, and Cirillo took him out with a couple of shotgun blasts. Heat of passion. Case closed."

"Any idea what happened to Eddie Hudack and Jolene Mrozek?"

He shrugged. "They'll turn up sooner or later."

Unless they'd disappeared down the same hole Phoebe and LaShonda had. I said, "I can't help wondering, though."

"Isn't that what got you into this clusterfuck in the first place? Wondering about things?"

"Don't *you* wonder?" I asked. "Did somebody grab Phoebe and LaShonda or did they take off on their own? If so, where? And why? Don't you want to know who hurt the baby, and how that happened? Did Eddie and Jolene take her from the mother? Is that how the baby got hurt and how the mother got killed? Or did Kennaday have a hand in this? Did you find out anything about him, anything at all about where he came from or who he is or—"

"Jesus on a crutch, Silvis," he interrupted. "Who built the pyramids? What was Göbekli Tepe for? You have to know every damn thing there is to know?"

The fact that he had even heard about Göbekli Tepe told me a great deal about Smathers—a great deal more than I ever would have expected.

"Yes, I would like to know everything," I answered. "But, as the years go by, I'm growing more and more reconciled to the fact that I never will."

"Nobody ever will," he said. And then, in a surprisingly conciliatory tone, "Whether we like it or not."

Again I nodded. Put my hands on the armchair's. "That's it, then?"

He nodded toward my report. "Take that with you."

"You don't want to keep a copy?"

"A copy of what?" he said.

Aha, so that was it. As far as anybody knew, he had never seen my report. Had never read a word of it. Had never even heard of it. Maybe he had never even heard of me. I stood and picked it up.

And once again our gazes met. My eyes were tired and bloodshot, his were merry but sad, eyes that had seen too much but weren't ready just yet to close. "You got a fireplace back home?" he asked.

"I do," I said. "Why do you ask?"

"Supposed to be a cold night."

"Is it?"

He shrugged. "Maybe not tonight, but soon enough. Howling winds, snow a foot deep, the windows so frosted up you can't see a thing outside. On a night like that you'd better have a nice big bundle of dry wood ready to go. Just in case your power goes out. And something to help you get the fire started," he said with a little jerk of his eyes toward the papers I held. "Keep the house toasty all through a miserable night like that."

And that was the end of our conversation. I nodded. We understood each other. I turned and walked away and went out the door.

The sun was sinking low, the air chilling quickly. I had barely stepped outside, had inhaled my first breath of unrecycled air, when a realization hit like a punch to the forehead: *Four people murdered.* That's what Kennaday had said to me at Joy Buffet. I had thought then that he had misspoken, but he hadn't. Faye, Burchette, Michelle Jordan murdered in the Burchette kitchen. And now Baby Doe's mother strangled and dumped into the river. Kennaday had known that from the beginning! The implications were staggering in their multiplicity.

I leaned against a parking meter, momentarily frozen in place as an icy snake slithered up my spine. The shadows of night would soon engulf the town and everyone in it. Nobody knew what morning would bring.

Nobody ever does.

42.

A willing suspension
of disbelief

For a few days after that meeting with Smathers, even though my health improved, I was incapable of anything other than sitting and staring, walking and staring, lying horizontal and staring. One part of me endlessly reiterated that there must be a rational explanation for what I had endured, some kind of technology, something that is in fact *ordinary* even if most of us don't know about it yet. The other part of me was just as adamant: Why are you fighting this, Silvis? It happened, just as you remember it, so believe it, man. As incredible as it might seem, believe it. You're only deluding yourself if you don't.

And why not? Is believing in extraterrestrials and djinn all that different from believing in the devil and the demons and angels and the God my Methodist Sunday school teacher exhorted me to accept? Is it all that different from believing that Jesus raised the dead and fed the five thousand from a couple of self-replicating fish? That he died and came back for a few last words with the gang, then levitated up into the ether like a hot-air balloon?

Every major religion *depends* on a world beyond this one. Every major player in every one of those religions has had at least one nonordinary experience. Christians, Jews, Muslims, Buddhists, Hindus, Mormons, and indigenous peoples throughout the world all believe in otherworldly beings and their magical activities.

Listen, if you subscribe to any religion at all, any belief in a higher power, you believe in ETs. You believe in interdimensional travelers and in other worlds and other levels of being. If you believe that your thoughts can affect your health, you believe in a magic that can be replicated but that science cannot explain. If you believe in the conscious mind's ability to create art and fiction and dreams and ideas, you believe in something that continues to slam material scientists up against a brick wall of inexplicability.

Consider your own beliefs. Consider the evidence upon which you base those beliefs. Do you *have* any evidence? Do you have any real, concrete, measurable evidence for *not* believing in the validity of what you have never personally experienced? Or have you chosen not to believe in something precisely because you have never personally experienced it? But is your inexperience a valid reason for denying what tens of thousands of others *have* experienced?

Isn't it more logical, more fair, more reasonable to believe that if any one scientifically implausible thing is worthy of belief, then all seemingly implausible things are worthy of consideration *until* an accumulation of verifiable evidence proves them otherwise? Isn't it fair to say that one needs as good a reason for disbelief as for belief?

This is what I believe, and not by faith or hope alone, but because I have had dozens of very strange experiences throughout my life, a couple of them wholly inexplicable except as either miracles or brief psychotic breaks. In terms of continuity and duration, though, the month that began with meeting Thomas Kennaday at Joy Chinese Buffet, then carried me through a hundred hours of research and conversations with Phoebe Hudack and others, only to culminate with my last visit to Detective Smathers's office, was the strangest experience of all. But the party wasn't over yet, boys and girls.

43.

The days, the nights, the highly unlikely

Halloween came and went, whimpering away on a rainy night that kept most of the kiddies at home, lobotomized in front of their screens. I had expected a finale of some kind, some coup d'état from the dark forces that had been beleaguering me, and Halloween seemed like the night it should have happened. But it didn't. Nothing happened. And over the next couple of days, I started to believe that maybe I could put October behind me without further injury.

On a day in early November, a clear, bright day but chilly nonetheless, I was already suffering from cabin fever. I still hadn't come up with a viable idea for a new novel, and you can play only so many games of FreeCell before you pass out and ram your head through the monitor, so around one in the afternoon, I kicked my butt out of the chair. The sky was now unblemished by a single cloud, a flawless dome of blue. For the first time in a long time, not a single chemtrail marred the heavens. I hated to waste what was left of such a day. Three good hours of sunlight remained. And there was only one way I wanted to spend them: astraddle Candy.

On the other hand, the windchill on Candy would hit me at about thirty-five degrees. And the body loses heat fast at that temperature. I have returned home after biking on chilly autumn nights so stiff with cold that my legs and fingers were numb, my nose and ears feeling in danger of breaking off. So the notion of taking a bike ride on a forty-nine-degree day was patently absurd.

But sometimes, perversely, I enjoy doing what others, and even I, consider absurd. Blame it on faulty wiring in the brain, deprivation of oxygen during childbirth, too much caffeine, whatever. I got myself all bundled up and suitably masked and prepared to discover how long it would take for the human body to turn into a Popsicle.

Maybe it was the lingering effects of a concussion and humiliating beatdown that made me eager to push my limits, I don't know. I only knew that I wanted to feel alive again, if only through the discomfort and pain of freezing my ass off. And that I was in desperate need of an experience that would jump-start my imagination.

Most of the routes out of my little town lead to other little towns, and I didn't want that this time. I craved the comfort of a road seldom taken, of negligible traffic, of solitude and silence, trees and hills, and long panoramic views of sleeping fields and river valley. Only one route nearby could provide that, a narrow country lane with lots of ups and downs, lots of swings to the right and rolls to the left, but also with lots of frost heaves and potholes and potentially disastrous ruts carved into the pavement by Amish buggies. I would have to pay attention and keep the speed down on that road, no ninety-mile-per-hour sprints to get the adrenaline up. But that was okay. Candy never failed to shoot me up with oxytocin and dopamine every time I slipped my legs around her.

And for a while the ride was just as salubrious as I had hoped it would be. Perforations in the foam face mask allowed me to inhale deep drafts of fresh air, often with the pleasant aromatic hint of woodsmoke from Amish chimneys. For some reason, having a warm face seemed to keep the rest of me warmer too. And almost immediately I felt my mood buoying, felt good health coursing back into my lungs and limbs. Every now and then, when I could do so safely, I lifted my eyes to the vast blueness and thanked it for this moment, this great good fortune of the life I was enjoying.

During one of those skyward glances, as I cruised at a leisurely speed past Amish farms surrounded by acre after acre of resting fields, everything changed. Far off in the distance, a small dark cloud hung well above the horizon, looking even darker for being such an anomaly. A vague gray curtain of squall lines appeared to be falling from it. It was not the first time I had experienced rain falling in only one small area, but it was the first time in such an otherwise perfect sky. And the speed with which the cloud was moving toward me was alarming. To be caught in a downpour at this temperature could be deadly.

I pulled onto the shoulder to calculate the cloud's probable path. Yep, it was coming straight toward me. I looked to the left, saw nothing but corn stubble, then to the right. Up ahead forty yards or so, a dirt lane ran alongside a scraggly stand of third- or fourth-growth hardwoods, ending at a barn and small farmhouse a quarter mile away. It wouldn't be the first time I'd sought sanctuary from bad weather in a farmer's barn or other outbuilding. I headed for the lane and the barn beyond.

Dirt and loose gravel can take a bike down as quickly as ice can, so I crawled down that lane at about ten miles per hour, shooting quick glances over my left shoulder. Because I didn't want to intrude on the family's privacy unless I was in real danger of being flash frozen, I traveled only far enough to be, I hoped, out of the small cloud's path. I stopped, put the bike in neutral, and allowed it to tilt onto its kickstand. Then sat there poised to make a beeline for the barn if Mother Nature deemed it necessary.

The cloud was not only coming straight at me again but was now descending at a sharp angle. And the curtain of rain dangling from it was not, I now saw, rain at all, but thick, writhing tendrils of gray-green fog—a fog that did not dissipate.

Because an accident was a certainty if I drove too fast down the rest of the lane, I leapt off the bike and started running hard for the barn. Within seconds I was knocked to the ground and, as incredible as it sounds, seized by the smoky tendrils first and then by the entire cloud. It felt like I had been body-slammed by a mammoth, sulfur-stinking grizzly with twenty arms. My face was shoved into the cold ground, where there was no air to breathe. And soon the inevitable happened; I stopped struggling against the weight atop me and passed out.

Consciousness returned in gradual increments, and eventually I could form a thought again. The cloud had lifted. My body, every inch of my body, throbbed with pain. I raised my head off the ground, turned it so that my left cheek scraped the earth. All I could see from that perspective was a gray sliver of ground and, in the distance, gray tree trunks.

Wincing with pain and disbelief, I managed to get to my feet. The world as I had known it was gone. The barn and small farmhouse and woods and field of corn stubble were all still there, Candy still there where I had left her, but every inch of visible landscape had been devastated. Even Candy. In horror, and needing to confirm what I was seeing, I pulled off my face mask. Nothing got better, only worse.

Not a single tree or building or other object in my field of vision had been spared the devastation. But it did not look burned; it did not look bombed or demolished or subjected to any comparable type of destruction. It looked as if it had been sprayed with a strong acid of some kind. There was no color to any of it, nothing but shades of gray, every object stunted or somehow compressed. *Desiccated* was the word I finally seized upon. Everywhere I looked, it was the same—every big and little thing made gray, dried up, sucked clean of every drop of color and moisture and life.

I had to assume that I was hallucinating or dreaming. But when had I taken anything that might have been spiked with a delayed-action psychotropic? My morning coffee? The kefir I drank with my vitamins? Or had the cloud itself been psychotropic?

I yanked the glove off my right hand and reached into my pocket for the cell phone, planning to take some photos of my hallucination; if the photos were still on my phone when the drug wore off, well then…I was in serious trouble. But when I raised the phone to eye level, my hand too came into view. And it, too, was desiccated and gray. A small, mummified hand made of wrinkled gray parchment stretched over brittle gray twigs with long, cracked fingernails.

The world was dead, and I was dead in it.

And again the inevitable happened; I crumpled to my knees, swooned, and fell onto my side, unconscious again.

You're way ahead of me by now, I'm sure. None of that could have actually happened, you're thinking. Strange clouds don't just appear out of nowhere, and if they do, they don't have the intelligence to target somebody, nor the mass to knock him for a loop, nor the ability to send him into some kind of whacked-out nightmare. And you're right.

Maybe.

44.

The definition of WTF

I was awakened a second time, again facedown in the farmer's field, by a brown-and-white collie licking my face. Joyously, I could see and smell and feel the dog, and it looked just fine, wholly doglike and properly colorized. Its tail throbbed back and forth as its raspy tongue kept slapping my cheek. I sat with the dog for quite a while, petting and thanking her, scratching her belly and wondering, as you might guess, *What the fuck happened to me?* I ran through the possibilities: the cloud had been an alien spaceship in disguise, and those crazy aliens had decided to have a bit of fun with me; the cloud itself was sentient, and malicious to boot; the cloud was a remote-controlled hallucinogenic-vapor dispenser that took aim at me as a warning to stop poking around in secret things, or so as to provide me a glimpse into the future; or it all happened just to mind fuck me.

But if mine had been a vision of the future, it was of a very near future, or else the buildings and woods would have been affected by the passage of years. But they weren't. The landscape I was shown was the very one I had been riding through, but utterly desiccated, including myself.

The simplest explanation seemed to be that I had suffered a psychotic break with reality—that the last thing that had *really* happened to me was that I had looked into the distance at a small rain cloud, and then *bam!* my brain misfired and I went into la-la land. I was, after all, suffering from too little sleep and too much stress, plus a noggin that still ached from time to time. *Come to think of it*, I told myself, *you haven't been very good to your head.* Four years of high school football, a couple of sailor dives into a too-shallow swimming pool, a couple of headfirst skiing crashes, a fifteen-foot fall off a ladder, one adolescent head-on collision with a tree while running down a steep hillside, one boyhood tumble through the hay chute and into an empty stall, one recent headbutt, one recent fist to the side of the head, a long history of exploding head syndrome. Considering all of that, wasn't it about time I started having visions?

Depending on whom you ask, I had already suffered two similar breaks with reality. The first one happened when I was nineteen; the second when I was thirty-two. Every moment and detail of those two inexplicable incidents remain as vivid to me now as the third one. So yeah, that was it. I was brain damaged.

But no. Personally, I long ago rejected the possibility that I had ever experienced a break with reality. My opinion is that what I experienced when I was younger, and what I experienced most recently, were not breaks with reality at all, but brief glimpses of a much larger reality.

Zen Buddhism recognizes such moments and calls them *kenshō*. A corollary in Western culture would be the epiphany, a sudden understanding or realization, originally thought of as a gift from the divine. My favorite description of the epiphany comes from William S. Burroughs's psychedelic *Naked Lunch*, in which the author describes it as "a frozen moment when everyone sees what is on the end of every fork."

Such insights are all considered a necessary step to enlighten-ment. But what I experienced at the hands of an apparently sentient cloud, or a chemtrail gone mad—where was the enlightenment in that? Had it been another warning, like the man in black who tried to intimidate me, and the intruder who walked through my house leaving nothing behind but an odd sense of his presence and a dead bee, and the bogus Lou Burbage who lured me behind a church to be beaten up?

Then who was responsible for all of that? A clandestine government agency hoping to keep the future intact and more or less beneficent? A group aligned with ETs and intent on world domination? A psychotic god? A sadistic fourteen-year-old pimple-faced boy getting his jollies by creating our *SimCity* world of misery and travail?

It could be any of the above. My money, based on what I had learned through Thomas Kennaday via Phoebe Hudack, and because I wanted to retain enough hope to avoid hooking up the hose to my car's exhaust pipe, was on the first option. Problem was, if the good side of humanity is willing to resort to the same barbarous, murderous actions as the bad side, is there really a good side at all?

45.

The proof is in the puddle

Inveterate researcher that I am, I wobbled home as fast as I could after that incident and scoured the internet for other stories about strange clouds, fogs, and mists. I was surprised—not to mention relieved—to discover that I was not the first to be knocked catawampus by a cloud. Although rare per capita, the victims are numerous enough to be accorded at least a moderate credibility. Several encounters with green, red, yellow, gray, and other mists, clouds, and fogs have been chronicled online. Many of those encounters resulted in sightings of ETs, Bigfoot, dogmen, men in black, ghosts, djinn, and more, while others produced episodes of missing time for those who experienced them. Many of the incidents came with substantial verification in the form of numerous witnesses.

I kept tunneling through the anecdotal material for a facsimile of *my* experience, and I did find many more encounters with an unusual cloud or mist or fog, a high percentage of them resulting in disappearances that had been witnessed by others. Nor were clouds the only meteorological phenomena being experienced. Cities in Missouri, Greece, Minnesota, and England have been blanketed with frogs that fell from the sky—frogs sometimes not even native to the area. Fish have rained down in Singapore, England, Australia, and

Alabama. Sometimes the fish were alive and flopping, sometimes dried—i.e., *desiccated*. Blood, flesh, fat, and/or muscle tissue have fallen in Tennessee, California, Italy, and elsewhere. Periwinkles and hermit crabs in England, baby jellyfish in Tasmania, red fungal spores in India, and alligators in South Carolina. Some of these have happened during or after a storm, sometimes under clear skies. History is, in fact, filled with strange, inexplicable aerial phenomena, from Biblical times to the present.

One mysterious encounter in particular set my spine to tingling. In 1963, three Japanese men were on their way to the golf course. For much of the drive they followed a black car. When the golfers' vehicle pulled up alongside the black car, they could see only an old man seated in the rear, reading a newspaper; the other windows were all darkly tinted. Within seconds, the witnesses said, a white fog completely enveloped the black car, then, seconds later, dissipated. The black car and its occupants were gone.

A black car with tinted windows that disappeared completely? This sounded eerily similar to Dan Aykroyd's encounter with two men in black, and to encounters experienced by hundreds of others, from UFO investigators and experiencers to those who are neither, such as actress Catherine Oxenberg, who as a child allegedly suffered a kind of telepathic strangulation from a man in black. Later in life, she learned that the father of her child had also been subjected to similar threatening visits.

A commonality shared by Aykroyd and Oxenberg is that both had become whistle-blowers of a sort, Aykroyd on the subject of UFOs, Oxenberg on the subject of pedophilia in Hollywood. As it turns out, researchers agree that becoming too interested in the dark side of reality leads, almost inevitably, to the dark side becoming interested in you. In other words, if you pull at the threads of evil, it will start trying to pick you apart.

Knowing too much does indeed appear to be a high-risk profession. From JFK forward and backward through time, hundreds if not thousands of political figures and investigators and whistle-blowers have been disappearing or turning up dead under suspicious circumstances. Many of them knew they had been targeted and warned friends or family that the threat was imminent. A few of the lucky ones, like Snowden and Assange, managed to find refuge. As for the ones like Ray Gricar who disappeared without a trace—who knows? Maybe he's living in Sweden now with a leggy blond and their three children. Maybe he's sharing a plot with Jimmy Hoffa in a toxic landfill beside the Hackensack River. Maybe ETs and abductions and disappearances and pedophilia and men in black and Baby Doe and the Burchette murders *are* all connected in some twisted, perverted way. Maybe that's what Thomas Kennaday wants me to know. Maybe that's what he wants *you* to know.

Suddenly, everything seems possible. Every damned and dire thing.

46.

Final thoughts

Because Cara is mentioned several times in these pages, I felt a responsibility to allow her to pass judgment on my depiction of her, and on my recollections of experiences we shared. By necessity, she read the entire manuscript and was appropriately aghast. She had a unique take, however, on the last experience chronicled here—my encounter with the psychotropic cloud. Here is the conversation that ensued after she read the passage:

Cara: I've seen that place.

S: How? Where?

Cara: During one of my shamanic journeys.

S: I don't remember you ever telling me about that.

Cara: It was before we met. I didn't want you to think of me as a crazy lady.

S: That ship has sailed. So where is this place? The upper, middle, or lower world?

Cara: None of those. Those are the only places I go to *now*. Now that I have better control.

S: I thought those are the *only* places a person can go.

Cara: Not hardly.

S: So you're saying that I went on an astral journey?

Cara: Sort of, yeah. An involuntary one. You slipped out of one reality and into another one.

S: So it was like a time slip, but...

Cara: A reality slip.

S: Okay. Then I guess the question is *why*. Because it was *not* an accident.

Cara: I can only speculate.

S: Go for it.

Cara: Somebody wanted you to see it. The future, maybe. Or a possible future.

S: But who? And why me? Am I supposed to do something about it? Stop something from happening?

Cara: You told me that Phoebe was supposed to stop Cirillo from shooting LaShonda, right? So that Shonnie could do something important in the future.

S: And?

Cara: And Phoebe did. So maybe they, whoever they are, were showing you what would have happened if she hadn't.

S: But she *did*. Which means that whatever might have happened, never happened.

Cara: Not in this reality. But there is a separate reality for every possibility.

S: I'm getting another headache.

Cara: I'm sorry, babe. But you can't explain other dimensions with a third-dimension vocabulary. No matter how much you might want to.

S presses the palms of his hands against his forehead, hoping to crack his skull and let some of the pressure out. But no luck there.

S: So, when you went there, you saw the same Amish farm and the dog and all that stuff too?

Cara: No, I was in Florida. Driving south through the Everglades. I'd been driving all night, and now the light was coming up, and I sort of nodded off, I guess. But then I jerked awake, and I was in not the same place as you went to but a similar place. Everything that was so lush and bright a few seconds earlier was now all gray and dried out and...I don't know. Just like the way you described your place.

S: And then what happened?

Cara: Nothing, really. I mean somehow the car had gotten parked along the side of the road. So I got out and looked all around and just sort of wondered, you know, what the fuck?

S: My thoughts exactly.

Cara: Then a mosquito or something bit me on the neck, I slapped at it, and *snap!* Everything was back to being just like it was supposed to be.

S: A reality slip.

Cara: So it seems. I got into the car and drove the rest of the way home.

S: And what was it all about? Yours and mine both? What are they supposed to mean?

Cara: What I took *mine* to mean was that I didn't really belong in Florida. It wasn't a good place for me anymore. So two months later I quit my job and moved north. And here we are.

She had said all this with a placid smile, as if she found none of it out of the ordinary. Her implication, though, was clear: I had to find my own meaning for my own experience. She couldn't give me that meaning; only I can give it to myself.

I am still waiting for my contrary self to do that.

Based upon my own experiences over the years, and Cara's, and those of people we have spoken to, I have come to suspect that all of us are surrounded, at all times, by entities we cannot see. Because they move about on slightly different planes, each reality intersecting or overlapping our own, we get glimpses of them only briefly. Some of these entities are watchful and protective of us, some are playful, others mischievous in a less compassionate way. Some have no interest at all in human beings. Others are just passing through, others are curious. And some have evil in their hearts. They despise us; we are of the Light, and they are not. Some, being creatures of energy, feed off our despair, our anger and fears and hatreds. They prey on the weak, though they will also torment those who radiate with the Light. Altogether these invisible entities share our world with us, permanently or only from time to time. Were they all at once to become solid three-dimensional beings, we would find ourselves in a world overcrowded beyond imagination.

Anyway, that's what I believe, and it is a belief that cannot be definitively confirmed or refuted. The true nature of reality remains a mystery. The only person I know who might be able to unravel a thread or two of that mystery is Thomas Kennaday. But after what a single brief encounter with him brought my way, I really don't want to ever see him again. Unfortunately, I have a very uneasy feeling that he might not be finished with me yet.

These days I carry Aunt Sara's miracle medal in a pocket wherever I go, just as I wear the archangel medallion around my neck. I installed security lights and cameras all around my house, with shrieking alarms at every possible entrance. I obtained a concealed carry permit and the necessary armaments, and I am fully prepared to defend myself and my home. I will be most vulnerable when wandering through the woods I love, but I refuse to abandon that love out of fear.

I court the light, though I do not shun the darkness. Fear can bring me down, but I'm just stubborn enough, child of an ex-Marine and a tough-as-nails blue-collar antiauthoritarian mother, to refuse the easy seduction of that emotion. I want the truth, and I won't stop searching until I dig up a little more of it.

If only it were a tiny bit easier. Beholding the truth of reality is like watching a drive-in movie through a passing fog. Fleeting glimpses of truth appear, usually one at a time and in different parts of the screen, colors muted by the limitations of human eyes and minds, sounds dulled by human ears, a fragment here, a suggestion there, none of it making much sense, chimera after phantasm after nightmare, but every snatch of truth whetting our appetite so that we lean forward and squint hard and silently beg for more.

And that, in these final years, is my quest: to navigate my way from one kernel of truth to the next, again and again, by whatever means necessary.

Every day I pick up that little bag of wrinkled mushrooms on my desk and stare through the plastic. Their shriveled brown skin reminds me of the way my hand looked during my hallucination. I've grown convinced that just as they were a gift from Kennaday, so was the dobro. But the mushrooms were not intended as a diversion, something to soothe me when my savage breast needs soothing. No, they are surely intended to deepen or otherwise illuminate the message of what I saw during my hallucination, and of what I have only begun to learn about the true nature of this world and those beyond it. Or am I so fixated now on the notion of connections that I am seeing them where none exist?

I know this much and this much only: I know that there are people who can see things I can't. People who know things I don't. And because of the things that I *have* seen and the things I *have* experienced, I am not arrogant or narcissistic or stupid enough to believe that this material world is all that exists, or even that it is the most important part of all that exists.

Everything that humankind now knows is but a thimbleful of all there is to know.

47.

Sort of a postscript, sort of not

Hmm. Just when you think a story is over...

A couple of things happened to me a few minutes ago. It's spring now, and the tips of the twigs and branches on my naked trees are turning red with new buds. The sun is just now clearing the horizon and throwing a pink patina over those trees and the yard and my deck and the geese out on the water. There's a newness in the air.

What's more interesting, though, are the two things that happened to me before I stepped out onto the deck. I had just finished my morning meditation, which consists mostly of a prayer of gratitude to the universe, my thanks for another day and all the blessings that have been bestowed on me, followed by a period of "watching the breath." This is meant to be a period of nonthought, a quieting preparation for the day. But this time, I suddenly remembered something from the distant past. I remembered a couple of dreams I had regularly as a boy. The first was of me flying over the landscape, a boyish Superman on cruise control, leisurely skimming the treetops and bursting with love for the beauty of the fields and woods and hills and valleys. In the second dream, I was standing out in my family's backyard at night and watching the stars slowly move and reform as spaceships, from a sparkling few to hundreds then thousands of ships glimmering from horizon to horizon. My family and neighbors were all outside too, all chatting and enjoying the evening, but I was the only one looking up, the only one aware of the wondrous sight taking place above us.

I must have had those two dreams a hundred times each before they stopped coming to me. I haven't thought of them for the past fifty years or more. Not until this morning, when the memory returned to me as vivid as ever. And now I wonder: What if those dreams were not merely dreams? What if they were, as many have suggested, the soul's travels?

The second interesting thing to happen was a text that buzzed in from Cara. It was a photo of an online meme, followed by a kissy face:

Love someone you can be weird as hell with who at the end of the day still wants to get naked with you. 🎀 🥀 🐚

I don't know why, but those two things, one on the heels of the other, filled me with energy and a quiet exuberance. It was in that spirit that I walked out onto my deck to behold the sunrise and another new spring.

And it is in that spirit that I now sit at my desk. I think about the Graham Greene quote with which I opened this book: And I wonder...

Because yes, there is a lot of evil in this world. Greene was right about that. What he failed to mention is that there is a lot of good too, a lot of white light marbling the darker shades.

I also know that my miraculously complex body is comprised of forty to fifty trillion cells, each one of them acting independently as well as collectively with other cells to keep my body functioning, each one of them evincing the qualities of consciousness by storing, processing, and sharing information. I know that those cells are, at their very essence, light. I know that all matter is light, and that light is energy. Consequently, I know that there is no such thing as objective reality. What I do not know, and have always ached to know, is *what else* there is. Because if this reality is nothing more than a construction built out of photons held together in sundry forms by particles of energy, then somebody or something, singular or plural, had to come up with that idea and do the building.

Yes, there is much white marbling the gray and black of human nature. And that white is light. And there is light inside all of us.

I keep an old Bible on my desk, the one I was given at the age of four and made to memorize verses from. In I John 1:5, the author wrote, "God is light." And the author of Matthew 5:16 wrote, "Let your light so shine before all, that they may see your good works."

I am a father, and my sons are the light of my life. I am a writer, which means that my words are the flints with which I attempt to strike a light. Cara is my lady with a light, and her light is love, and I must try to be a brighter light for her as well. We are all lights of the Light, and it is our job, one and all, to illuminate the dark in whatever way we can.

As to the vast unknown, for every veil lifted, another waits beneath it. Were the mystery ever to end, existence would end with it. You can choose to be frustrated by that truth, or enchanted by it. I am both, though I am doing my best to erase the frustration.

I have a hundred more stories to tell, and I will tell them all. I have more truths to learn, more love to give, more work to be done.

Near the end of his seventh decade, Henry Miller, that old hedonist, wrote in *Big Sur and the Oranges of Hieronymus Bosch*, "A man writes in order to know himself, and thus get rid of self eventually." I think that's where I am now, where I am trying to be.

To embrace writing as a profession is to embrace solitude, a decision I made a half century ago. And I did so knowingly, for precisely the same reason Nietzsche did. To my mind he wrote the most succinct explanation for such a decision: "In his lonely solitude, the solitary man feeds upon himself; in the thronging multitude, the many feed upon him."

After fifty years of solitude, I think I have just about gnawed myself into extinction. The goal is to get rid of the chaff and leave nothing behind but that kernel of divinity that gave birth to the self, to sacrifice self for the All.

It's ironic, isn't it? God created billions so as to eradicate loneliness, and some of we humans embrace loneliness so as to better understand God.

On the other hand, maybe there's no irony in that at all. Maybe that was the intention from the very beginning.

To continue on this exploration is dangerous, I know. But what is life without risk? Besides, what do I have to lose? My sons no longer need me. Truth is, I need them. I need their love, a bit of their time now and then, an occasional phone call or text. Sometimes I get so lonely for them that my whole body aches and my eyes well with tears. It's a tricky trek, this fatherhood road. You raise your children to be self-reliant, to make their own decisions, to be nobody's fool. And when they turn out exactly as you wished, or even better, they move hours away from you and go on about their lives as if you are already dead. Well, that's a bit of an exaggeration, I guess, but sometimes it feels that way. You positively ache for those days when they were small and needed you at every turn, needed you to stand up for them against all manner of bullies and villains, to cuddle and tickle and kiss them into happiness, to reassure and encourage and teach and provoke, to shell out a few bucks or a lot more than a few, to be their Daddy, their Dad, their Pops. You lie awake in bed sometimes and wonder what they think of you now. Have they already forgotten your unflagging devotion to them, how you gave over your every day to attend to their needs? How you set your own career on the most distant back burner, just to be sure that they never once had to look around and ask, "Where's Dad?" Never once had to make an excuse for your absence. Never once went to bed without hearing the words, "I love you, my son."

But boys become men, and men do not want their old man slobbering all over them. They don't even much want his advice anymore. They know what they want and they know how to get it better than he ever knew of his own wants and methods.

All of which leaves me precisely where I am today, with the fatherhood road grown over and weed-choked behind me. There is no going back. Not ever. The only options are to stop dead in one's tracks and never move again, or to venture on ahead, into the darkness of the unknown.

Dark but beguiling. A last frontier. The truth behind the veil. The beckoning, seductive, tantalizing knowledge that waits for me to push my way through to it. To be embraced or ripped to pieces. Nullified or multiplied.

As for that little bag of dried mushrooms on my desk, snuggled up as they are between the Bible and my Blue Yeti microphone, what am I waiting for? Why should I *not* court every source of knowledge and enlightenment that is offered to me? Why should I *not* take a leap of faith, another joyous lunge for the golden ring?

I have heard that psilocybin can bring life-altering visions. That it can open a person up to deep knowledge, even a rapturous gnosis. I *should* try one of the mushrooms. But just a taste to start. There's a fine line between courage and foolhardiness.

Cara will have a fit if I do it without her standing by with a defibrillator and a hypodermic needle full of adrenaline. But she worries too much. I'm a grown-ass man. Grown and done grow-ing, except for this possibility, this dangerous but beguiling growth spurt. So if I want to have a nibble, I should have a nibble. What can a nibble hurt? Am I right?

Read on and discover Randall Silvis's bestselling mystery *Two Days Gone*

One

The waters of Lake Wilhelm are dark and chilled. In some places, the lake is deep enough to swallow a house. In others, a body could lie just beneath the surface, tangled in the morass of weeds and water plants, and remain unseen, just another shadowy form, a captive feast for the catfish and crappie and the monster bass that will nibble away at it until the bones fall asunder and bury themselves in the silty floor.

In late October, the Arctic Express begins to whisper southeastward across the Canadian plains, driving the surface of Lake Erie into white-tipped breakers that pound the first cold breaths of winter into northwestern Pennsylvania. From now until April, sunny days are few and the spume-strewn beaches of Presque Isle empty but for misanthropic stragglers, summer shops boarded shut, golf courses as still as cemeteries, marinas stripped to their bonework of bare, splintered boards. For the next six months, the air will be gray and pricked with rain or blasted with wind-driven snow. A season of surliness prevails.

Sergeant Ryan DeMarco of the Pennsylvania State Police, Troop D, Mercer County headquarters, has seen this season come and go too many times. He has seen the surliness descend into despair, the despair to acts of desperation, or, worse yet, to deliberately malicious acts, to behavior that shows no regard for the fragility of flesh, a contempt for all consequences.

He knows that on the dozen or so campuses between Erie and Pittsburgh, college students still young enough to envision a happy future will bundle up against the biting chill, but even their youthful souls will suffer the effects of this season of gray. By November, they will have grown annoyed with their roommates, exasperated with professors, and will miss home for the first time since September. Home is warm and bright and where the holidays are waiting. But here in Pennsylvania's farthest northern reach, Lake Wilhelm stretches like a bony finger down a glacier-scoured valley, its waters dark with pine resin, its shores thick on all sides with two thousand acres of trees and brush and hanging vines, dense with damp shadows and nocturnal things, with bear and wildcat and coyote, with hawks that scream in the night.

In these woods too, or near them, a murderer now hides, a man gone mad in the blink of an eye.

The college students are anxious to go home now, home to Thanksgiving and Christmas and Hanukah, to warmth and love and light. Home to where men so respected and adored do not suddenly butcher their families and escape into the woods.

The knowledge that there is a murderer in one's midst will stagger any community, large or small. But when that murderer is one of your own, when you have trusted the education of your sons and daughters to him, when you have seen his smiling face in every bookstore in town, watched him chatting with Robin Roberts on *Good Morning America*, felt both pride and envy in his sudden acclaim, now your chest is always heavy and you cannot seem to catch your breath. Maybe you claimed, last spring, that you played high school football with Tom Huston. Maybe you dated him half a lifetime ago, tasted his kiss, felt the heave and tremor of your bodies as you lay in the lush green of the end zone one steamy August night when love was raw and new. Last spring, you were quick to claim an old intimacy with him, so eager to catch some of his sudden, shimmering light. Now you want only to huddle indoors. You sit and stare at the window, confused by your own pale reflection.

Now Claire O'Patchen Huston, one of the prettiest women in town, quietly elegant in a way no local woman could ever hope to be, lies on a table in a room at the Pennsylvania State Police forensics lab in Erie. There is the wide gape of a slash across her throat, an obscene slit that runs from the edge of her jawline to the opposite clavicle.

Thomas Jr., twelve years old, he with the quickest smile and the fastest feet in sixth grade, the boy who made all the high school coaches wet their lips in anticipation, shares the chilly room with his mother. The knife that took him in his sleep laid its path low across his throat, a quick, silencing sweep with an upward turn.

As for his sister, Alyssa, there are a few fourth grade girls who, a week ago, would have described her as a snob, but her best friends knew her as shy, uncertain yet of how to wear and carry and contain her burgeoning beauty. She appears to have sat up at the last instant, for the blood that spurted from her throat sprayed not only across the pillow, but also well below it, spilled down over her chest before she fell back onto her side. Did she understand the message of that gurgling gush of breath in her final moments of consciousness? Did she, as blood soaked into the faded pink flannel of her pajama shirt, lift her gaze to her father's eyes as he leaned away from her bed?

And little David Ryan Huston, asleep on his back in his crib— what dreams danced through his toddler's brain in its last quivers of sentience? Did his father first pause to listen to the susurrus breath? Did he calm himself with its sibilance? The blade on its initial thrust missed the toddler's heart and slid along the still-soft sternum. The second thrust found the pulsing muscle and nearly sliced it in half.

The perfect family. The perfect house. The perfect life. All gone now. Snap your fingers five times, that's how long it took. Five soft taps on the door. Five steel-edged scrapes across the tender flesh of night.

Two

DeMarco took the call at home just a few minutes after kickoff on Sunday afternoon. He was halfway through his first bottle of Corona. The Browns, after only four plays, had already driven inside the red zone. Pittsburgh's Steel Curtain appeared made of aluminum foil. DeMarco was settling in for an afternoon of mumbling and cursing when the call came in from Trooper Lipinski, who was working the desk at the State Police barracks.

The bodies of the Huston family had been discovered approximately twenty minutes earlier. Claire's mother and father had driven up from nearby Oniontown, just as they did every Sunday through the fall and early winter, "to watch the Steelers beat themselves," as Ed O'Patchen liked to say that season. The O'Patchens went up the walk and onto the covered porch as they always had, Ed lugging two six-packs of Pabst Blue Ribbon, Rosemary cradling her Crock-Pot of cheese and sausage dip. As always, they walked inside without knocking. Rosemary went searching for the silent family upstairs while Ed tried to figure out how to work the remote on the new wide-screen Sony.

The Browns scored while DeMarco was taking the call. He saw no more of the game.

Later that day, DeMarco and three other troopers began

interviewing the Hustons' neighbors up and down Mayfield Road. Not a single resident along the tree-lined street had anything negative to say about the family, and none were aware of any financial or other marital problems between Thomas and Claire. All were stunned, most were grief-stricken.

Available now from Poisoned Pen Press

Reading Group Guide

1. How did the author's presence as a character change your experience of the story?

2. What was your first impression of Thomas Kennaday? How did your opinion of him change throughout the book?

3. Why does Silvis get involved with the Baby Doe and Burchette murder cases? If you were approached in the same manner, would you listen to Kennaday?

4. Why was it so important for Phoebe to tell Silvis things in the correct order and in small pieces? Why do you think she was willing to follow directions so meticulously? Who did the interview strategy protect?

5. Silvis's research quickly takes him into the realm of conspiracy theories. Which of these theories seems most plausible to you? Do you think looking into them helped or hindered Silvis's investigation into the murders?

6. Silvis considers abandoning the investigation several times

but finds himself too stubborn. Where does that stubbornness come from? Is there a point in his investigation that would have made you give up?

7. What did you think of the way Detective Smathers responded to Silvis's narrative? Do you think he'll do anything with the information either officially or unofficially?

8. The note that comes with the dobro indicates that the instrument is a reward for a job well done. What exactly do you think Silvis is being rewarded for accomplishing?

9. Do you believe in a reality beyond our own? Is it possible to research that world or access it?

A Conversation with the Author

The Deepest Black **is a unique project. How did the writing compare to your Ryan DeMarco mysteries or any of your other work?**

Some of the difference applies to the next question, so I will postpone that information for now and address here the primary differences between writing in first person and in third person.

Hemingway once said that writing in first person is easy, and that anybody can write in first person. That might be a bit of an overstatement. First person is both easier and more difficult than writing in third person. Easier because presenting the narrator's emotions and thoughts seems quite natural to a reader, just as it is when you tell a friend a personal anecdote. Consequently, it is easier to pull the reader into the narrator's world, and to make the narrator's motives, fears, suspicions, and so forth tangible. It can, if done correctly, add a certain intimacy to the story, bringing the reader and the narrator closer together, so to speak.

But writing in first person can be more difficult for a writer who, like me, loves more descriptive and evocative prose. That kind of prose in first person tends to sound artificial and stylized, mainly because we don't usually speak that way. It's a different level of diction not often heard spoken aloud. Writing in first person forced me to write more straightforward prose, with fewer modifiers and a more conversational style. So a compromise had to be found between coming off naturally yet evoking atmosphere and setting sufficiently that the reader could imagine and envision those elements of the story. I did my best to find a good balance, but I will admit that it took nine revisions on my part before I was satisfied with that balance.

You present yourself as a character in the book. How did it feel to write about yourself that way? How do you and your book counterpart differ?

I have written about myself many times in personal essays, and writing about myself in *The Deepest Black* presented the same challenges—to depict the action and the characters' interactions authentically while still keeping the narrator as likable and sympathetic as possible. Unfortunately, likability is a very subjective assessment. Does the reader like a narrator better if he is strong and bold and confident, or if he admits to uncertainty and doubt and often has to blunder his way through a scene? The truth, I think—and literary studies seem to bear this out—is that readers like an imperfect narrator better, someone who makes mistakes, has regrets, and frequently second-guesses himself. Fortunately, that's me. Unfortunately, I also tend to be a smart-ass sometimes, and that, too, can be either amusing and likable in a narrator or it can be off-putting. I find myself relying on smart-ass remarks when I am angry or wanting to avoid the subject or just plain frightened, as in the spirit attack scene in the Scottish Rite Cathedral.

I also wrestled with revealing my interest and involvement in the paranormal. But, as I mention in the book, I have been having paranormal experiences ever since I was a small boy, and, because of those inexplicable experiences, I have never ceased to question the true nature of reality. Some people will pooh-pooh those beliefs, and if I were thirty years younger, I might have downplayed mine for the sake of my career. But I'm getting too old to live my life based on what others think of me, and besides, what happened, happened. Why hide it? I have no plans to run for political office, so no reason to take up lying as a vocation at this stage of my life. Fiction, however, is the art of lying convincingly. I do some of that too.

In answer to the final part of this question, there's not a lot of space between Silvis the narrator and Silvis the author. Yes, I learned late in life that several of my "eccentricities" are associated with Asperger's syndrome, what some people call being "on the spectrum." I continue to use the word Aspie because it designates a certain point on that spectrum, and because I was so happy, in my sixties, to learn that word as an explanation of why I am as I am. Throw in introversion, misophonia, and a blue-collar contempt for authority, and that pretty much explains Randall Silvis, in the book and in real life.

There is, however, an even more important element to Randall Silvis the author and man, and except for a few references, I decided to leave that part of my life out of *The Deepest Black*. Being a father, and now a doting grandfather, has been the most important part of my life since 1985. I write about my sons frequently in my personal essays, and especially in my memoir *From the Mirror*, because their presence in my life has truly shaped me into the person I am today. I raised them to be self-sufficient and independent, and that's who they are. Unfortunately, that independence has taken them to brilliant careers conducted hours away from me, but we still talk almost daily by phone and text, and I am always ready to undertake a full day's drive at a moment's notice to come to their aid. Nothing I have ever done or ever will do can equal the sense of pride and accomplishment or the love I feel for my sons. One of them will likely shake his head and mutter when he reads *The Deepest Black,* and the other will chuckle, but they know me and accept me well enough to shrug off any criticism the book might bring me. They do not appear in the book because none of the action involved them in any way. And they still know next to nothing about the contents of this book. I do not discuss a work-in-progress with *anybody* unless they are associated with the book's future development and publication. My belief has always held that one can be the kind of writer who talks about his work or the kind of writer who writes. In my experience, not much is ever accomplished by those who choose the first option.

Thomas Kennaday is a crucial character, but he only appears in person once throughout the book. Why did you decide to keep him so removed?

Thomas Kennaday is the one who made the decision to appear only once in the narrative. I assume he did so, egotist that he appears to be, to make himself a central question in the book, and a constant source of the author's consternation. Did he have some other motive for being so elusive? Is he finished with Silvis now, and done jerking him around? Or will he show up again in Silvis's life? And if he does, will it be to bring answers or more mystery? I wish I knew.

Do you have plans for what's next in your writing career?

By the time *The Deepest Black* hits the shelves, I will have finished two more novels. As of January 10, 2022, the first full draft of the mainstream novel *The Long and Winding Road* is complete. I hope to send the polished version to my agent by the end of March or sooner. Also as of January 10, I am twelve thousand words into another mainstream novel, this one set in the Florida Panhandle in 1962. Its working title is *Hurricane*, though I sometimes think it should be called *Twisted*, not only because the hurricane spawns a tornado, as they often do in the Panhandle, but also because there are a few twisted characters in the story. After that, who knows? Maybe Thomas Kennaday will show up again.

What are you reading these days?

As of today, I am still reading Greg Isle's *Cemetery Road*. I have about a hundred pages of the six hundred-plus to go, and it seems at this point to be turning into a soap opera with its unlikely scenarios and outcomes, but I will stick with it to the end just to see if my predictions about the denouement prove true. Next on the stack are Michael Ruhlman's collection of three literary novellas, *In Short Measures*; Patrick Hoffman's *Every Man a Menace*; and Larry McMurtry's *Cadillac Jack*, not necessarily in that order. Ever since reading Sebastian Barry's hauntingly beautiful *Days Without End* a few years ago, I have been searching for another book that will command my attention, and earn my respect and admiration, with every single line. I haven't found that book yet, but I will keep trying.

By the way, for those of you who might be interested, my free monthly newsletter always includes a review of whatever I have most recently read. You can sign up for the newsletter on my website at randallsilvis.com. I try to pack every installment with not only a book review but also photos, news, maybe a video, writing tips, and anything else that irks, amuses, excites, or confounds me. As a thirty-third-degree card-carrying introvert, it took a long time for me to be convinced that readers might actually want that kind of thing. But solitude can get awful solitary sometimes, and I have learned to enjoy that connection with my readers.

Thank you for reading *The Deepest Black*. If you, too, are interested in the unknown, the strange, the hidden, the monstrous, and the mystical, my addendum to *The Deepest Black* is just a click away on my website. Not only do I provide links to the sources that inspired *The Deepest Black*, but to the many others that have informed my beliefs. Depending on your own stance on the paranormal, you might find that information startling, annoying, comforting, terrifying, infuriating, or revelatory.

I wish you all peace, love, good health, and a decent night's sleep now and then.

Acknowledgments

I have spent my entire career as a writer, and therefore my entire adult life, hopscotching through the fiction and nonfiction sub-genres, and in so doing giving massive headaches to certain agents and editors. But where's the creativity in writing the same thing time after time? What's *creative* about that? Some stories are not meant to be mysteries, or strictly literary, or slipstream, or thrillers, or even all fiction or all truth. Some stories are meant to be a little of this and a little of that. So why should writers be only this or only that? If forced to write by the numbers, I would rather be an accountant. They make more money. They have more time off. And they can leave their jobs behind at the end of the day. I write because I love writing, and I love it because it is the most exhilarating daily challenge I can think of, short of being fired out of a cannon every day. But even that, after a while, would become routine: Climb the ladder, slip down into the barrel, pray, fly through the air, look for the net. Writing isn't like that. Writing is unpredictable day after day after day. And there is no safety net. You land safely or you don't. Now *that's* what I call exciting.

I have been blessed these past few years to be assisted by two individuals who, despite their probable misgivings and headaches, have made no attempts to stop me from climbing into my own personal cannon book after book. My gratitude to Sandy Lu, my incomparable literary agent, and to Anna Michels, my peerless editor, has never dimmed.

You're the best. Thank you.

I also want to thank Tamra Lyn Bessette, who, besides being my prodigiously talented and grossly underpaid social media manager, website designer, publicist and promoter, was my first reader of the manuscript in its earliest draft. She told me what she liked and, more importantly, what she didn't like. And I, of course, ignored the second category of remarks. But with each succeeding draft I got a little bit smarter, and eventually I made most of the changes she suggested. Because she was right.

You're a jewel, Tamra, and I am blessed to have you in my corner too.

About the Author

Photo © Tamra Lyn Ressette

Randall Silvis is the multigenre author of nineteen critically acclaimed novels, three story collections, and two books of creative nonfiction. A former contributing writer for the Discovery Channel magazines, he is also a prize-winning playwright, a produced screenwriter, a prolific essayist, and an amateur songwriter. His many literary awards include the Drue Heinz Literature Prize, two literature fellowships from the National Endowment for the Arts, a Fulbright Senior Scholar Research Award, and a Doctor of Letters degree awarded for "a sustained record of distinguished literary achievement." A link to subscribe to his free monthly newsletter, which includes photos, news, book reviews, and writing tips, can be found at randallsilvis.com. His book trailers, songs, and Ask Randall video series can be found on YouTube at Author Randall Silvis. An addendum to *The Deepest Black*, which includes source citations for material referenced in this book, plus links to other relevant material, can also be found on his website.